NUMBERS

Like *City of Night,* with which it has much in common, *Numbers* takes the reader on an unforgettable journey through the limbo of hidden sex between men to chronicle a way of life barely imagined by those outside its boundaries. Its hero, Johnny Rio, is an angel of dark sex on an obsessive return trip to Los Angeles, to test himself anew in the arena of male love. He stalks the balconies and men's rooms of the all-night theaters, the erotic beaches and shaded glens of the city's parks, to attract the shadowy sexhunters in an implacable contest against time. An explosive sequel to *City of Night,* the runaway bestseller that propelled Rechy into the front ranks of American writers.

Other Works by John Rechy

Published by Grove Press

City of Night

Rushes

The Sexual Outlaw: A Documentary

The Vampires

NUMBERS

by JOHN RECHY

Grove Press, Inc.
New York

Acknowledgments: "Wild Thing" by Chip Taylor, copyright © 1965 by Blackwood Music Inc., reprinted by permission of Blackwood Music Inc.; "Summer in the City" by John Sebastian, copyright © 1966, reprinted by permission of Faithful Virtue Music Co., Inc.; "Hungry" by Barry Mann and Cynthia Weil, copyright © 1966 by Screen Gems—Columbia Music, Inc., New York, reprinted by permission of Screen Gems—Columbia Music, Inc.; "Dirty Water" by Ed Cobb, sung by the Standells, reprinted by permission of Equinox Music, Publisher.

First Black Cat Edition 1968
Ninth Printing 1981
ISBN: 0-394-17130-6
Grove Press ISBN: 0-8021-4125-0
Library of Congress Catalog Card Number: 67-28972

Manufactured in the United States of America

DISTRIBUTED BY RANDOM HOUSE, INC., NEW YORK

GROVE PRESS, INC., 196 WEST HOUSTON STREET, NEW YORK, N.Y. 10014 for Bill, Bob, and Bill

It was always so; during the day
the Dwelling was covered by the cloud,
which at night had the appearance of fire.

Numbers 9:16

ONE

HE LEFT PHOENIX in the morning, in the early dawning moments when the world is purple; and he saw, on the highway, bands of spectral birds clustered on the pavement searching for God knows what—certainly not food, not on the bare highway and so near the sleeping city.

Expecting them to take flight quickly, he did not reduce his speed; but even as the car dashed dangerously toward them, they remained there as if mysteriously involved in some suicidal ritual—until Johnny Rio, who would have brooded grayly about killing anything (he would prefer to swerve off the road), smashed at his brakes and sounded his honk—the long sound spreading emptily, lonesomely, into the caverns of the still morning.

Only then did the strange birds scatter—but very, very slowly, reluctantly; they flew away—gliding like pieces of dark paper abandoned suddenly by an erratic wind; gliding, but quite low, just barely above the hood of the car: as if in a deep trance.

Again and again, as he drives now much more slowly (the car hardly moving, Johnny himself caught in the hypnotic mood this phantasmal morning has spread over the birds and the highway), he encounters other, similar birds, always small, always shadowy, always in groups of eight or nine, always as if courting a harsh, inevitable destiny, either reluctant to move away from or unaware of the crushing path of the car.

Within a distance of perhaps a mile, the birds were gone.

Once again, Johnny can slash the desert in his speeding new car, as he has done from Texas to New Mexico, into Arizona—the country he has traveled from Laredo, through the burned desert, the level lands leprously spotted with dried bushes; and he's rushing to Los Angeles for a reason he does not know: knowing only that he's returning for ten days.

Exactly ten days.

To avoid the yellow heat of the Arizona desert, a heat remembered from other, distant times, he left Phoenix early (after arriving there yesterday afternoon: renting a room in one of those synthetic "luxury" motels which seem to be made of layers of colored sugar; and he lay by the pool glancing admiringly and often at his slenderly muscled body stretched sensually turning dark tan under the raging summer sun, the hairs on his legs gold despite his dark-brown hair); but already, now that he's many,

many miles into the desert, the heat is panting at the windows in recurrent smothering breaths.

He removes his shirt. He never wears underclothes, and so his chest is bare. He feels free and sexual.

The sun has whitened the desert, transforming it paradoxically into that snowy, icy spectacle created by the sand and the trembling waves of steam released by the pavement in the distance. A car ahead of Johnny (but not ahead for long: he has a compulsion to pass) augments the sense of unreality which has not yet been lifted; that car seems to float on the horizon as if on a frozen lake.

Deliberately to shatter the mood, Johnny turns the radio on, hoping for one of those miraculously lunatic stations that spew out the blessedly mesmerizing wailing of young groups with lovely names, the hopped-up disc jockeys making bad jokes; or hoping for a biblestation from which a Negro preacher will moan out ineffable rocking blue damnation. But Johnny has already traveled too far from the cities, and all the radio picks up is one of those square stations you inevitably get so inappropriately as you speed frantically in the daytime along the highways of America toward an urgent destination.

He's going 90 miles an hour.

The amorphous heat is fierce.

Far, far away he sees a shadow slice the air before him sharply like a scythe ripping the sky: perhaps a vulture swooping down on something dead in the desert. Johnny imagines it perched humped over the bleeding flesh. Appalled by the cruel image, he futilely tries the radio again.

But death, which he avoids thinking of, seems determined to permeate his awareness; it does like a knife in his flesh.

Behind him are memories of dead birds smashed by other cars along the highways—of the red, red freshly spilled blood smeared on the concrete pavement. The crushed feathers.

And already his windshield is speckled heavily with those tragic moth-creatures that descend from the sky to crash against the glass—each tiny life transformed mercilessly in one instant into a powdery smear, perhaps a dot of blood on the pane—to be wiped off with a moist paper towel at the next gas station.

Are those dusty insects aware of the windshield? Do they lunge from the sky, welcoming their destruction? Or are they trying to enter the car to escape the powerful currents created by the plunging cars? Deceived by the glass, they crash against an invisible destiny—a destiny unperceived until the fatal moment.

Not that Johnny would equate destiny with death, which may be only an anticlimax in the curve of life; no, his awareness is not so much of death as of a *welcome* extended to fate, of the suicide that doesn't involve the taking of life: of the infinite ways in which your "number" (so many penultimate numbers!) comes up every single day.

Thinking that, Johnny accelerates his speed to 95—as he lunges toward the foggy city of lost angels.

Unconsciously, he's begun to count the number of bugs slaughtered by his speeding car.

Splash! . . . One. . . .

Two . . . three. . . .

He's about to count four, but the tiny fluttering speck veers away from the windshield, escapes. Its number wasn't up.

But when it is— . . .

He imagines a roster, with everyone in the world—past, present, future—numbered (as in that book of the Bible in which Moses is commanded by God to take a census of his people): all listed neatly in long, thin, tight columns. Say that your number is infinite-billion, six million, eight hundred and sixty-six thousand, three hundred and seventy-three. That means you'll go immediately after number infinite-billion, six million, eight hundred and sixty-six thousand, three hundred and seventy-*two*. If you could only determine the numbers of those before you, then you'd know almost to the instant when your own would come up. (A sure way, Johnny can't help thinking with amusement, of insuring that you will, indeed, be your brother's keeper!)

Splut! . . . Four.

He imagines God poised behind an automatic rifle sniping each "number" down—though on occasion He might, for expediency, use a machine gun to topple the ranks like dominoes.

Johnny notices the fifth crushed bug since he began counting.

When your number comes up— . . .

Six!

Suddenly aware of what he's been counting, and angered by it, he tries once again to shut off that area of his mind obsessed with death and self-destruction—that area opened by the shadowy birds outside of Phoenix, the crushed feathers glued with blood to the pavement, the mothy bugs on the windshield.

And this is how he tries to shut those thoughts off: He looks down at his shirtless chest, which—deeply, deeply

tanned—gleams with sweat. Pleased by the sight, he runs
his hand over it, brings that hand to his mouth, and he
licks his own perspiration, feeling excitement burgeoning
between his legs. He spreads his knees, arches his body.
His foot on the pedal accelerates the speed still more:
one hundred miles an hour.

Triumphantly, the thought of sex has driven away the
thought of death, at least for now.

He has counted the number of cars he has passed on
the highway from the time he began to encounter some
light traffic. Three cars so far. The fourth now coming up.

Whooo-*oosh!*

Four. He's passed four cars.

And not one has passed him!

He sees the fifth ahead, approaches it. Now he inches to
the left, to begin passing; but the driver in front of him,
challenged, accelerates his own speed. Johnny sees the
blond head of what appears to be a youngman—he too
shirtless. Johnny Rio is about to steer sharply to the left,
to force the other to allow him to pass—begins to do so
in a swift, swerving arc; but a car rushing in the opposite
lane—its panicked honk blaring, echoing itself into the
desert—forces him to retreat. The driver of the car which
Johnny is even more determined now to pass is keeping
to the left, almost flush with the line dividing the highway; he's seizing strategic advantage of the narrow, single
lane to block Johnny's car. Enraged, Johnny watches his
speedometer wavering uncertainly beyond the 100 mark.

A distance away, on a gradual ascent, a heavy truck
moves slowly like an enormous red-striped insect along a
no-passing stretch. Approaching it, both Johnny and the

driver of the car ahead—brakes protesting shrilly—are
forced to decelerate suddenly: 95 miles . . . 90 . . . 80 . . .
70 . . . 65 . . .

Now the driver in front turns to look at Johnny. In that
swift instant they see each other, and what Johnny sees is a
blond youngman in his 20's with wild, wind-tossed hair.

I've got to pass him! Johnny thinks urgently.

He notices that only a few feet ahead, beyond a curve
on the ascending highway, the double, no-passing line
breaks for a short distance. There are no cars on the opposite lane. At exactly the right instant he depresses the
gas pedal, moves quickly into the left lane, is now parallel
with the car he's been trying to pass (the two drivers
glance at each other once more, swiftly, like charioteers),
moves ahead of it (wishing strangely for the wild beat of
rocking music on the radio to accompany the speed), is
parallel with the truck, passes it—and glides into the right
lane feeling almost sexually released.

I've passed five cars, one truck! he exults.

The number on the speedometer is 105.

He tells himself to slow down, but he doesn't. He feels
carried on a current—not so much he who is driving as
he who is being driven—as if the highway is pulling him.

Faster than time!

He leaves his foot pressed tightly to the pedal.

Yet despite the urgency, at the thought of his destination (I am returning to Los Angeles after three years!),
his heart protests in terror, his body chills the perspiration,
his mind howls with echoes.

As he speeds ineluctably to the foggy city of dead angels
(even when he lived there, he often thought of Los

Angeles—with its ubiquitous advertisements for inter-
ment—as a "swinging cemetery," a "graveyard of fun";
have-a-ball-on-your-own-gravesite!), Johnny Rio appears
moody, almost sinister, like an angel of dark sex, or death.

He looks like this:

He is very masculine, and he has been described recurrently in homosexual jargon as "a very butch number"—
a phrase invariably accompanied by a great rolling of the
eyes, a nervous, moist flitting of the tongue along the lips.
A supreme accolade in that world, "butch" means very
male and usually carries overtones of roughness; a "number" is a potential or actual or merely desired partner in
vagrant sex.

But Johnny's is an easy masculinity—not stiff, not rigid,
not blundering nor posed—although, when he wants to,
he can look tough: unapproachably tough when he carries
it to a self-defeating extreme. The fact is that, as with all
truly sexually attractive men, there is something very, very
subtly female about him; and only at first does that seem
a semantic contradiction: because, although, yes, there is
that something which is vaguely female, there is nothing
feminine, there is nothing effeminate.

He walks gracefully, weightlessly, like a panther—and
with just the slightest trace of a cocky swagger. (A girl he
went out with told him once that she waited at her door
to watch him walk away.) His eyes are green—but if he
wears blue, they assume that color, become unbelievably
azure; and they're rimmed by thick, full, curled, almost
ridiculously long lashes. He constantly flirts by glancing
down through sleepy lids, then looking up quickly. He
has dark-brown wavy hair. A slight crook in his nose keeps
him from being a prettyboy and makes him, therefore,

much more attractive and masculine. He has a tremendous smile, which he has often observed himself while looking into a mirror—but only after many people had commented on it (so it is not "studied"): It begins, his smile, almost shyly as the barest hint of a grin—then, disappearing entirely for an instant as if he has decided not to smile after all, it spreads suddenly—bursts radiantly—very wide, revealing white, even, dazzling teeth.

So the "femaleness" has to do with the fact that he moves sensually, that his eyes invite, that he is constantly flirting (although this is not conscious), and that he is extremely vain.

And, also, it has to do with a harrowing sensitivity about age.

One should therefore merely say that Johnny looks to be in his early 20's. He has even been asked for identification when, on very rare occasions, he has bought liquor during the past three years. (And he's firmly convinced that—largely through sheer determination—he'll never age.)

Neither tall nor short (though closer to short than tall), Johnny has a slender, muscular body. In the past few years he has exercised diligently with weights—not in order to become one of those rigid grotesques with coconut muscles that bear no relation whatever to the natural lines of the body, but to keep lithe and hard. This he has accomplished eminently.

There is at least another reason for his determined exercising. Stripped down to trunks, alone in the room where he works out in his apartment in Laredo, he becomes acutely aware of his body—at first in opposition to the weights (himself overcoming the resistance), then in fusion and harmony with them (strength and power existing only in their actual manifestation, in the kinetic activity). His muscles pumped, flushed tight, rigid and filled with blood, the perspiration flowing in relief, he's aware of whatever mysterious thing it is that makes him alive.

Johnny's father, now dead, was Irish. His mother is Mexican. ("Rio" is not actually his last name—it's not even his mother's maiden name, although hers is really Mexican. He assumed the name in Los Angeles because, especially in a world where no last names are given, it sounded romantic—like a gypsy's.) From them he inherited a smooth complexion which sponges the sun's rays easily, almost, one could say, adoringly: When he lies stretched under the stark gaze of the sun—and he does so religiously each summer—he feels that the heat is making love to him, licking his body with a golden tongue. Each summer his skin becomes like brown velvet.

Many people have told him that he's very handsome. He likes to hear that, and he never denies it. But he knows that the designation is not exactly correct. Precisely: he is much more sexual than he is handsome; and that, for Johnny, is even better. There is something about him which exudes sensuality. He knows it, he may even have cultivated it. He has been told that there is a promise of "dark sex" that hovers about him.

Again, as with all truly sexually desirable men, he attracts both sexes—even, among his own sex, some who will never recognize that attraction, who will feel it, disguised, only as a certain anger and resentment toward him. Johnny is used to a type of man, usually married, who will try to quarrel with him instantly.

Added to the various paradoxes of his being, as well as to his attractiveness—there is—or so he has been told (but only by people who have not known him sexually)—a suggestion of something that remains pure and innocent about him, something of uncontaminability.

This perplexes Johnny because he has not—since he was a child—felt "pure."

If you approach Los Angeles on the highway turned freeway, as Johnny Rio will soon be doing, you're aware, perhaps as far as a hundred miles away, of the Cloud. It enshrouds the city. In the daytime and from that distance, the Cloud, which is fog and smoke, creates a spectral city: a gray mass floating on the horizon. At night, lit by the millions of colored lights with which the city attempts futilely to smother the dark, it becomes an incandescent, smoking halo; dull orange: as though the city were on fire.

In a curious trance at the awareness of his imminent return—sailing automatically, effortlessly, unconsciously, between cars, ahead of them, assuming a waltzing rhythm as he does so—Johnny Rio hasn't yet noticed the ominous Cloud. He hasn't even noticed that the traffic has thickened considerably for the last few miles on the long, long . . . long . . . entrance to Los Angeles.

He tries the radio once more . . . the electronic murmuring.

Suddenly, with a blast, a rocking L.A. station shatters the static. A male voice groans:

> *Wild thing, you make my heart sing—*
> *You make everything groooooveee. . . .*

The music, by a group called the Troggs, with its persistent beat (like life imbedded in the record's groove, to be played over and over—the same; what changes between the beginning and the end?), acts as a catalyst for Johnny's buried despair; and despair flows in a confused mixture of panic and excitement which burrows between his legs; his cock begins to swell.

The moaning voice on the radio imitates the dark sounds of Negroes:

> *Wahld thang . . . Ah thank Ah loooove yew!*
> *But Ah wanna know foh SUUUUUUURE! . . .*

As he speeds into that mushroom of gray mist ahead of him (the car devouring the highway), the foggy, smoky Cloud reaches out for him, begins to surround him more and more closely—although he's still not aware of it, partly because it seems to recede as one nears it.

> *"Wahld thang— . . ."*

The sky is still clearly blue; but the scenery ahead has begun to fade, buried beyond that foggy veil; the mountains appear unreal, like movie props. Each mile farther inward, the Cloud perversely shuts out more of the sky; and the spotty verdure assumes that patina of gray that settles on the city.

> *Wahld thang, Ah thank yew moooooove me! . . .*

Enveloped by the grayness, Johnny Rio suddenly realizes he has entered the Cloud.

On a Friday afternoon in summer.

TWO

"JOHNNY! JOHNNY RIO!"

The man calling him has just stepped out of a bar and into the dirty yellow afternoon. He waltzes up to Johnny, who has just turned the corner of 5th Street into Main—three blocks away from where he parked his car. Johnny and the man meet before the men's store there, its windows an insane clutter of flashy, tacky clothes, bright colors battling each other for prominence.

"Lord-uh-*me!*" Hand-to-heart. "*Where?* have *you? been,* Johnny Rio?" Striking a languid pose, one hand wilting on his cheek, elbow supported by the other, the man stands before Johnny, openly appraising him.

Knowing that he's being studied, Johnny tries quite

urgently—but unsuccessfully—to read the man's reaction to him by an expression, a look.

"Now *tell* us: Where? have? you? been?" the man goes on. Like the small bulbs that wink in response to each tap on a pinball machine, his eyes blink, twice, as he punches each word out lightly.

Johnny remembers the man, vaguely—from a dim bar, a yellow-lit gray street, a smothered room. "I've been— . . . Away," he answers.

"Well, of *course* you have! But *where?* I bet some absolutely mad, rich queen just *snatched* you away from us— like a *vulture*—and *kept* you away—all these *years!*— until *now!*"

Johnny remembers the imagined vulture feeding on the carrion in the desert. "No," he says, trying to place the man more definitely. "It wasn't like that. I've just been Away."

And he has been Away.

"Away" means Laredo, in Texas, his hometown in the beautiful purple, blue, and golden Southwest: Laredo— which, on one side—toward the border—is still very Mexican, as colorful as a spread sarape; and, on the other, toward the highway as you leave the city, is all imitation-rainbow motels. Though it has unpleasant memories for him (a dreary fatherless Mexican Catholic childhood: poor, poor years and after-school jobs in a laundry call-office, a department-store stockroom, and on a newspaper as copy boy), Johnny has lived there for three years since fleeing Los Angeles one day, fed up; has lived there alone in an apartment (except for a few weeks with his mother at her home soon after his return). He could have found turbulence in Laredo, too, of course—though not in the abundance of Los Angeles; but he could also retreat, and did: working hard (for his father's brother in the evenings), saving all his money; in his leisure time exercising compulsively with weights or listening to music in a darkened room; avoiding people (except his mother and a few others who wouldn't remind him of the world he left behind); and, often, having to drug himself to sleep, to stifle a stunning fear of the annihilating darkness.

Then—precisely one day after he told himself he was completely rid of the need for the life he'd fled—that day, as he stood looking at himself in the mirror, he felt curiously that he had ceased to exist, that he existed only in the mirror. He reached out to touch himself, and the cold glass frustrated him. Before, others had confirmed his existence with admiration.

Johnny was driven back to Los Angeles not unlike the apocryphal criminal driven to return to the scene of his crime.

But he set an exact limit to the time of his return: ten days. He announced this to his mother, his uncle, and his very few friends.

Ten days.

"*Well!*" the man says. "So you don't *want* to tell me where you've been. You always were *quite* the mysterious one!" He takes a short step back, to view Johnny more strategically. "Let me *look* at you!"

Johnny stares at the man as a defendant will at the jury that decides his fate.

And the verdict is read: "Why, you haven't changed at all!" the man says.

Johnny's heart opens gratefully.

"No, wait!" the man says. "I take it all back; you *have* changed!"

Johnny feels like a man whose reprieve has been withdrawn.

"You've gotten *sexier!*" the man says. "And, you know, you always were one of the sexiest numbers around."

Now Johnny smiles, radiantly. He exists again in the admiring eyes of the other, the apprehension has evaporated. He feels more sexual, handsomer than ever. He relaxes.

"I just bet you're *madly* broke and in need of money," the man says gleefully.

And so I'm really back, Johnny thinks. He shrugs indifferently, playing the role he knows so well. (Though he's taken money in exchange for sex over and over and over, Johnny Rio has never felt like a whore.)

"I've rented a room at the hotel nearby *just* in case something like this happened." The man giggles naughtily. "And it *has!*—lucky me I *saw* you!"

"How much?" Johnny asks automatically from the past.

"I'll pay you the usual," the man sniffs, as if somewhat offended that Johnny hasn't taken that for granted.

Johnny nods, wondering what the usual is now. Almost unconsciously he reaches behind him, touches his wallet. I've got about seven hundred dollars here, he thinks, and I'm going with this man for maybe ten. He follows the man, who ambles merrily crossing the street toward the hotel Johnny remembers only too well. Johnny walks this familiar street—past stores displaying hundreds of magazines showing naked bodies in garish color; past the rancid fried-chicken counters ("You hungry?" the man asks.

Johnny's stomach turns in revulsion. "No thanks"); past the leathery army-and-navy outlet stores.

Johnny stops abruptly. Is this why I've come back? To prove to myself I can still hustle? Once, it had been the most liberating of experiences—to be desired enough to be paid for lying as motionless as possible on a bed while a man burrowed his head between Johnny's legs.

With a tilt of his head, the man motions Johnny to come along. He doesn't.

"What's the matter, honey?" the man says. "Ooh, you are a cute number!" he exclaims.

"I don't want to go to that hotel," Johnny says; and although that's true (he remembers the rooms there: a bed, a table, a chair, a tin can for an ashtray, the smell of loneliness), his main reason for hesitating is that a nebulous plan is forming. "I'm staying at another one, just a couple of blocks away. Let's go there." What he just said isn't exactly true. It's true that he has rented a motel unit, but it's not nearby.

"Okay," the man says, somewhat bewildered. "It's highly irregular, of course," he adds.

They walk together. Away from Main Street. Along trashy, ugly downtown Los Angeles. A distorted checkerboard of afternoon shadows.

The man is saying: "Oh, Johnny Rio, you *should* have been here a few years ago—when that *stir* happened! (I think you had *just* left.) *Well!* You probably remember him—this young number that used to hang around the *bars* and *Pershing Square? Well!* He wrote a *book* about *Main* Street and *hustling* and Pershing *Square* and *queens,* and tourists came down looking for Miss *So*-and-So that he'd written about! And that trashy big picture magazine did an article with photographs of *Main* Street. . . . It's calmed down again, however."

Johnny is walking so fast, impatiently, that the man is having a difficult time keeping up with him. One block.

"Can you *imagine?*" the man continues. "I *knew* him— the author. Knew him *quite* well, I might add," he adds suggestively. "Who would have thought he was going to write a *book?* Why, he looked like any *other* young vagrant!"

It's a smoggy, livid afternoon. The Cloud has taken possession of the city. Two blocks.

The man goes on: "Now *every* time I pick up a hustler, I wonder if I'm going to end up between the sheets of a *bed* or the sheets of a *book!*"

Three blocks.

"Why, doll," the man says incredulously, "where are you *going?*—and *whose* car is *that?*" Mouth-ovaled-in-alarm. "My *God!*—you're going to *steal* it! In broad daylight!"

Johnny has deliberately led the man to where his own car—new and shiny and goodlooking with just the touch of subtle flashiness that he likes—is parked; he proceeds to unlock the door. Looking at the man over the black vinyl top of his car, whose lower body is prairie-gold, he says coolly: "I'm going back to where I'm staying. In a real expensive motel. Alone. And this is my car." The car has suddenly become a symbol of his not needing that man, of no longer needing the man's ten bucks.

"What— . . . ?" The man is visibly bewildered, and this is exactly what Johnny has hoped for. "This is *your* car? But I thought— . . ."

Johnny gets into his car, starts it, drives away, engine

roaring. Instantly he feels very sorry for what he did to that man, but he thinks:

It wasn't that. That isn't why I've come back.

But he's still not sure.

And so, that evening, he went to Pershing Square.

He's dressed like this:

In a thin, pale-yellow silk shirt, perfectly tailored to show off his body (even his nipples are lightly outlined)— short sleeves rolled even higher, two buttons open at his neck; faded Levi's; and scuffed tan (not at all tawdry) boots.

Years ago, he had first arrived in Los Angeles by Greyhound bus. Less than half an hour later he was in Pershing Square. This time, it took him longer; but here he is again.

In the light, warm early evening, he sees it has all changed.

It is no longer the Pershing Square he knew. Vengefully, the enemy, known as "The City Authorities," had removed the benches and ledges that outlined the park, had cut the trees that sheltered the old and pensioned from the sun in the afternoon, and the young and indolent from the cops in the evening. Now it was a concrete skeleton. In two pitiful little squares surrounded by grass and no trees, a handful of the old denizens of a freer Pershing Square—preachers, winos—still gathered intrepidly, sitting crowded on the few benches situated in the glare of the sun and any hostile eye.

But looking more closely at the tight groups, Johnny spots a male hustler here, an interested man there, a potential queen; and he thinks: Soon it'll be the same. They could dig a hole to replace this square (and probably will, in time), and its usual inhabitants would fill it up. He doesn't know whether he thinks that with sadness or satisfaction. Perhaps with some of both.

And look at this: An obvious queen (a very, very, very effeminate youngman, all windmilling, busy hands) has strolled into the park—like the unafraid advance guard, or scout, of a soon-invading army—only temporarily vanquished. With "her" is a hoody-looking youngman, obviously a hustler. The queen spots Johnny, says something to the youngman, and saunters toward Johnny. Her youngman waits a few feet away.

She wastes no time.

"I'm having a party tonight, out on Vermont, baby," she says. "I'm issuing the invitations right now. And *you* are invited!" She points a reedy finger at Johnny. "My 'sisters' and their 'aunties' are furnishing lots and lots of liquor, and I'm rounding up the— . . ." She makes her voice deep, throaty, husky; she tilts her head, looks at him sideways, suggestively growls: ". . . —and I'm rounding up the *meat!*" Now she indicates the youngman waiting for her and says: "The number over there will drive you to the house when we have a carload."

Johnny can "see" the party (just as he could see the room the man who picked him up earlier would have taken him to). It will be in an enormous old house— once elegant—in a rapidly deteriorating neighborhood; the palmtrees will be yellow. The shades drawn, the lights dim. Queens in drag: makeup, high-heels, sequins . . . like colorful ghosts. And very-masculine-looking, very-masculine-acting youngmen picked up from the streets and bars and outside the U.S.O. and in the Greyhound bus-station will strike overtly "butch" poses on couches and chairs, as if completely indifferent to the scene ("I-came-here-for-free-drinks-and-food, man!"). And incongruous, well-dressed men, rich and not-so-rich voyeurs, will expect all kinds of orgiastic spectacles, which may or may not happen. . . . All permeated by the odor of marijuana. . . . And later a queen (drunk or high) will make a pass at the wrong youngman (drunk or high) in front of his friends (drunk or high), and he'll hit her to assert his "indifference"; and a queen will threaten to scratch another's eyes out for carrying on with the number she herself wants; someone will burst into the restroom at an inopportune time ("Excuse me, Miss Mae, I didn't know you were brushing your teeth!"); and one of the queens and/or the well-dressed men will discover a wristwatch gone, a wallet picked. . . .

"I'm waiting for an R.S.V.P., honey, which means: Will You Come?" says the queen.

"Sure, sure," Johnny says. "But not right now. I'll see you in the park. Later." He walks away.

The queen stays behind, evidently annoyed—but only for a short while: When Johnny is leaving Pershing Square a few minutes later, he sees her talking to two youngmen with close-cropped hair, obvious servicemen though in civilian clothes.

Something has saddened Johnny immensely.

Of course, he had known all along he would do it. (Is this why I came back to Los Angeles?) It was just a matter of determining when—although why he should hesitate, he didn't really know. When he did do it, he did it on impulse—right after leaving Pershing Square.

He saw a telephone booth, went in, searched his pockets
for the right change, couldn't find it, stepped out abruptly
before a well-dressed man walking by, and actually said,
"Buddy, could you spare a dime?" Quickly, the man gave
it to him and in evident disbelief remained staring at
Johnny, who is already back in the booth.

"Johnny *who?*" said the voice on the other end of
the line.

"Rio. Johnny Rio. Is this Tom?"

"Yes." Pause. "Where are you, Johnny?"

"In L.A.!" He said that as if the announcement were
a present.

Pause. "No!"

"Sure. I got here— . . . just now," Johnny lies.

"But *where* are you?"

"Downtown." And because of what that might imply,
he adds: "I got lost on the freeway."

"You have a car?"

"Sure! And I can be over in a few minutes."

"You know how to get here?" said Tom.

"Sure," said Johnny, feeling warm—and somewhat
cocky: like a person who knows he's loved.

He drives up Sunset Boulevard, perhaps a third of the
way toward Hollywood. How often—in the last months
before he left Los Angeles—had he ridden, walked, hitchhiked these same blocks!

He made me feel like a prince, he thinks.

Now he turns into one of those side streets that lead
into shady, crooked, peaceful lanes and hilly landscapes,
all heavily treed, into an old, attractive section of the
city: sturdy two-story houses perched on hills like fat satisfied wealthy ladies looking down on the newly arrived.

Tom's house. Johnny parks. Remembers:

I met him one night when I was hitchhiking on Wilshire, by Westlake Park. I had been in Hollywood earlier. The night was very hot. He told me later he had driven by me, had seen me, wanted to stop—but he was in the inside lane, other cars were in the outer. So he turned as soon as he could shift lanes—anxiously because he was afraid someone else would pick me up—but I was still there (only a few minutes had passed), and he offered me a ride.

Johnny had nowhere specific to go that night—which was no different from other nights—or days. Working only occasionally—once even three weeks in a row—but mostly not, he had become accustomed to diving daily into one of the many rivers of the city's life and letting it carry him along. So when Tom invited him to come to his home and take a swim in the pool, Johnny gladly accepted. Later Tom told him he had thought he was so young that that's why he didn't try to come on with him as they sat by the pool that evening, Johnny Rio in borrowed trunks much too large for him. Tom had thought Johnny was perhaps 18—which he wasn't; he was older.

Tom didn't come on with him until late that night, and this is how it happened: Johnny remained in trunks, Tom dressed; and they sat watching television. Then it was that Johnny reached out rashly for Tom's hand—sure of Tom's interest—and put it on his own—Johnny's—thigh. Tom did the rest, and Johnny lay back.

An architect then in his late 30's, Tom had intense dark eyes and a fine, intelligent face. He kept his body slender by swimming daily in the pool added incongruously to the proud old house.

From that first night, Tom made Johnny feel like a prince. Johnny saw a lot of him—but he saw others too. Thinking he did so only because of what those others gave him (so did Johnny), Tom was very generous with him—he took him to eat, gave him money to spend, bought him presents (including a handsome silver identification bracelet engraved with Johnny's name). One weekend, after Johnny had admitted liking filet mignon, they had it three times a day.

When Johnny, guarding his freedom, resisted moving in with him, Tom nevertheless set aside a room for him in his home: "This is your room, whenever you want it," he told him. He also paid Johnny's rent in the hotel downtown where he stayed. Tom even offered to send him to school so he could: "learn-a-trade" . . . not knowing that Johnny had finished high school, had made straight A's in math, and was much smarter than he sometimes pretended to be: often slurring words and using bad grammar in the required style of the street hustler.

In return, Tom asked nothing of him except that he let him make love to his body. Johnny let him: Tom licked every inch of Johnny's body, and Johnny came in his mouth—sometimes several times a day. On weekend mornings Tom would go into "Johnny's room" silently and wake him up by kissing his body lightly all over.

Still, Johnny kept seeing other people who gave him money.

Now it isn't that Johnny was insensitive to others' feelings. (In fact even in hustling he tried not to hurt anyone: If he mentioned money to someone who was affronted by being sized up as a payer—though Johnny didn't make this mistake often; he was usually instinc-

tively *positive* who'd pay—he'd try to right the situation
something like this: "Oh, gee, *mano*," using the hip
Mexican appellation, "I knew you weren't the paying
kind; I just mentioned it to you so you wouldn't waste
your time—and if I didn't really God's-truth need the
bread, I'd make it with you just for crazy.") What some
might call insensitivity was, rather, a condition arising
from the fact that Johnny's needs were so enormous: In
those Los Angeles years, he longed, craved, needed to be
admired, wanted, adored (and he was—abundantly); and
as the symbol of his sexual power he "chose" (or perhaps
it chose him) the act of men paying him to love his body
without his reciprocating.

Knowing or sensing or tolerating all this, Tom still
continued to treat him like a prince.

Finally, Johnny saw what may have been a vision of his
own corruption. Returning to his rented room one afternoon (to take a shower before meeting Tom for dinner)
—a ten-dollar bill crumpled in his pocket (given to him
earlier by someone he immediately forgot)—he looked in
the mirror to dazzle himself with his smile; and he saw,
instead, a depraved distortion of himself. He washed his
face, looked again in the mirror. Once again, he was the
Johnny he liked so much to look at.

Soon after that—three years ago—he returned to Laredo. That was on a gray Los Angeles morning before the
mist had lifted as much as it ever does. Johnny said so
long to Tom, explaining only that he was very confused.
(He didn't tell anyone else he was leaving. For those
others he was only a body.) He returned to Laredo by
Greyhound bus, just as he had left.

During the next few months, Tom telephoned him long-

distance very often—once five times in a single day. He
wrote him many letters. He sent him money (each month,
for more than a year), a subscription to a Los Angeles
newspaper, and many other presents. Johnny wrote him
back at least once a week. He told him how well he was
doing working for his father's brother; that he would
soon be moving into an apartment alone (he was staying
temporarily with his mother); he also told him that here
in his hometown he was keeping entirely to himself: which
was true.

After about a year, Tom's calls dwindled, then stopped;
the letters waned, they stopped. The money stopped too.

He made me feel like a prince, Johnny remembers. He
rings the bell of the two-story house and smiles: prepared
to be greeted.

"Hello, Johnny," says Tom, at the door.

"Hello, Tom."

"Come in."

Johnny walks through the door.

He sits on the couch in the living room; everything
here is as it was.

Tom sits on a low chair. "Well, what brings you back
to Los Angeles?" he asks.

"I don't know," Johnny says truthfully. "I'm trying to
find out."

"Well, maybe a drink will help?"

"No, thanks," says Johnny.

"And where have you been all these years?"

"In Laredo," says Johnny. "You know that. You used
to call me."

"Of course," says Tom. "You were staying with your

mother; then you moved out. And how is your mother?"

"Fine and dandy," says Johnny.

A long, long, long pause.

"And what do you do there, in Laredo?" asks Tom.

"I wrote you. My uncle. I've got an uncle there—my father's brother; he's finally got his business going big. I take care of his figures for him—inventory, stuff like that; I do it in the evening at home. That way, I keep away from people. I've wanted to be alone—till now. My uncle understood. And I was always good at numbers."

"Were you?" asks Tom.

"I've even saved money," Johnny says hurriedly, "and I just bought this crazy new car. It's got a wooden steering wheel, wooden paneling—and— . . . Well, you'll have to see it."

"I want to; it sounds nice," says Tom. His eyes are dark on Johnny when Johnny suddenly looks up from cupped hands. Tom quickly averts his glance.

Abruptly, Johnny stands up. "I've been weightlifting," he says. "On a split routine—that means I exercise different parts of my body on different days—and I never skip a session," he goes on nervously. "I've even quit smoking, and— . . ." Impulsively, he removes his shirt, revealing his chest, which he knows tapers impressively from broad shoulders to narrow waist. He flexes.

"My, you have got muscular," says Tom. "You used to be flat as a board."

"Yeah—but I'm still slender as a— . . ." He was about to say "tiger," which is what Tom used to call him when he was about to lick Johnny's body. ". . . —slender as a panther," he finished.

Tom has looked away.

Almost sheepishly Johnny puts his shirt on again; he even buttons the second button from the neck, which he usually leaves open.

"Can I see the room I used to stay in?"

Tom doesn't move at first, then he gets up. "Of course." They walk upstairs.

"It's completely different," says Johnny, looking at the room.

"Yes, I had the furniture changed—all of it. About— . . . about two years ago." Then he says: "A friend of mine — . . . He stays here sometimes."

"In this room?" Johnny asks.

"Yes."

"Oh," says Johnny.

They go downstairs.

"But you *are* all right?" asks Tom.

"Yes, oh, yes, sure, great!" Again, their eyes meet. Again, Tom looks away. "How long will you be staying?" he asks.

"Exactly ten days," Johnny answers quickly.

"That's nice," says Tom. "It isn't too hot yet; the weather's been good. You have a good tan already."

"Yes, I like the sun."

"I remember."

"I'd better go now," says Johnny.

Tom gets up quickly. "Well, it was fine to see you again."

They walk to the door.

Is there really someone else? Has he really turned off on me? Johnny wonders. Or (he glances at the possibility for the first time ever!) is it that I hurt him so bad before?

"Goodbye, Johnny," says Tom, a dark shadow against the door.

"Goodbye."

"Johnny," Tom calls, "good luck."

"Thanks," Johnny says. He walks to his new, shiny car —a symbol that he no longer needs other people's money.

He used to treat me like a fucking prince, Johnny remembers.

THREE

IT'S NOT YET 9:00.

He'll go to Main Street, find someone who'll want him a lot (perversely, he can't help thinking: maybe the man I walked away from this afternoon)—or go to a party; on weekends there are always many like the queen's he rejected.

He parks his car on Broadway. An enormous loneliness is choking him. And so: Will it all be the same? Just as it was before? he wonders. Those three years I was away —what have they meant then? Didn't I learn anything from the time I lived here? (Often he thought of the crowded incidents of those years as battles he survived.) Yes, I have; I know I've learned a lot.

He walks along Broadway, on his way to Main Street.

At the corner of 7th Street, a white-haired Negro woman with a face wrinkled like a raisin is prophesying the world's end—for tomorrow. Do or die, she's really calling it close, Johnny thinks, admiring her gambling spirit: Tomorrow, if she's wrong, she may be out of the preaching business; in fact, she'll be out either way! Curiously, she lacks passion. A black Bible open in one hand, the other hand raised, she's saying (not shouting it, not crying, not howling it)—just simply saying:

"We awll doomed—we awll go tomorrow."

She's pitifully failed to attract even a small gathering. People passing ignore her. (What if she turned out to be right? At the very moment of the eruption, the holocaust, the explosion, the judgment, would they say: "My God— the woman on the corner of 7th!—she was right!"?) Touched by her aloneness at this moment (how sad if she really believes it's going to happen tomorrow), Johnny stands and listens for a few moments. But the woman seems unaware of him, of anyone else.

"We awll doomed."

Johnny walks away.

Lights scurrying like electrified mice, a bright movie marquee proclaims that the theater is:

* O *
* P *
* E *
* N *

ALL NIGHT *** ALL NIGHT *** ALL NIGHT ***

Two technicolor hits. And Smoking In The Balcony. It's open all night, and there's a balcony. Johnny knows—

just as anyone who has hung out in gay bars knows—what that means. The hunting shadows in the dark . . . the frantic moving in and out of the toilet.

He buys a ticket.

But he doesn't go to the balcony. He sits under the dark dome of the theater on the lower floor.

On the screen a loony woman is offering to pray for everyone's soul. (Johnny thinks: We awll doomed, we awll doomed. He's trying to follow the movie, but his mind keeps slipping away like a fly; he forces his attention to return.) A man is getting beaten up severely. (Johnny's mind slides away again. The awareness that he's in an all-night theater with a large balcony is making him feel tense; almost, ironically, like when he was a kid and applied for a job as usher—and then impulsively turned it down.) A ball of fire is cascading down a hill toward what must be a used-car cemetery; the sound is very, very loud —as if the technicolor, being so bright, has burst into sound.

The balcony. So near.

Johnny tells himself insistently he doesn't want to go upstairs.

But already he's gotten up, already he's pushing the door to the lobby—and he pauses at the candy stand, buys an Almond Joy (pointing to it under the counter because he can't bring himself to say the campy name); but he knows all this is just a matter of marking time, because: already he's walking up the stairs. But he stops suddenly . . . pauses . . . descends—starts hurriedly to walk toward the exit, decides not to leave, and goes down the stairs toward the head instead.

Quite probably this theater once housed elaborate pro-

ductions—vaudeville, perhaps even opera. Its men's
lounge has all the tattered elegance of such a house—
carpets (large chunks missing; like an uncompleted jig-
saw puzzle), stuffed chairs (lopsided lumps where the coils
threaten to spring through), even a statue-lamp of a naked
woman (she's so old-fashioned-looking that she appears
curiously clothed). Beyond—the door open—is the fluo-
rescent-lighted restroom.

A man sitting smoking idly in the lounge stares at
Johnny as he walks by. Another man is making—probably
only pretending to make—a call in the phone booth; he
also looks at Johnny.

In the restroom, Johnny stands before the urinal; but he
can't pee.

Even before he hears footsteps, he knows that one of
the two men—or both—will soon be here. And here's one:
standing only one urinal away from him. In his anxiety
the man has even forgotten to pretend he's standing there
for any purpose other than to see Johnny's prick; he hasn't
even opened his fly in the charade of pissing. What he's
doing is staring down at Johnny's cock, Johnny can see, although he's not looking directly at the man; no, not at all,
is looking, instead, slightly up—to indicate what the man
probably already knows from just having seen the way he
swaggered past him, the way he stands there with his
shoulders so defiantly squared: that he has no interest in
him, that whatever interest exists is his in Johnny. Still
looking up, Johnny nevertheless allows his eyes to shift
slightly toward the side where the man is standing. He
sees the man looking down in abject fascination, licking
his lips.

Johnny still can't pee.

The man moves over to the urinal immediately next to him. Johnny can hear his own heart pumping—rather, two hearts, one pumping in each ear. . . . He has stood like this before, in toilets of bars and bus stations, of Pershing Square—luring interested men by shaking his cock before the urinal long after he was through—but only to entice, only preparatory to leaving and expecting to be followed, propositioned, paid—never consummating the implied contact in the restroom, however. But that was three years ago.

So long ago.

Emboldened by the fact that Johnny hasn't moved away, the man lets his hand fall, preparatory to touching Johnny's thigh. Next: He'll hold my prick—then a blowjob in a public head, Johnny thinks. At the precise moment when the man's tentative gesture would have become sure, Johnny withdraws before the man can touch him; he buttons his pants, hurries out of the head—past the other man, who had been standing by the door all along quietly watching.

"Why-don't-you-let-him-suck-you?" the second man says to Johnny; "I'll-watch-out-for-you."

Johnny dashes out of the theater.

Reflecting the city's brazen lights, the Cloud, shutting out the stars, is orange tonight.

By the motel pool. Sunbathing. Saturday morning.

In brief white trunks, his hands stretched over his head, toes pointed as if to offer even more of his body to the sun, Johnny lies on a beach chair. He has a mental picture of himself: the white of the trunks contrasting sharply with his dark, dark skin; and this picture nestles comfortably, warmly, in his mind.

Constructed about the pool and as if incidental to it (the pool must have come first; *then* they said, "Let's build a motel around it!"), large rooms with sliding glass doors as front walls are tiered in two white layers like a wedding cake, each line of units linked by a narrow, long terrace and a balustrade of imitation-Creole curled-iron grillwork. At the head of each stairway leading to the lower level, and at the foot of each, stand two statues facing each other happily: an Egyptian woman with a sash, and an Egyptian man with a loincloth. They hold torches which at night turn into orange electric lights, and they both look like movie extras in a De Mille epic. Stubby palmtrees guard the walks that lead across the grass (more like a carpet than anything produced by nature) toward the area of the pool, which is shaped like a four-leaf clover, its shallow "stem" evidently intended for children to wade in. About the pool are fringed peppermint umbrellas, white iron tables and chairs matching them—other chairs in flowery designs, still others like giant cups—others long and lazy. All Disney-contemporary.

Johnny is the only one by the pool right now—others apparently prefer the beach on the weekend. The sun is warm, almost hot.

Here and there, along the rooms, cleaning women dump bunched sheets into their carts, soon carrying away last night's secrets. A little boy of about five or six years sits on the grass away from the pool; he seems to be playing idly with something on the ground, perhaps a bug.

Tap . . . tap . . . tap.

Heels on the cement walk.

Johnny closes his eyes quickly.

Scraping of a chair being moved.

Shwooosh! A large table umbrella being opened.

Tinkling of ice in a glass. Someone is drinking, and that someone is not too far away from where Johnny is lying.

"Excuse me, do you have the time?"

Johnny opens his eyes and smiles (always ready to charm). He sees a youngwoman sitting only a few feet away from him under one of the enormous mushroom umbrellas. Squinting against the glare of the white sky reflected by the water, he looks at his watch. "Five minutes after 11."

"Thank you," she says in a velvety voice. She tinkles the ice in her glass, almost as if it were a signal for his attention. Holding the glass out for Johnny to see, "Breakfast," she says.

"Orange juice?" Johnny asks; he has remained propped on an elbow.

"Orange juice and . . ." she sniffs at the glass " . . . and vodka," she says. "It doesn't smell."

The little boy on the grass is looking intently at them, as if wondering what game *they're* playing.

Because she wears an enormous wide-brimmed hat (her hair tucked under a tight cap that's a part of the hat) and impenetrably black sunglasses like Batman's mask, Johnny can't really tell what her face looks like. He can, however, see her body; and it looks like this:

Quite tall: very long-limbed and perfectly proportioned. Like Johnny's, it's the color of dark honey. She wears a bikini—blue-and-white zebra-striped. High-heeled shoes support slender, well-curved legs and thighs which flare softly from her hips in the continuation of gentle parentheses. Johnny's eyes slide from the squeezed split between her breasts to the flat belly, to the part where her hips—rudely intercepted by the lower half of her bikini—begin to widen. A fine, velvety, all-but-invisible down of tiny blond hairs gleams below her navel on her oiled body—that portion not shaded by the umbrella or hat.

Johnny imagines the triangle under the zebra stripes. Would her pubic hair be blond?—those tiny hairs say so; they might be bleached by the sun though. He imagines her opening, just slightly swept with fine blond hairs.

He pictures his dark pubic hairs meshing with her blond ones.

But Johnny isn't a hunter; he's used to being hunted—and this is true even with women (part, again, of the "femaleness"). He may invite with smiles, with all his charm—and does; but the proposition must always be made by another. He could never, never allow anyone—male or female—the pleasure of feeling he wanted him/her enough to initiate the pursuit.

So he leans back on the lounge chair, closes his eyes, and waits for her to—hopes that she will—advance.

Now the question may occur: Does Johnny Rio consider himself heterosexual? He would answer the question like this, as if putting it to a jury to draw its own conclusion: First, I have never *desired* another man, I'm aroused only by what another man *does*—and not by *him*; second, I have not reciprocated sexually with another man—nor have I ever let a man come on with me other than with his mouth—and of course his hands—on my body; and third, I've done it for money. . . . Johnny himself will agree that all that is part of the Myth of the Streets (primarily the myth of male hustlers): a curious myth which says that a man may go with other men, over and over—especially to make money—and with as many as he wants—and still be "straight" (that is, heterosexual) as long as he doesn't reciprocate sexually. Whether all that is true or not—self-knowledge not being one of Johnny's characteristics, he's content to leave the Myth intact.

Now Johnny would probably hesitate to admit this; he might even exaggerate: But the fact is that he's been with only a handful of women (though many more have wanted him)—compared to large numbers of men.

Not counting the ordinary child-sex experiences with girls, he has been with five—though he'd quickly point out: "With most I made it more than just once though."

First, there was the pretty blonde in high school (the one who said she liked to watch him as he walked away because he walked so sexy).

Second, there was the high-school teacher in her 20's, very highstrung, who asked him to come up to her hotel room to discuss his grades. She greeted him in a nightgown.

Third, there was the girl he met when he was in the army and stationed at Fort Sam Houston in San Antonio. Again. she was blond, and she had a new car; and it excited her to think that her family would be very angry if they knew she was dating a soldier who was only a private.

Fourth, there was the strange, terrified, lonely, lovely girl he met in Los Angeles. Later, she turned into a junkie and a prostitute and her pimp was a woman.

Fifth, there was a mad married woman of 30 or so whom he met in, of all places, a homosexual bar in Hollywood, when she swept in by mistake, all covered with mink, and sat next to him at the bar, thinking (Johnny is sure of this): "How great!—all men and I'm the only woman!"

The first one, he made it with only once.

The second one, twice—the two semesters she was his teacher.

The third, only three times; she was too busy wanting to be seen by her parents.

The fourth— . . . Johnny prefers not to count.

And the fifth, the red-haired married woman, he made it with at least seven times for slightly under two weeks— the time that remained of her California visit from Washington, where, she said, she was married to: An Important Man. (It amused Johnny that, being a Southerner, she pronounced "important" as "im-POH-tent"—exactly the way she would have pronounced "impotent.")

And, in those years back again in Laredo—Away—there have been neither men nor women. Because, Johnny would explain, I *had* to be alone—completely and away from sex!

"Hey!"

Johnny opens his eyes lazily, as if he's been dozing.

The youngwoman sitting near him pushes her giant hat back. With one shake of her head, she unfurls her shoulder-length blond hair, which curves swiftly into a tilt at the ends. As if to show Johnny Rio what her face looks like, she removes her sunglasses too—slowly and dramatically. Still, the shadow of the umbrella hides her somewhat, so that the only real parts of her face appear to be the unreal ones—the ones she's painted on: the fuchsia mouth, the thick long eyelashes, the blue lids, the arched eyebrows.

"Did you call me?" Johnny asks her, sure of her interest.

"Yes. . . . Sip?" she asks him, extending the glass of orange juice and vodka to him.

Johnny stands up—his turn to exhibit himself; stands before her, looking down between her full breasts, like navel oranges. He has a fantasy: his prick between her breasts while she presses them with her hands. He's so carried away by the image that he hasn't yet looked at her face, which is turned up to him as if for inspection. Now he sees it. Her face matches her body; she's a blond beauty.

He takes the glass, swallows from it, returns it to her. Her gestures slow and deliberate for him to perceive and interpret, she rotates the returned glass 180 degrees in her hand so that she will be drinking from the place his lips touched. Preparatory to drinking, she runs her tongue along the rim of the glass, looking up at him, smiling a strange-hybrid smile that is innocent and enticing.

Almost with apprehension, Johnny—who feels very protective toward children—looks around for the little kid who's been playing on the grass. The kid is looking at Johnny and the youngwoman quizzically. Playfully, Johnny cocks his finger at him in imitation of a gun and "shoots": "Bang-bang!" But the kid didn't "shoot" him back nor play dead, didn't even seem to want to be involved in a game. Sad kid, Johnny Rio thinks.

"My name is Tina," the youngwoman says, drawing his attention back to her. "What's yours?"

"Johnny Rio," says Johnny.

"You're dripping wet, Johnny Rio," says Tina.

"I haven't even been in the water," he says, knowing she knows it. Intrigued by her, he wants to make it; he also knows that for it to happen she must take the initiative, and she's doing it already:

"You're perspiring though," she says. "Cummere." He sits on a chair, leans toward her, and she wipes his chest lovingly with her pink towel. She does it slowly, rubbing the towel over his shoulders, looking straight into his eyes. Her lips have the pout of a child's—but he can't determine her age; she could be 19, she could be 30. She's too tanned, too made up to tell. "Betterrr?" she purrs.

"Better," he says, feeling good. Yes, he wants to screw her; wants to very, very much—because— . . . Well, because, after so long, he wants sex—and, yes, with a woman; and because she's really gorgeous and has indicated she'll do all kinds of crazy things in bed; and because— . . . because— . . . Because he wants to erase— . . . something . . . something about last night. To cancel it. To put it away finally.

As if understanding that whatever will happen must be initiated by her (or must it be like this for her always; is this *her* scene?), Tina says bluntly, "Want to see my— . . ." suggestively, sleepily, her heavy eyelashes lid her blue eyes ". . . —my room?" she finishes.

"Crazy," says Johnny, *his* heavy eyelashes lidding *his* eyes sleepily.

"Cuhrrrrrazy, baby," she growls, huskily; wiggling her butt as if she's being pleasantly goosed. She gets up. Actually, she hardly reaches Johnny's ear—despite the high heels. She looks now like a tiny Amazon. "Cummon," she says, playfully pinching a coiled cluster of hair on the lower part of his stomach.

He follows her toward her room.

On the way he notices the lonesome kid looking down forlornly at the grass. As they pass him, he looks up at them. A cute kid. Sandy hair. Blue, blue eyes. But sad.

At her room, which is on the ground level, Tina slides the glass door open.

Johnny notices the DO NOT DISTURB sign on the door. Was it there from last night? Or had she hung it up this morning, knowing he would come here with her—that he would or someone else would?

I won't let that turn me off, Johnny thinks. Already, his trunks are tightening at the crotch.

As in every other motel of this kind, the rooms are very much the same. This one has a large bed, the table lamps with shades like extravagant hats, other lights hidden somewhere about the curve of the ceiling, the fake rubber plants, the water-color prints, the small brown-enamel refrigerator convenient for drinks, the small bar, and the three stools standing on ostrich legs.

Johnny Rio sits on a stool at the bar while Tina gets a tray of ice cubes from the refrigerator. She moves sensually; each movement ends in a pose. She reminds Johnny of one of the stars in the movies on Main Street, the kind in which all the girl does is remove her clothes while she:

Pouts.

Sits.

Stands up.

Lies down.

"I bet you're an actor," Tina says.

That turns Johnny off badly. He's often asked that, and it annoys him, associating a certain prettiness with actors. "No," he says curtly.

"Sorrreee," she says, realizing he's offended. "I only meant because you're so goodlooking . . . and I like only goodlooking men . . . Johnny Rio," she explains, hugging his name.

That pleases him, and he mellows.

"Same?" she's asking him, indicating the drink.

"Uh-huh," he nods.

"I love vodka for breakfast," she says.

"*I* had waffles and sausages," Johnny ribs her rigid pose of sophistication.

"Ah used tuh hayve them on th' fawm." She assumes a hickish accent.

"I *knew* you were a farm girl!" Johnny came back.

She wrinkles her nose cutely at him—forgiving him the dig—brings him the drink (having filled hers), slides onto the stool next to him. She moves her bare leg, brushing his. Both face ahead. Then, as if on cue, they swing in a quarter arc, and their legs lock like two sets of prongs.

But, now, neither advances further—as if waiting to establish, by the next move, on whose terms who will have whom. Knowing this, Johnny forces her to act; like this: He jumps off the stool, breaking the contact; and—perversely—he moves away from her in deliberate indifference, to the sliding door, even unlatching it as if to walk out unless she moves quickly.

And she does: She floats toward the door to him. "Silly," she says silkily, standing very close to him. "Sill-leee." She's barely inches away from him, looking up at him. "Close the door," she says.

"Please?" he insists, perversity flaming at the prospect of making her beg.

"*Please*," she says, adding a heavy, suggestive emphasis to the word.

He slides the door.

Fingernails long and red, like weapons already bloodied in other battles, she holds his shoulders.

On tiptoes, she brings her mouth to his; their mouths are barely touching, lips tingling at the promised contact, cherishing the promise before the act. He embraces her, his hands on her hips; but he's waiting for her to move first.

And she does. She rolls his trunks down, slowly, her hands inching them down over his hips, first in back, then in front—just enough to free his cock. Now he does the same to the lower part of her bikini—just to the very point where the opening between her legs begins to show. He leans back deliberately, and he sees that her hair is indeed blond there—delicate and blond, just a puff. She holds his hardening prick lightly in her hands, rubbing it, then drawing it slowly into her—while he puts his hands on her buttocks, which are firm and tight; pulling her body to his.

The glass door slides open.

The little boy who loitered outside stands there watching them. Nervously, hurriedly, he says, "I thought you were through, momma."

Desire smashes inside Johnny like glass on tile. He raises his trunks, his cock quickly limp.

Adjusting her clothes, Tina yells at the child: "Get the screw out of here, you little bastard! Haven't I told you— . . . ? Haven't I?"

Visibly trembling, the little boy says, "I thought you were through, momma; you said— . . ."

"TO STAY THE HELL OUT!" the woman shrieked. "And I've told you to call me Tina. *Tina! Tee-nuh!* I've told you that a hundred times!"

She reaches out to slap him, but he rushes out before she can touch him. Instead, her hand slams against a table. "Ouch!" she yells. "I broke my nail! Look what he made me do! I broke my nail!" She sticks the wounded finger in her mouth as if it were a placating lollipop.

Johnny merely looks at her.

"Damn crazy kid," she says, trying to smile now, evidently intending to resume where they were interrupted. "I told him to stay out until I called him. I sent him out earlier—when I saw you outside. I've told him to act like he doesn't know me when I'm with a guy. He's done it before. Sometimes just beats on the door. . . . Why didn't you latch it again? . . . Crazy kid. I should put him in a home, but I guess I love him too much." She said that easily. "He's ruined more— . . . Crazy kid! Sometimes I think I ought to take him to a psychiatrist," she said in a rough, scratchy voice. "I should've let his old man keep him. But I guess I love the kid too much," she repeated, again easily. "But we're wasting precious time, Johnny Rio, baby." Once again her voice is furry. "Checkout time's at noon, and there's a lot of things to be . . . done." Again she places her hands on his shoulders.

Johnny suddenly imagines the kid 15 years, say, from now: sitting dejectedly in one of the many gay bars in Hollywood (as dejectedly as he sat on the grass earlier), hating women, searching for men.

He looks down at the woman he would have entered a few minutes ago. Her face is brutal.

"Cummon, Johnny Rio," she says, grinding against him.

He moves away from her, her hands drop suddenly to her sides. He walks out.

The kid is sitting desolately on the grass.

"Are you through with Tina now, sir?" he asks Johnny.

FOUR

JOHNNY HAS GHOSTS TO PURSUE.

Years ago, when he hitchhiked to Santa Monica from downtown Los Angeles, he'd ask whoever gave him a ride to let him off as close as possible to where Wilshire runs into the welcoming arms of a statue of Saint Monica on the strip of gaily flowered park, where old people sit on benches under the benign attention of solicitously hovering palmtrees.

From there Johnny would walk across the bridge to the honky-tonk stretch of the pier. Calliope music (tunes squeezed out like smoke signals) floated in heavy puffs from the arcade. He would pass the curtained box where the gypsy woman told fortunes. Always tempted to go in,

54

once he did—and dashed out quickly when her voice called through the flowered curtain, "Come in, come in, don't stand there waiting for fate, which is: *rushing!*" . . . After walking the pier, he'd retrace his steps, heading toward the beach.

The beach then seemed almost deliberately divided into fraternal, protective groups. The first few laps were taken over by heavily muscled men who got together ostensibly to work out with weights under the sun; clearly, though, they came to pose for each other (oiled gleaming bodies assuming poses the body rejects) and for the people who gathered, sometimes derisively, sometimes admiringly, as at a sideshow. From there, followed a kind of limbo of children, families, youngmen and women on the beach. Thinning out, they gave way to another distinct group: brown pulpy-skinned men and women drenched in perspiration, wearing loose trunks and bathing suits, perpetually playing a game in which a ball is struck with small paddles back and forth across a net. Beyond the private wire-enclosed courts, another limbo, and then a pocket of high-school and early-college students, many surfers, separated by a further limbo from the "gay" part of the beach.

There, inevitably, Johnny would sit on the concrete ledge or lie on the sand or go to the male-bar or the hamburger stand—until someone spoke to him. Later, if he was still around or had made it near enough to come back—he'd walk through Pacific Ocean Park with all its carnival attractions and make-believe juxtaposed with the row of shabby bars catering to old sailors, arms such a tangle of tattoos they look like blue-and-red maps . . . past the blond mousy children roaming in tribes . . . past

Lawrence Welk playing for The Folks; and Johnny would move on to Venice West, to the bar which attracted exiles of every breed: dikes, queens, hustlers, "heads," even famous movie stars.

It became a ritual for him—from Wilshire to Venice West—until, one summer, he moved into a fantastic old house a block or so from the beach. One of those flimsy old wooden two-story buildings that give the impression of actually swaying (a bony porch nervously attempting to "anchor" it to the sandy, tentative ground), it sheltered a squadron of vagrant youngmen.

You didn't check in, you didn't ask for a room, you merely moved in. The mad old queen who owned the building and lived in it would look in on each new "occupant"; if he was "cute and butch," he could stay—but she never made a pass at anyone. Its occupants changed so often you hardly knew who was living there at any particular time. There were hustlers, beach idlers, two or three bodybuilders. It was referred to as "the place" by its inhabitants. Although rent was cursorily mentioned from time to time by the queen ("Every boy should help his mother"), no one took it seriously; and no one ever paid. A skinny, wonderful, unbelievably swishy old man— who wore false eyelashes and a hat laden with artificial fruit—the queen had apparently said fuck it, opened all the rooms of her house, and left them open for the "cute and butch."

Periodically, something would set her off—a careless remark perhaps—and she'd threaten loudly: "Unless she starts getting more respect from the tenants around here, your mother's *really* gonna start collecting rent!" Nobody believed her; they just kept away from her during her sulking times ("her periods"). After that, she'd quickly make up by announcing a house dinner for "the guests"; that meant she'd toil for hours like a witch over a cauldron of stew—"for my boys so they can go out, strong, healthy, well-fed, and make money to help their dear mothers."

Today, parking his car in a lot a few blocks away, Johnny will walk from Wilshire to Venice West: in a tribute to the Past.

As soon as he reaches the narrow park and heads for the familiar bridge, he removes his shirt. He pulls his Levi's very low, slung on his narrow hips.

Just like he used to.

But the gypsy woman on the pier is no longer there. The curtained box is sealed, boards crisscrossed in stark X's. (Did she one day see her own future, dark, and just give up?) The calliope is silent.

He walks on the beach.

Where muscle beach had been, there is now a playground. Here and there some of the bodybuilders hang on intrepidly—not unlike the old-time denizens of Pershing Square in their raped park. True, even before he left, there were hints of the demise of this part of the beach. A scandal: Three white weightlifters were discovered shacked up with two Negro girls, aged 12 and 13. And something else: A house nearby, where bodybuilders and stray girls gathered, turned out to be a voyeurs' delight, with spyholes in the walls. . . . And so the omnipresent enemy known as the City Authorities had waged a concerted drive To Rid The Beach Of Undesirables.

Walking on, he sees that the members' courts are still there. The same brown-leathery types feverishly beating the ball back and forth, back and forth.

And in tight clusters—unchanged—are the frozen-blond teenage girls in bikinis; the yellow-colored, long-haired young boys like wet birds. Surfing boards propped against a wall like defiant shields.

Now Johnny is on what had been the gay section of the beach. The bar and the hamburger stand are gone. Not even a trace of them—not even an outline on the ground. There is a concrete parking lot instead; to accommodate the cars, they've even narrowed the beach. Again like the denizens of Pershing Square and the bodybuilders of muscle beach, there are about a dozen homosexuals (scattered among the families and the children) still clinging tenaciously to their part of the beach.

And so the City Authorities haven't really won. The original squatters will return. Already the advance guard is restaking the territory. In the meantime, where are all the others? The people who laughed so loudly, so euphorically? Ghosts drowned in Johnny's memory, who nevertheless wail to be remembered. People and places existing now like marks erased from paper. Where are they now?

Somewhere.

Another beach.

They'll come back.

Johnny moves on.

Even Pacific Ocean Park has felt the nearly fatal blow of the City Authorities. Desolate and sad. Like an abandoned movie set after the movie is completed. You have the feeling that if you go behind the restaurants and shops —most of them closed—you'll find stilts supporting cardboard buildings.

The scrimmed sky augments the feeling of desolation. Bewildered as if after a bitter battle that left few survivors, some of the old sailors and beach types still hang around; but their bars—the beat-up bars without doors, bars with only three walls—have disappeared. The cheap fried-shrimp and hot-dog counters are closed.

Perhaps it's only because it's still early in the season, Johnny thinks. Perhaps in a few weeks— . . .

But no.

In the distance, beyond the beach, Johnny sees the enemy's weapon—the hideous machines that have already swallowed, digested, and thrust out as dust so many familiar places. It's Saturday, and even the machines rest now; but they sit there like monstrous dinosaurs, heads bent but ready to resume their fatal devastation, giant claws ready to scoop up the earth. Jagged outlines of demolished buildings create gutted craters. That portion of the city—a part of Santa Monica, a part of Venice West— looks as though it had been ravaged by bombs. Without searching it out, Johnny knows the building he lived in has been scooped up and turned to dust. (Where is the mad wonderful old queen with the fake eyelashes and the hat like a basket of fruit?)

It will all be replaced with slick glassed rectangular "luxury" apartments, lined up uniformly like giants defying the ocean.

Johnny walks on.

The dark old Jews of Venice West still cling to their places on the rococo benches that face the row (still mostly there) of stores and kosher delicatessens. But Johnny can imagine the machines, now idle but waiting, scooping them up too, hauling those old people away—still sitting on their benches.

Closed . . . the large building with thick columns, where

messianic bearded men read fiery poems to the accompaniment of bongos.

Turning away, Johnny looks futilely for the bar where he spent so many, many afternoons and nights. It doesn't exist any more. Was it there?—where a new crackerbox building two short stories high has gone up? (Rooms identical, all glassed facing the ocean—the building is an insidious hint of what the whole beach will look like in a few years—if the City Authorities win the war.) . . . No, there's not even a hint of where the bar was. (The laughter has been buried in the ocean; the wind wailed at its wake.)

Suddenly Johnny wishes he'd parked nearby, so he could get in his car and leave this sad cemetery of memories. He wishes that instead of coming to the beach he had gone to see a writer friend who lives nearby in the canyon. He feels like someone who goes to church for a wedding and finds a funeral.

But wait! Another encouraging sign. Out there on the pier—and milling about the walk in their smiling groups: the beautiful saintly-looking longhaired girls and bearded youngmen, decorated with beads and flowers and rainbow ponchos: lovely barefooted hippies, flower children. Soon they may help bring back a wild, loving sanity to the beach —if the Enemy doesn't crush them.

Hey, Johnny! Hey, kid! Hey, man!" A man in yellow trunks is advancing toward him.

Although he doesn't recognize him, Johnny waves at him. "Hiyah, *mano!*" he calls.

In a few seconds, the youngman is facing Johnny on the walk. About 28 years old, his hair blond and curly, he's as tall as Johnny; but he looks much, much shorter

because of his excessive muscles. His body, once undoubt-
edly goodlooking, is now so vastly distorted by the bulging
pectorals and deltoids that he looks inflated. Broad as they
are, his shoulders nevertheless sag under the weight of
enormous biceps and forearms—arms held curved as if he
were carrying two heavy buckets. Each hugely muscled
leg is a parody of a Mae-West doll. All this makes his
head look smaller than it should be. He has a handsome
face—white teeth gleam starkly out of the dark tan; but
his exaggerated body, calling shocked attention to itself,
all but obscures the good looks.

"Where ya been, kid?" he's asking Johnny, who still can't
place him definitely. "Donya recognize your old buddy
Danny?" He stands very straight, spreading his "lats" like
batwings. "You don't remember? From 'the place'? You
usedta live there too, remember?"

At last Johnny remembers him. Much bigger now, he's
one of the two or three bodybuilders who stayed at the
mad-queen's house: always flexing their biceps, adopting
a weird pose (a leg out and twisted, the toes pointed) to
show off their thighs. Johnny remembers: Danny was always putting his arm about him warmly, always affection-
ately calling him "kid." But they hadn't been "buddies."
Johnny has never been "buddies" with anyone.

"Oh, yeah, sure, *mano*, sure; I remember," Johnny says,
glad to see someone from those earlier years.

"Gee, man, you sure look great!" Danny says, looking
Johnny up and down. "You've got nice and husky—used
to be kinda skinny, dinya? I bet you been workin out!"
he says enthusiastically.

"Yeah, yeah, man," Johnny says, "but just to keep in
shape—you know." He's embarrassed Danny may think

he wants grotesque muscles like his. Abruptly silent, Danny is probably waiting for Johnny to comment on his appearance. So Johnny says: "You've gotten lots bigger; that's why I didn't recognize you at first."

Danny evidently takes that as a compliment. "Thirty pounds heavier!" he announces. "I got a 17½-inch neck now!" He strains it so that it flares from his ears toward his shoulders in a squat trapezoid.

Obviously, he wants to impress Johnny; but Johnny can't think of anything tactful to remark. "Gee," is all he can bring himself to say. Danny shouldn't be encouraged to work for an 18½-inch neck!

"Hey, cummon, kid, let's take a walk along the beach," Danny says eagerly. "I wanna show you where the guys work out now."

The prospect doesn't excite Johnny; but the thought of walking back alone now, with the memories that will be opened by each desolate strip of beach, pushes him to agree.

"I always used to look at you and think, That kid's got a real good frame on him—slender but real good," Danny is saying as they walk along; he's also twisting each wrist alternately, exercising his forearms. "Thirty more pounds and you'd really have a body and a half!" He takes a deep breath, his chest rolls out. "Yeah, just 30 more pounds—that's all you'd need—and a good six-day-a-week lifting routine with heavy weights," he proselytizes.

Johnny imagines himself 30 pounds heavier: the slender sensuality coated over, the lean sexiness smothered, the panther grace turned bearish. Ugh, he thinks. "I don't think I'd like to gain all that weight," he says tactfully.

Danny unflexes, as if Johnny's words have punctured

the bulky flesh. "Well, yeah," he says dejectedly, "I guess maybe you're right. Some people should carry a leaner body."

"Yeah," says Johnny Rio, sorry if he's hurt Danny.

A girl is walking toward them. She's not particularly pretty; in fact, Johnny would say she's something of a mess; but Danny whoops: "Wow! Ain't she sweet? Shake it! Wow!" He makes a complete turn, whistling after her.

Slightly embarrassed, Johnny remains silent.

A stretch of beach ahead, Danny announces excitedly: "Here's the new queer beach, man!"

Yes, definitely this will soon become an exclusively "gay" section, Johnny thinks. Groups of men, groups of women cluster tightly on the sand, staring at everyone who arrives. Instinctively Johnny looks to the side. Yes, already there's a bar nearby.

"I wonder if she's a lez," Danny is saying. He's looking at a blond youngwoman lying alone several feet away. "She sure looks nice; but you never can tell, man—some queers look just like us." He's still ogling the girl as Johnny moves ahead.

"Queers," says Danny, catching up. "They hang out a lot where the guys work out. See that one over there? He's just crazy about guys with big muscles. He hangs around always asking everyone what exercise is good for this or that, but you never see him touch a weight—no sir!"

Johnny sees a very skinny man staring at them, the man Danny pointed out. Johnny is, of course, convinced the man is looking at him, not at Danny.

"Then there's this other one," Danny is going on compulsively. "He talked to me the other day, wanted to take pictures of me—that's all. Naked, you know. He'd pay, of course. . . . Queers," he says as if it's all beyond his comprehension. "He asked me did I have a buddy; he'd take duos—you know, two guys. Queers like that. I got his number at the pad. I told him maybe. You know—so what? Just stand there, get paid. He might ask us to make out like we're wrestling—but so what? *Guys* wrestle. Doesn't mean nothing. So I said yeah I'd keep it in mind. Say— . . ."

Johnny deliberately changes the subject quickly. "Everything sure has changed around here," he says.

Danny merely says yeah and goes on doggedly: "Lots of the guys here, they go for the three-B's scene—you know, blowjob, bed, breakfast. Most of the guys in that weird house—where you and me stayed that summer—that's how they made out." He said that as if he had just found it out. Maybe he's sounding Johnny out about his scene.

Johnny says nothing.

"But those fruits, man, I wouldn't lettem touch me. I don't have to. I'm doing real good in the movies. Bit parts—you know, gladiator pictures, stuff like that. And this Italian director—he might take me to Italy to make a flick there. Say, maybe you saw me in *Bloodsuckers of the Moon versus the Crabmen of the Red Sea?* A muscle-science-fiction-horror movie about the son of Hercules? With Rage Storm? (He's a muscle gay—I mean guy.) Did you see me in it?"

"Yeah, yeah," Johnny lies. "I did see it, *mano!* Jeez, you were great!"

"Been making good bread in the movies," Danny says proudly. "And I got a real swell pad. Right now, though, I'm on unemployment. In this weather, who wants to do anything but be in the sun?"

"Right," says Johnny absently, drenched in memories of the beach.

"You know, it must be something about me that attracts the fruits," Danny is returning relentlessly to the same subject. "I bet you attract 'em, too, kid, goodlooking like you are. Anyway, I was staying at the Y once, and this guy kept following me in the showers, wanting to cop my joint. Finally, I said, 'Look, fag, I got nuthin against you; what you do is your own damn business; but I saw you in the showers on the third floor just a while ago, and here you are on this floor— . . .'" He caught himself too late. "See," he tried to explain hastily, "the reason I was in the showers on *both* floors is that this guy had been bugging me; so I went to another floor."

Johnny says nothing, wanting to make him believe he didn't notice.

They've reached the place the musclemen have taken over. Perhaps half a dozen are working out on a platform, appropriately like a small stage. About it on a square of grass another half dozen or more idle about. Usually quite short, they seem to want to compensate for their lack of vertical dimension by growing horizontally. There are three youngwomen milling about in bikinis; they resemble big warm-water doll-bottles: all hips and bust and ridiculously tiny waists. Both men and women are like a distinct, incestuous species. Like most of the men—who would be handsome—the women would be pretty if their bodies, like the men's, were not literally "stacked"—part by part developed with no visible relation to the other.

An enormous-chested man on an exercise bench presses a bar heavily loaded with discs. Another stands behind him, almost over his head—to "spot" him if the one pressing can't complete the lift. On another bench a youngman is doing situps rapidly, while his partner sits on the lower part of his body straddling him—in order to enable the one on the bench to perform the waist movement strictly. Another man is doing "donkey raises"—for the calves: Leaning with his hands on the edge of the platform, he rises on his toes; another man sits on the buttocks of the one exercising—in order to add weight and resistance to the movement.

When you first come on it, the spectacle is startling: Each couple—in brief trunks—appears to be performing a distinctly recognizable sex act.

One of the men on the grass has been lifting a woman; she holds her body prone while he presses her overhead, twirls her around in adagio movements. Catching sight of Danny and Johnny, he dumps her unceremoniously on the grass. He calls out: "Oooeee, there's my one-and-only favorite, Danny-boy. Howya, sweetheart?" Although the words are clearly a parody of "gay" jargon, they're spoken in a deep, masculine tone, which is intended to make it All Right. Others are now waving and calling endearments to Danny. The man who was lifting the woman comes up to him. Bored, the woman lies face down on the grass.

"Hiya," Danny says to the man, introducing Johnny. The man's muscles are like armor plates pasted on his body. He wears an imitation leopard-skin bikini. Realizing that this man is quite obviously appraising him, Johnny feels proud of his own shirtless, tightly muscled body. Danny and the man begin talking about the relative merits of "frog kicks" for the "abs" as opposed to regular situps—which may or may not actually make the waist wider by enlarging the obliques. Danny says yeah, man; the other says no, man.

Turning his back on the whole scene—deciding to say so long to Danny and walk away—Johnny looks toward the walk; and he spots a thin, wispy, very swishy young queen about half a block away. "She's" looking bewilderedly about her, evidently "lost"; probably trying to find the part of the beach she's heard has turned gay.

As if realizing that Johnny is about to split from him, Danny breaks his conversation off abruptly. "Cummon, kid," he says. "Let's sit over here."

As they're moving to a bench nearby, one of the men in the exercising arena calls out to Danny, "Blow us a great big goodbye kiss, beautiful." The faggy words, the determinedly masculine tone—the latter again meant to obviate the former and render it acceptable.

"Say," Danny says suddenly to Johnny as if it just occurred to him, "why don't you work out with me this afternoon, kid?" His eyes are fixed on Johnny's almost imploringly. "There's a gym downstairs where I live— it's got pulleys, racks, everything. You got a great build now, and you gotta keep it that way. But you need a partner, everybody does."

Johnny imagines the scene: He'd want me to sit on his butt while he does "donkey raises" like that guy on the beach . . . for his calves. I'd "spot" him on the bench press, standing over his face . . . for his chest, triceps, and deltoids. I'd sit on his legs to keep his movements strict . . . for his abdominals. And then he'd want to do all that for me. And we'd rub each other down afterwards, all sweaty and breathless. Thanks a lot.

Before he can answer, a great tide of hooting, catcalling, and whistling is coming from behind them. Without yet looking, Johnny knows that the musclemen have caught sight of the young "lost" queen.

And so they have: There she is, trying to ignore them, dredging up all her dignity, her face set, fixed straight ahead. She's very meek, Johnny can tell. Another queen, more brazen, would have put them all down in an instant with something like: "Well, look at all the topless lesbians"; or: "Fuck you in the ears, muscle-ladies"—and she would have dashed—skipped—merrily away. But not this poor fluttery creature; she's too young, too inexperienced, probably wearing eye makeup (very lightly) for the first time.

Noticing that Danny has joined in the derisive whistling, Johnny feels a twist of anger.

Now that the queen has passed and the nasty ritual hooting has stopped, "Wotdayasay, man?" Danny is asking Johnny. "Wanna go work out?"

Johnny sees the queen, safely past the mocking group, pause to mop her forehead; he hopes she noticed he didn't join in the derision.

"No, thanks," Johnny tells Danny. "I'm real tired right now. And I'm used to working out alone. I think I'll just go lay down on the beach a while."

"Swell!" says Danny imperturbably. "I'll go with you. Wanna go to my place and I'll lend you some trunks?"

"No, thanks," Johnny declines again.

They begin to walk back toward Santa Monica.

When they've reached the soon-to-turn-gay part of Venice West, Johnny says, "I think I'll stay here." A few feet away the lost queen is now sitting on the sand, trying to compose herself.

"Man," says Danny, "this is the *queer* beach."

"I know," says Johnny.

Bewildered, Danny insists: "Ya sure you wouldn't rather come work out with me?" He looks so helpless and pitiful standing there, with that body exercised way out of control; so isolated by it: doomed to the coterie of his "fans" at Mr. So-and-So shows, and to his "buddies": to those who will adore his very grotesquerie: doomed always to surrogate sex.

"I'm sure, Danny," Johnny Rio says, with kindness; and he is very, very sure.

Already, the clusters of men on the beach have noticed them, are looking on interestedly.

"Okay, then," Danny says sadly. "Seeya around. Be cool, kid."

"You, too, *mano,* you be cool, too," Johnny says.

Danny walks away, flexing his "lats."

Johnny moves toward where the "lost" queen is sitting.

"Hi, honey," Johnny says to her. He winks at her.

"Huh-*eye!*" she drools at Johnny; she's entirely composed.

Now Johnny Rio is not coming on with this queen— although he spoke to her and winked. The fact is that even the Myth of the Streets allows a "butch number" to flirt with a queen—as long as he leaves the ultimate sexual pursuit to her. Beyond that, Johnny did what he did for the same reason he stopped last night to hear the Negro woman preaching: merely because she was so alone, because he wanted to make her feel better.

Seeing Johnny already moving away from her, the queen calls out, "Why don't you stick around?"

"Some other time," Johnny says; "I gotta be somewhere else soon, and I'm late. Another time."

"When*ever* you say, doll," she says. (Oh, Mary, she'll tell her "sisters," I'll simply *die* all my life thinking of that living *dream* on the beach—the sexy number who *saved* me from those muscle queens!)

At least she's honest about what she is, Johnny thinks suddenly.

And he thinks: Poor Danny, poor guy. Jesus, have I ever sounded like that? Don't ever let me!

A harsh, unexpected glimpse of The Myth makes Johnny force himself to stop thinking at that point.

Dark, dark like a gypsy, with long straight black hair and yellowish eyes that jump out at him from the smooth, brown-tanned face, a gorgeous young sea witch with a turned-up nose is bending to retrieve a beach ball that rolled toward the bench on whose back Johnny sits moodily on one of the limbo-stretches of beach. "Hi!" she says.

"Hi!" Johnny answers.

She moves away from him, wiggling her tiny cute butt, lovingly emphasized by a series of red-polka-dotted ruffles on the lower part of her bathingsuit. Glancing back twice, she joins a group of three young men and two other girls. They're all tanned and goodlooking, all 18 or 19 or in their early 20's. A guitar on the sand near them; a transistor radio turned up—rocking music raiding the air.

Johnny watches the girl closely.

Her back is to him for the first few moments as she plays with the others thrusting the ball back and forth—but not in a real game. Too cool for that, too hip, they're using the ball simply to localize their restless movements. Slowly, the girl is maneuvering herself so that, now, she's looking in Johnny's direction.

He's interested in her; yes. She might even be able to cleanse the stagnating memory of Tina. But she's with those others. Probably nothing would come of waiting, he tells himself. So he jumps quickly off the bench preparatory to leaving.

Watching him, the girl misses the ball tossed at her.

Johnny remains standing by the bench. His eyes follow her as she goes after the ball. On her way, she turns around as if to make sure he's still there. Ignoring the ball, she stands over it and waves at him. A welcoming, perhaps beckoning, wave.

Johnny waves back at her. But in farewell.

FIVE

THE NEGRO WOMAN with the raisin face is standing at the corner of 7th and Broadway again. "We awll doomed," she's saying, except that her voice is even less emotional now; "we awll go tomorrow"—although it's already yesterday's tomorrow, and there she still is.

"We awll doomed." Johnny Rio repeats the words, imitating the way she said them. Soon they'll become like a recurring tune grooved into his mind.

Because it was a decision made without deciding (his mind shut itself off, his body moved), Johnny will try to insert his "reasons" later in attempting to discover—when he looks back on what will happen tonight—what finally set it raging.

Tina and her sad, sad child. The anger. Yes. And Tom, too—the shattered yesterdays. And someone else. Who? Danny. Yes, somehow Danny! And the feelings of loss on the once-familiar, now haunted, beach. And the Negro woman proclaiming—no, stating—doom . . . for tomorrow. So near.

Yes, all that.

Yet by then he was already in Los Angeles—and so he will try to search even further back. To the moments outside of Phoenix, perhaps—when he witnessed the ritual of death; the spectral birds in his path, seemingly rushing to welcome destiny that tenebrous morning; the moth-creatures on the windshield, their "numbers" up . . . so quickly. But he was already on his way here. So: Try further back. To Laredo. To a mirror . . . We awll doomed.

(So soon!)

But Johnny still doesn't understand.

All he knows is that from the time he left the beach he moved like a somnambulist.

Johnny pauses in front of the bright marquee of the theater he walked out of only last night—pauses like someone about to descend into the turbulent city from a remote mountain. Lighted dots chase each other frantically:

OPEN ALL NIGHT

The ticket seller hardly looks up.

Still like one hypnotized, reacting to some awful demand beyond his consciousness, Johnny Rio walks into the lobby.

Up the stairs.

To the balcony.

Suddenly, the heavy mood lifts. Instantly it's converted to euphoria. He's like someone reacting to a powerful stimulant—like an alcoholic returning to his liquor, an addict to his drug: spuriously renewed, as if the storm that raged is over but within the calm, the manifestations of the devastation remain.

He stands at the upstairs landing and looks at this balcony for the first time, as though it were a foreign country that must be conquered. It's an enormous cavern of dark at first—so enormous that he can't tell how far up it goes, nor how wide its last rows stretch at the top. The dark becomes heavier, thicker, gathering clouds of cigarette smoke as the rows of seats ascend—until, toward the vanishing top, the blackness, erasing everything, swallowing itself, could go on forever.

Like the flailing wing of some icy bird, something passes over Johnny, smothering the euphoria. An internecine clash between his charged body and his numbed mind is taking place. He waits at the landing for the struggle to end. He tries to focus his attention on the screen.

The movies are the same as last night's. But the one with the loony woman isn't on. It's the other feature. A mousy man is claiming to have seen a ghost in an abandoned house.

Directly below Johnny in the loge several people are scattered about. Between its last row and the first row of the balcony, there's a wide aisle. In the lower rows of the balcony, people are sitting, carefully spaced several seats apart—unless they've come here together in the first place. Then, not unlike the limbo stretches of beach that separated the distinct groups, there's a thinning beyond those first few rows, a bare sprinkling of people. This is the boundary, the division—an invisible separation tacitly accepted. Beyond that boundary is the deep, dark throat of the balcony.

Square and squat like a huge gravestone, the projection room in the center splits the highest section into two pits on either side; an amber light hangs over each, without visible suspension: the lights are like yellow space saucers floating in the dark.

Johnny welcomes those lights. He knows that when he finally moves up and his eyes adjust, he'll see perfectly in this balcony. Its top rows will be just dark enough to be obscured from the sight of the people sitting in the lower rows, and light enough, within that uppermost area, for him to be seen clearly. He will not be—he would not want to be—a shadow.

Now in those years he had spent earlier in this devouring city, Johnny never came specifically to dive into the black sea of the balcony's last rows. That is usually not the turf of hustlers—and, then, Johnny considered himself "strictly a hustler." Especially in the area of the hustling bars and of Pershing Square, it would have hurt him crucially—as it would have hurt any other hustler, financially—to join the free scene of movie theaters. Johnny had never even been tempted.

When he went to theaters, it was to see a movie. Someone might sit next to him and make an advance, true; and if that person was interested enough to pay, they'd leave the theater, Johnny making sure to add the price of admission to what he asked for so he could return to finish seeing the interrupted movie.

Tonight, though, he has come for another purpose. He

still has almost seven hundred dollars, in his wallet—and some more in a bank in Laredo; so he can't tell himself he needs money. Just knowing—from that man yesterday on Main Street, and indirectly from the queen in Pershing Square—that he can still make it that way—hustling—continues to satisfy that side of his ego.

He moves under the halo of dim yellow light fallen on the landing. Eyes are looking down from behind the curtain of dark; he knows that—and so he stands there for long moments, allowing himself to be seen, wanting those on the top rows to hope he'll make himself available. He can feel that tide of darkness flowing toward him to claim him. He moves slowly. Eyes in the black pool follow him. He stands in the aisle as if undecided whether to sit in the loge or the balcony. But there's really no decision to be made now. He walks up. Slowly. The first row. The second. The third. Higher. Midway—at the "boundary" and still in the aisle—he waits again. I want them to want me, I want them to . . . love . . . me, he thinks. But of course he means "desire me"; there has always been a severe confusion between "love" and "desire" for Johnny Rio.

He sits within the "boundary"—almost exactly halfway between those on top, waiting, and those below, watching the movie. Despite the trance leading him, he wasn't able to walk all the way up. Not yet. Nevertheless, he can be seen clearly here from those upper rows. An image of how he will look from above guides him into a casual, sexually inviting pose; he sprawls on his seat, legs propped on the back of the seat in front.

He's acutely aware of the stares from the dark cave. He knows they're on him.

He's been sitting there only a few minutes when a shadow melts from the darkness, flows along the row where he's sitting, and materializes as a man only one seat away. He's carrying a coat, which he places partly on his lap, partly on the empty seat. Johnny has seen all this without turning; he's aware that the man's face—an opaque oval at the extremity of Johnny's vision—is fixed sideways toward him. That man's interest established, Johnny looks at him openly now, sees him clearly, as he knew he would be able to in this light. Not yet 30, the man is well dressed, attractive.

Johnny invites: He stretches his legs, both arms behind him—exhibiting his body as he often does instinctively, but, now, deliberately. Instantly, the man's right arm encircles the back of the seat between them, the fingers of his hand—a smaller opaque object—moving up and down as if restless to find a place to settle. Finally, the hand drops to the empty seat, awaiting a sign from Johnny.

Johnny gives it. Left elbow on the armrest, he allows his hand to dangle bare inches over his own crotch.

The man's fingers crawl toward Johnny's thigh.

Abruptly, Johnny moves his leg away, removes the invitation harshly.

Obviously bewildered, the man doesn't withdraw his hand yet; it remains glued there—as if the action will call attention to the thwarted movement. After a few seconds, he does remove it, like a thief.

The moment he does so, Johnny invites again. Lightly, and only for an instant, he cups his own groin. Perversity has seized him (a perversity he'll regret later, because he isn't really cruel—but, now, his own needs are roaring):

Leading this man on, he'll force him to withdraw, encourage him again: Johnny is playing a sinister, exciting, brutal game, testing his desirability.

Emboldened by Johnny's gesture, the man drops his hand quickly into the empty seat, his fingers reaching out to brush Johnny's thigh.

Deliberately looking tough, Johnny turns to face the man in a manner designed to throw him into a further quandary—looking at him with contempt—a warning not to proceed any further. The man draws his hand away, gets up to leave.

And Johnny lets his hand drop openly between his own legs.

The man sits down again, just as Johnny knew he would; sits this time immediately next to Johnny, who has removed his hand from his lap and leans back arching his body.

Acting quickly—perhaps apprehensive that Johnny's erratic mood will change again—the man lets his hand glide over the armrest, over Johnny's thigh. The game he's playing is arousing Johnny, and this shows through his pants. The man's fingers hover anxiously over Johnny's groin; now they barely brush his hardening prick, lightly. Since Johnny hasn't moved, they explore more openly.

Moving his jacket so it extends over Johnny's lap in order to hide his own motions from the penetrating eyes focused on them like radar, the man begins to unbutton Johnny's fly. Apparently expecting to have to work through shorts, he's evidently surprised (he starts) to encounter bare skin immediately as he explores inside Johnny's fly. His hand encircling Johnny's hardening prick, he draws it out; his hand slides up and down on the now-stiff cock, jerking it under the jacket.

Unexpectedly, Johnny twists his body away. Abruptly, he pushes his prick back into his pants, buttoning up as hurriedly as he can—with some effort because of the bulge. Suddenly he stands up. The man has withdrawn his hand in almost-fear. Is Johnny going to hit him? Maybe he's a decoy. The man sits there rigidly. And this is what Johnny does:

Moving out—but his body facing the man—he pauses in front of him so that the man's face is only inches from Johnny's crotch. In one rash moment—which is what Johnny counted on—the man pushes his head forward, his mouth on the bulge showing through Johnny's pants— this time ignoring the certainly staring eyes. Johnny feels the promise of bursting pleasure as the man's mouth tries vainly to suck him through the cloth of his pants.

As suddenly as he stood up, Johnny moves away—but only into the aisle, waiting there. The man gets up, moves down the stairs, expecting that Johnny will follow him to the restroom, where they can finish the act implied.

Instead—though he doesn't know why—Johnny walks up, deeper into the roiling dark. Still in the aisle, he waits for his eyes to adjust to the denser black. Soon, faces begin to bob out of the darkness like objects rising to the surface of the sea. There are perhaps two dozen people, or more, scattered about the last few rows of this side of the balcony. It's Saturday, predictably it's crowded with sex-hunters. The atmosphere of sex is as thick as the dark. Like gray moons, faces turn toward Johnny, who can see perfectly even here—and so, importantly, he can be seen perfectly. In the eye of the darkness, the darkness doesn't exist.

To the side of the second-to-the-last row, there's a stretch of about five empty seats. Johnny sits there. He wants them to come to him.

Now as he walked along this row, he noticed a young-man lean forward toward him from the last row, inviting him to sit next to him; and he's still straining to look at him. Johnny glances up at him, then turns away, looking down at his own groin.

Instantly, the youngman climbs over the back of the seat. Already his hand is on the armrest next to Johnny; already his fingers extend over the edge. Even in this light his faun eyes reveal his infatuation with Johnny. Some-what thin, he's in his early 20's.

Not even going through the preliminary movement of allowing his hand to float over Johnny's thigh preparatory to letting it descend—quite openly, hurriedly, frantically, as if Johnny will get away from him, he touches Johnny's cock, which is still semihard. Oblivious of everyone else, he struggles with the buttons on Johnny's pants. The more frantic he becomes, the more the buttons resist.

Johnny won't help, his hands at the back of his own head—to make sure that those certainly looking on know that *he* isn't touching the other; that it's the other who desires *him*. Glancing behind him, he sees several men staring down hungrily from the upper row, mouths open as if vicariously preparing to experience what they know the youngman wants to do with Johnny. This multiplying of desire augments Johnny's craving ferociously.

Having succeeded in opening his fly, the youngman fondles Johnny's balls and then takes the stiffening cock

out. In one sudden unexpected downward thrust of his
head—rashly ignoring any possible danger of hostile eyes—
he swallows Johnny's prick to the very rim of his balls.
Johnny feels a fierce, shooting, incredible pleasure as his
cock swells in the moist mouth; feels that miraculous pull
of the body as if his whole being is draining to the tip of
the sexual organ—as the youngman assumes a perfect
rhythm, up and down, in the sliding movements.

But even as he feels these exciting sensations, Johnny
is searching the row above—this time not for the eyes that
will multiply his pleasure—but:

Because—bewilderingly—he's suddenly anxious, inex-
plicably anxious, for this youngman to move on—and for
someone else to take his place!

He withdraws his cock from the youngman's mouth.

The youngman remains bent over him. "Don't you
wanna come?" he whispers.

"No, man, no, I can't. Cool it," Johnny whispers back.

"I'll wait, I'll make you come," the youngman pleads.

Johnny doesn't want to hurt him. How can he explain
that all at once, in a way that confuses him too, he needs
someone else? "No," Johnny says, "I just don't want to
come."

"Please," the youngman begs—so urgently that Johnny
opens his legs as a signal that he'll let him.

The youngman's mouth pounces as if starved—sucking
him expertly. He knows how to keep Johnny exactly at the
very edge of release without carrying him over: contracting the muscles of his throat, relaxing them to reduce the
pressure just enough to stem the tide, knowing uncannily
when he can thrust down again, stopping just in time.

Johnny's whole body seems to be flooding to that one

area of feeling. Even cramped as he is, he can ride to release in a moment. Now the youngman wants to prolong it. But Johnny brings both his hands over the other's head. His body contracting, his cock pushed all the way inside the other's mouth, Johnny comes in an exploding spurt, another, another, sailing to another, while the youngman drains his cum.

Through, Johnny's body relaxes in the seat; but even now the youngman won't unglue his mouth from his prick, which begins to grow soft inside the warm mouth. Despite the discharge, Johnny feels a lingering pleasure. Finally he withdraws his cock with his hand. The youngman sits up—still obviously hungry, still wanting him.

Others here have witnessed this scene—a scene not rare but not common even in such a balcony, where the groping is usually done as an end in itself or as an invitation for completion in the restroom. Now, as if Johnny's sexual release has made them restless, there's a silent moving among those others—as if they're playing a game of musical chairs without music. They move in the smoky darkness as if in a dream. The imitation of a dream.

The youngman next to Johnny still hasn't moved. Johnny turns his body away, tries to concentrate on the movie.

Minutes pass.

Suddenly he realizes with a fusion of excitement and apprehension that he's far from satisfied. The youngman next to him would be only too glad to repeat the act— already he's reached out tentatively twice to see if Johnny will respond again; but Johnny doesn't want the same person. He wants—needs—someone else.

Perhaps an hour passes. The youngman has given up—

finally has moved dejectedly out of the balcony. Several others have sat next to Johnny. But for one reason or another, he didn't encourage them, and they moved away. Although he still needs someone else—yes, very much—he's being particular.

He's tempted to explore the other side of the balcony—partly blocked by the projection room; but he knows instinctively that those who come together for a mutual purpose congregate in one area. So he remains where he is, alternately wishing that this flaring sexual excitement would abate, alternately glad it doesn't.

Sitting there waiting, he feels—he knows he is—more desirable than ever.

And he feels alive.

Intermission.

Warm yellow lights melt the cold darkness. The surreptitious movements stop.

Johnny is aware of eyes focusing on him anew—to see him better in this light. There's no doubt he's the central point of attention. Fresh desirable bait among the fish circling the dark sea hungrily. Johnny stretches his body.

A handsome dark-haired youngman is coming up the steps, slowly as if, like Johnny earlier, he wants to exhibit himself. Seeing him, Johnny feels his heart sink as if into a frozen lake: The thought that at least some of those who wanted him—even one of them—may—just possibly may—now prefer this youngman frightens him (although he's of course convinced that he, Johnny, is much better looking, much, much more desirable). One rejection—real or imaginary—can slaughter Johnny Rio, even among 100 successes. If he can lure that dark-haired youngman to sit next to him, to come to him on his—Johnny's—terms, then— . . . As before, he sprawls invitingly, convinced that this youngman won't be able to resist him—if he's come to join the hunt.

The dark-haired youngman sits in line with Johnny, yes—but on the opposite end, many seats and an aisle between them—in a section of the balcony where, for now at least, he's alone. Again like Johnny, he seems to expect others to come to him. Maybe their scenes are the same.

The lights off, the theater is again a cavern of dark.

Someone is moving down from the upper row. Will he sit next to me or next to him? Johnny wonders anxiously. Neither. The man walks downstairs. No test.

Then Johnny sees the thin youngman who sucked him off earlier returning to the balcony. Ineluctably, he moves toward the dark-haired youngman and sits next to him.

Motherfucker, Johnny thinks. Cocksucking mother-fucker! He feels depressed, rejected—although he's already explaining defensively to himself: After all, he *did* want to come on with me again, and I didn't let him; if I had encouraged him, he'd *still* prefer me.

But the doubt festers. Instead of his earlier triumphs, this possible rejection dominates his thoughts. Son of a bitch, he keeps thinking, that son of a bitch preferred that other guy to me—but maybe he didn't see me this time, didn't expect me still to be here; yes, that's it! He locks the thought in his mind—tightly. *That's it!*

He decides to try this—although he knows that, if it doesn't work, depression will crush him: He slides down the back of the seat in front and sits on a lower row, where the thin youngman (and the dark-haired one, too—but Johnny is convinced he wants someone to come on with him) will be able to see him clearly. Johnny places his hand between his legs and lightly outlines the bulge there —in this way announcing to the thin youngman that he's ready again.

And why is he doing this if he doesn't want that same youngman?—if he needs someone else?

Because, Johnny would answer, he just *has* to prefer me!

And what he did worked. The thin youngman has left the other one and is once again sitting next to Johnny. Johnny lets him touch his cock again; but when the youngman tries to take it out, Johnny twists his body, having— yes, cruelly—established all he needed to know—that he was preferred over the other. In a quandary the thin youngman disappears out of the balcony once more, per- haps still expecting Johnny, or even the other youngman, to follow him to the restroom.

Instead, the dark-haired youngman moves across the aisle, nearer to Johnny but still on the upper row. He leans forward, obviously staring at Johnny, who is now sure of. the other's interest. He's coming to me, Johnny thinks triumphantly.

But this happens: Another man has moved up the stairs and stands in the aisle as if choosing whom to sit next to. Before he decides, the dark-haired youngman slips over the seat in front and sits only three places away from Johnny. The other man moves into the same row, however—which is perhaps what the dark-haired youngman was trying to thwart—and sits exactly between Johnny and the other youngman. He can, therefore, be after either. For now, however, it's a draw. Again, although Johnny doesn't need that man, he does need to know the man wants him more than he wants the other youngman. Actually, of course,

Johnny would prefer the handsome dark-haired youngman to come on with him—*only* because (he would explain quickly), being goodlooking and desirable, he'd be much more of a conquest, especially since others evidently want him on the same terms Johnny needs to be wanted—one-sidedly. So Johnny once again invites by cupping his own groin. The man in the middle is looking at him with unmistakable interest.

If I want him, he's mine! Johnny thinks.

Suddenly the dark-haired youngman gets up, passes the man in the middle, passes Johnny, and sits next to him on the other side. Johnny has won. The two flank him; and then another man sits on the seat in front, where Johnny's feet are propped so that they straddle that man's shoulders, his head leaning back toward Johnny's crotch.

Johnny's conquest is complete.

Unexpectedly, causing Johnny's feeling of triumph to crumble, the dark-haired youngman thrusts his leg intimately against Johnny's.

Christ, Johnny thinks, he wants me to come on with him, too—mutually; he thinks *I* dig him too!

The thought disturbs him so sharply that he gets up hurriedly, walks down the stairs, leaves the balcony, goes to the lounge, into the restroom.

No one here. Johnny stands pissing. Though angry, he still needs someone else.

Footsteps. It's the dark-haired youngman. In a panic that he'll indicate once again that he thinks Johnny desires him back, Johnny is about to button his fly and walk out, when the youngman says, "Let me blow you."

The panic stifled immediately by that expression of one-way desire, Johnny remains standing before the urinal, his cock out. *My terms!*

The youngman kneels before him and sucks him. But he does it badly, merely slides his mouth back and forth on the tip of Johnny's cock. Obviously inexperienced, he's probably used to being the one standing. It will take a long time this way, others will certainly be coming downstairs—and Johnny is anxious to come again to still the fever. So he reaches for his own cock and jerks it in the youngman's mouth.

"Let me know when you're ready!" the youngman says excitedly; and he licks Johnny's balls.

"Now!" Johnny gasps. But the cum is already shooting out, the white liquid drips on the youngman's cheek, which he quickly wipes with his own hand, using that hand to jerk himself off.

As Johnny walks out, the two other men who sat near them moments ago are moving hurriedly toward the restroom.

Johnny rushes past them, out of the theater, into the night's shroud of fog and smoke.

SIX

THREE.

Johnny has just awakened. Still drowsy from the iron-heavy sleep, his mind said: "Three."

Three what?

He lies in bed naked with a hard-on. Since his midteens he's slept stripped. In warm weather, he doesn't even cover himself with a sheet, loving the sensuality of his nudity. He loves to wake in the morning to the sight of his body— so dark in summer on the white sheet.

The blinds closed only partly, the room is suffused in that golden light which magically brings out all colors as if they're on fire in their respective hues.

Three. . . .

Right on the threshold of recognizing its significance, his mind repeats the number insistently.

The drowsiness is melting slowly. Johnny's head is propped on his hands. He's staring down pleasurably at his body. In that yellowish light it glows like warm copper; the narrow strip sheltered from the sun by the trunks is now exposed stark white. The hair about his crotch looks darker than it is, in contrast to the sun-bleached hairs on the rest of his body. Johnny is fiercely aware of his body as he wakes.

Three?

Three!

It slips into his consciousness.

Three people.

I was in that movie about four hours, and three people came on with me, and many others wanted to, and two sucked me, and another tried to, and I came two times! He thinks that victoriously.

Now two things have changed for Johnny from the earlier time he lived here: Last night he didn't make himself available to men for money only—no, he went to that theater balcony for the experiences themselves. And: When he was "strictly a hustler," Johnny made it with those who paid him what he asked for—middle-aged men, young ones, it didn't really matter as long as they didn't absolutely turn him off; he hardly looked at them. Last night, however, with no intention of asking for money, he became much more selective. Several of those who obviously wanted him, he turned down. It amounted to this: Without himself desiring back (no, not at all, Johnny is quick to emphasize), he chose to be desired by the most attractive only—and Johnny has, of course, always been able to gauge another man's desirability, although the Myth of the Streets says otherwise.

Feeling a squeezing violence after he left the theater last night, he came straight to the motel, took a sleeping pill, and sank into dark sleep.

Now he feels the same fierce sexual excitement of last night, a continuation, as if sleep merely interrupted the sensation but didn't calm it.

To still it now, he jumps up from the bed quickly.

He has inserted in the high door sill between the bedroom and the small dressing room the portable chinning bar he brought with him (along with cables and iron exercise-shoes): to work out regularly while he's here; for exercise is such a beloved ritual he wouldn't think of laying off even for the ten days he'll be here—or going to a gym where others might distract him.

He does a set of very wide chins, performing each strictly, lowering himself each time to a full dead-hang, feeling the muscles at the sides of his chest (which give him the V he's so proud of) pull, contract, expand. Eleven repetitions. Another set: ten; then nine, nine again, then seven. Five sets.

Narrowing his grip and pulling himself up rigidly over and over, he pumps up his biceps like rocks; reversing the grip, he works his triceps.

Next with cables: He pulls the coiled wires stretching his chest. He follows this with wide-handed parallel dips between the backs of two bar stools; for his pectorals.

Immediately after, he does many frog kicks for his waist:

hanging from the bar, raising his legs sharply, squeezing his thighs against his abdomen, thrusting his feet out at a 90-degree angle, holding that position to feel the severe pull on his abdominal muscles.

Lying on the floor, the iron exercise-shoes strapped to his feet, he does 77 leg raises, very quickly, lifting his legs to a position over his head, almost touching the floor in back. Then 49 more. Then 42. (Seven being his lucky number, he often exercises in multiples of it.)

Although in Laredo he does many different exercises with barbells and dumbbells (presses, curls, squats, and their variations)—working out, each session, up to two hours, sometimes three—six days a week—now he has concentrated on a few movements. And he performed each with fury, as if the flushed blood and the flowing perspiration will bathe something away, out of him. He wants to become very, very tired, to feel a blessed fatigue, a physical satisfaction that will quench this thing inside.

But as the perspiration covers his body, he feels progressively more exhilarated. Weariness is determined to elude him. The more he pushes himself to exercise—repeating the same exercises for additional sets—the more hopped-up he feels—almost like when, years ago, he forced his endurance repeatedly by going on benzedrine pills to keep himself awake beyond the night, sometimes several nights in a row.

In the full-length mirrror on the bathroom door, his body gleams golden with perspiration as he breathes very hard, panting.

Staring at himself, he feels,—he knows with certainty— that looking like that he can make it wherever he wants in this vast city of doomed angels.

He tried the pool—although he was apprehensive that Tina or her child would be there. But an older man and a woman are sitting serenely on lawn chairs before what had been her room. I wonder if that poor kid's beating on another door, Johnny thought.

The first few moments sunbathing under the white sun Johnny felt somewhat calmer, but as the sun grew warmer, more passionately lapping at his body, Johnny felt the full return of excitement and craving: augmented by the fact that a man—who looked like a payer—kept hovering about him by the pool, but the man himself turned Johnny off badly; he just emphasized the ubiquitous erotic ambience of southern California.

By noon, having eaten in the motel coffeeshop, Johnny Rio is dressed and ready to go out. Loving the luxurious feel of that material, he's wearing another silk shirt—also tightly tailored; this one is grayish-green. He wears his Levi's a size bigger than his waist because he's become convinced that loose jeans are more attractive than too-tight ones—which are faggy. He's wearing the tanned, scuffed boots.

I'm an irresistible number, he thinks vainly, not at all embarrassed to wink at himself in the mirror.

But the cockiness wore off quickly.

Back on Broadway, he panics curiously when he sees that the Negro woman isn't preaching on her corner this Sunday afternoon—which would seem to be a very appropriate time. Is she here only in the evenings? Is Sunday her day off? Or does the awareness of doom hit her only at night when she's alone?

We awll doomed, his mind says with some wistfulness. He actually lingers at that corner, hoping she'll turn up, his heart responding in anticipation when, half a block away, he sees a small dark figure carrying a black book. But it isn't her; the black "book" is a black bag.

Johnny buys his third ticket in three days for the same two features.

Now he expects that, this being Sunday afternoon, the balcony will once again be filled as it was last night, but with different, new hunters who will want him like those others.

Inside, he realizes immediately that it's all different.

The balcony is filled, yes, but with Sunday-afternoon couples and families seated all the way from the loge to what was the "boundary" last night—probably, too, all the way into the back rows. Evidently That World stays away on Sunday afternoons—at least from this theater: a tacit agreement perhaps. It's actually possible that another theater nearby swings *only* on Sunday afternoons.

Still, he walks all the way up the balcony. Two or three men at the top eye him with interest; but the male-and-female couples, necking, extend even to the last row. Nothing really could happen here—not what Johnny wants: not a recurrence of last night.

Sitting in the crowded loge, Johnny tries watching the movie. Again. The thought occurs to him that he still hasn't actually seen either feature, but he's grown tired of them; it seems he's seen the same scenes over and over.

After about half an hour of trying futilely to follow the movie about the man who claims to have seen a ghost, Johnny is once again outside on the smoggy street. The warmth of today has intensified the smog. The Cloud looms heavily over the city.

Automatically Johnny walks toward 7th Street. He

pauses. Does he really want to find out if the Negro woman is there? If she is, it will make him feel mysteriously better. . . . After all, as long as she's prophesying doom, then we're still not doomed, he thinks; as long as she's there to talk about, it's all right.

She still isn't there.

In this area of Broadway, there are several movie theaters. Johnny remembers one with a restroom like a dungeon. His purpose thwarted so far, his need is increasing alarmingly.

Inside that theater, he goes straight to the restroom. A long row of stairs angles sharply at two different landings before leading to a narrow corridor which in turn leads to the restroom. Along the stairs several men, smoking or pretending to smoke, watch Johnny, perhaps trying to determine what purpose he's down here for. Johnny pegs them right away as sexhunters. In the corridor outside the head, two more men. Inside, another at the urinal.

Predictably, one of the men who was in the corridor comes in, stands near Johnny. Now another one, on the other side. Another one pretending to wash his hands, comb his hair—actually staring in the mirror at the reflection of the others' backs. Johnny picks up immediately on what all this would mean: the waiting. The halting movements. The interrupted acts hardly begun. The making sure those who enter aren't hostile—aren't vice cops. The attempts to outlast the others. The nervousness. And, possibly, after all that waiting, nothing will have occurred.

Frantically, the fever raging, Johnny tries the balcony. Another enormous cavern. But, to thwart the type of activities that occurred in the theater he was in last night, the whole upper third of the balcony is roped off. The bottom two-thirds of it is taken over by necking couples, families, children.

Johnny leaves this theater too.

Main Street. The smell of greasy fried chicken everywhere. The familiar bars he hustled. He's tempted to go into Harry's bar.

No.

He's in a hurry, and bars take too long: Someone would buy him a drink, make conversation, make an implied or overt offer of money, invite him to a place perhaps a long distance away. . . . I don't need money, Johnny reminds himself.

The burlesque-movie theater. Occasionally, years ago, Johnny would go there when he'd be too tired from hustling but wanted to come back to the bars and the street. He remembered the frantic activity in that theater —an activity of which he had not been an immediate part—being "strictly a hustler."

Something incredible has happened to that theater, Johnny discovers when he enters. Every other seat has been removed. It's a decaying mouth, with teeth hideously missing. A giant, crystalline light glares down rudely on the men—several servicemen—scattered about, separated like naughty children. Evidently the City Authorities discovered What Went On—and they conquered. For now at least.

Where are the groping ghosts? Ghosts then, they're now ghosts . . . of ghosts.

On the screen, a woman with long blond hair is removing her clothes casually, almost bored. She looks disconcertingly like Tina.

Johnny walks out. The third theater in about two hours.

Across from Pershing Square there was another one. As with the one on Main Street, he'd go there when he was tired and wanted to come back or when rumors spread that the cops were going to raid the park for vagrants. There was action in that theater, too; but, again, and for the same reason, Johnny wasn't strictly a part of it.

Now, three years later, it's become a girlie-movie house. The man who takes Johnny's ticket has a look of hatred stamped indelibly on his face—like that on the faces of the City Authorities. Then what the hell is he doing here?

Clusters of servicemen and others watch a cheap Grade Z movie made maybe 15 years ago, given a sexy new title that bears no relation to the story (*Rape of the Strawberry Blonde on Avenue F*), and redistributed. No sooner has Johnny sat down than the man who took his ticket is pacing the aisles with a flashlight (like a dog on a leash), up and down, pausing to look, hard, wherever two men are sitting together.

Now Johnny knows why he works here: He actually has to search out the object he hates. Poor man, Johnny thinks.

Coming here was another mistake.

The movie is such a gray drag that Johnny leaves after a few minutes.

Now where?

For a brief period—when he was living here and decided to get away from downtown Los Angeles—Johnny moved into a small apartment only a block or two from MacArthur and Westlake parks and a block or two more from Lafayette Park. To hitchhike on Wilshire, he often had to cross those parks at night; and he had seen shad-

owy figures prowling. Intuitively, he knew of course what
went on. But he also knew that such dark cruising parks
—like movie heads and balconies—are unreliable hustling
turf—too many there for free kicks. So Johnny would
walk through them only when it was necessary.

Once again on the street now, he decides he'll go there.
But first (glancing back at Pershing Square as at a house
one has moved out of) he walks back to Broadway and
7th Street.

The Negro woman isn't there.

Waiting for the evening to cloak the parks protectively,
Johnny drives back to the motel. In the trunk of his car
he brought a black-leather jacket—one he used to wear
those many years ago: molded to his body like his shirts.
Impulsively, when he was packed and ready to leave Laredo, he returned to his apartment and put the jacket in
the trunk.

He tries it on in his room, looks in the mirror. He
looks terrific! Like a black panther. Hustling, he wore
this jacket often at first; but after a while he wore it less
and less, along with the black, buckled engineer boots he
had, because the combination tended to attract masochists.
And that's never been Johnny's scene. Besides, it's his body
Johnny wants admired, not his clothes.

Reminding himself that Los Angeles nights are awfully
chilly, he'll wear it tonight; and he changes to black
Wellington boots.

Tonight Johnny Rio will look like a tough fallen angel.

Outside, darkness has begun to gobble the long shadows
of early evening. By the time he reaches Westlake, it will
be night.

Parking his car a few blocks away, Johnny walks up Wilshire—remembering (but he forces himself to stop quickly) that it was nearby that Tom picked him up that hot, hot evening. Deliberately, Johnny avoids that corner.

Now Wilshire Boulevard splits what is technically one park into two: Westlake and MacArthur. In the first side Johnny explores, a large lake is taken over by rented boats; young couples are certainly necking on the black glossy water. On benches along the paths, old men and women, speaking a foreign language, linger into the evening. Not for hunters, this side.

Emerging from a small tunnel that connects one side to the other, Johnny sees another lake, smaller—the lake he now remembers: a shallow one, no boats here. Ducks perch shivering on the grass. . . . There is an enormous shell—evidently for concerts; benches face the empty stage. It's hillier here, in MacArthur Park; there are more trees, more shrubbery, more dark places. And: On a slight hill and in back of a row of benches, two shadows stand idly.

At the rim of the park, along which Johnny will later discover is a walk ledged by flowers, other shadows glide slowly. Lone figures sit on benches in the darkest parts of the park. A man leans on the wooden railing on a small bridge. Two outlines separate from the dark and walk out of the park together.

As in the dark movie-theater balcony, there is here something of pantomime, something of a frozen dream, a trance, of something dazed, traumatized, unreal. A flowing dance of ghosts.

Johnny walks up the small hill nearest him, where benches curve in an arc; walks to the top—a symbolic position. One of the two men there moves toward him quickly. The other surrenders to another puddle of dark, disappears. Now Johnny walks down a few feet, sits on the back of a bench, his feet propped on the seat. He's chosen this bench deliberately because it's almost hidden by an enormous, shaggy tree, its tattered branches grotesque and gloomy in the moonless night.

The man who has moved toward Johnny sits about ten feet away. He appears slender and youngish.

As he did last night, for just a brief moment, Johnny lets his hand touch his own groin. Withdrawing it quickly, he glances at the man, determining his interest. In answer, the man moves next to Johnny's propped legs. Johnny repeats the gesture, wanting the man to reach up quickly and touch him there—needing that contact badly.

Instead: "Nice night," the man says.

He wants to talk. It'll take forever. "Yeah," Johnny answers tersely.

The man is staring between Johnny's legs. But he persists: "New in town?"

"Yeah," Johnny says again.

"Rode in with a gang? . . . I mean, you look like a motorcyclist; and they travel in gangs, don't they?" the man asks awkwardly.

"I drove in alone," Johnny says.

"Working yet?"

"Yeah." Hustling, Johnny would have answered: "Nope."

"I'm from Michigan myself," the man says, settling back on the bench, perhaps encouraged by what he thinks he's found out about Johnny—if he's answered truthfully. "I've lived in L.A. for years, though."

Now Johnny is very, very impatient. He wants this man

to make an advance—or move away. He's trying to sound me out, Johnny thinks; trying to figure what my scene is—hustler ("Working yet?"), mugger or decoy (". . . with a gang?")—as if I'd *tell* him if I was a mugger, for godssake! He'll take very long, Johnny determines, and *then* he'll ask me if I want a cup of coffee. I'll have to *make* him move, he decides, not wanting to abandon this place, which is so appropriate to his purpose.

His voice turns purposely rough: "Wahdayaaftuh, mon?"

"Pardon?" the man says.

"What? Are? You? After? Man?" Johnny repeats.

The man becomes very nervous right away. "Oh, well, uh, nothing, really, I just, well, I was just taking a walk, and I, uh— . . . Excuse me." He moves hurriedly away.

That's that!

Predictably, Johnny's sorry for the man. But I'm in a hurry! he explains to himself urgently as if that will justify what he's done, may do—no matter how cruel.

As the man leaves, other shadows shift course, pass before Johnny, to the side, in back. Occasionally someone sits near him, studies him, moves closer, sits down, stands up, moves away. Johnny realizes what's happening: He looks too tough—like the mugger or decoy that other man at first suspected him of being. And despite the fact that he isn't hustling, he's automatically assumed the hustler's stance, the look. The very same aspects that strongly attract those here to him also make them suspicious of him —and afraid. He considers removing the jacket; that might help. But it's cool, almost cold. The sky is gray and watery.

Boldly, a blond, curly-haired, well-made man in his 30's

approaches Johnny, almost defiantly. "Hell-*oh!*" he bel-lows—an angry greeting.

"Hiyuh," Johnny answers.

The blond man faces the shadows moving centrifugally. "Look at them!" the man says, and there's no disguising his outrage. "All those guys—out for a one-night stand!"

"And what are *you* doing here," Johnny asks quickly, to keep the scene moving and avoid another waste of time.

"Me?" The man faces Johnny, frowning as if greatly annoyed that the question came up. "Me? Hell, what I'm looking for— . . . Well, the chances of its being here— . . . well, they're one in a— . . . You name it: high odds." He laughs bitterly. "But you wonder what I'm looking for, right?" Before Johnny can answer, he goes on: "I'm looking for: Someone I Can Really Love!" the man blurts crazily.

"Oh, wow!" Johnny can't help deriding. "In *this* park? You're putting me on!" What the hell *now!* he wonders, struck by the man's fantastic approach.

"Precisely!" the man says. He raises a finger like a prophet. "You see, you think it's remote. You scoff at the very idea of love." He sounds like a poet from long ago. Very long ago.

"Yeah. Especially in this park," Johnny says. The man may be nutty, but Johnny is intrigued by him. More, he's touched powerfully by the man's tone of profound despair.

"But *why* not?" the man pleads passionately. "Why is it impossible for love to be . . . poised . . . waiting . . . in the dark? Why is it impossible for love to be hiding in the shadows?"

Why? Johnny thinks. And he answers himself: Because it isn't there, that's why.

"And look at *you!*" the man lashes abruptly at him. "Looking so tough and . . . desirable. . . . But desirable for what? For someone to take you home and blow you once and say goodbye when you say goodbye! Is that love! Is that *anything!* Just by the way you look, the way you strutted (I heard you across the park!), the way you swaggered—by all that—you do away with everything that *might* be possible between two people: decent emotions, friendship, real ties— . . ."

Oddly, Johnny isn't angered by any of this. Had someone else spoken in that tone to him, he would have put him down, or walked away, made a smart remark. But this person seems to be not so much attacking him as exploring his own frantic loneliness. Poor lucid madman, Johnny Rio thinks.

"If I sat here and said I just want to talk," the man says, "you'd probably think I was crazy; you'd walk away."

A few minutes ago—anxious as I was to make it—yes, I would have, Johnny thinks. But I wouldn't do that now. "I won't walk away," he promises. "You wanna talk? What about?"

The man looks bewildered, puzzled, as if he hasn't heard right—or as if he thinks he's being made fun of.

Johnny fumbles for conversation, feeling great sympathy for this man. "What do you do?" is all he can think to ask.

From the look of flaring anger on the man's face, Johnny realizes immediately he's misinterpreted the question. What Johnny meant is: What kind of work do you do? But as the words came back at him the moment he'd said them, he realized he'd asked what is a very common question in the world of vagrant sexhunters: meaning:

What kind of sex activity are you after? That is, are you looking to do what I want done?

"*You see!*" the man gasps. "Everything reduced to the physical act! The localized sensation. Instead of the mind and the heart stimulated, it's the *penis!*"

"Cool it, man," Johnny says. "That's not what I mean; I mean: What do you do for work?"

"So! You're trying to find out if I have a good job! You want to know if maybe you can ingratiate yourself with me! You probably want to get *paid!*"

"No, man," says Johnny patiently (although his mind says, Fuck it). "I'm not hustling."

"You're not?" the man asks.

"No," Johnny says. "I just wanted to make conversation." The man's franticness keeps Johnny here, keeps him deliberately calm. "That's what you said you wanted—conversation—and how the hell do you know that *I* don't want it too?"

"Because of everything about you!" the man goes on. "Because you want to be admired, desired—oh, it's so obvious!—because you're selfish— . . ."

"You wanna talk?" Johnny makes another attempt to cool him.

But the man has abruptly stopped talking. Suddenly, without warning, taking Johnny completely by surprise, he reaches out to grope him between his legs. Stunned, Johnny lets him. Now the man's got Johnny's cock in his hands; now he's bending over the bench blowing him. Bewildered, Johnny can't even get hard at first; but soon he does—very, very hard, perhaps in anger. As he sucks Johnny's prick, the man's hands move frantically in his own pockets.

Obviously the man came: He quickly removed his mouth from Johnny's cock, stood up—spitting contemptuously.

A wave of anger engulfs Johnny. He wants to hit the man—but he's already hurrying away. With real bitterness Johnny calls after him, smashing the silence so violently that the shadows stop all over the park, as if roused from deep slumber; calls after him loudly: "Say, friend— buddy! You forgotta say goodbye!"

Crazy bastard! Weird-ass fucker! That man's strange hypocrisy has made Johnny even more anxious for that fleeting contact again.

Impatiently he moves about the park—to the darkest places—the walk where a ledge of flowers conceals one's lower body; then to the place where an artificial waterfall creates a small alcove. People follow him everywhere, but they're still suspicious of him. Eventually they move away. Finally he walks out of the park.

Along Wilshire. To the other park he recalls a block or so away. This time he passes the remembered corner. He thinks of Tom—stops his thoughts.

Lafayette Park spills from a small branch library (now dark) on a slight hill. A balustraded terrace leads down a few steps to a landing with concrete benches. A row of concealing trees, then more stairs, and a small square lake, where water plants float prettily and tiny fish swim. To one side of the park there's a row of dark trees along a road. On a gradual slope from the road, those trees provide several guarded areas. On the opposite side, the park rolls in exposed hills.

There are few people here—Johnny has seen only three

—and so they will probably be more determined, more in a hurry, he thinks.

A man is sitting on a bench near the balustrade; he looks anxious, ready—staring after Johnny. Johnny walks toward the tree-covered area along the road. Legs planted firmly and spread, he stands before a thick growth of trees and shrubs, which create a hollow big enough for someone to squat in. Now his groin is *demanding* attention.

From God knows where, a swishy youngman—a pretty almost-queen—stands next to him. "Hi!" he says languidly.

"Howya," Johnny says. (I don't want conversation, that crazy fixed that!) He buries his hands in his pockets, to touch his cock and thereby indicate what kind of action he wants.

The youngman walks away quickly, almost running. Now he *is* running!

For chrissake, Johnny thinks, he probably thought I was going to pull a knife on him and roll him!

Someone else is approaching: the man he saw on the bench.

"Wanna come with me?" the man asks Johnny quickly.

"Don't wanna go anywhere," Johnny says.

"I got some fuck-movies at home," the man tries to entice him, "and all the beer you can drink—and you can stay if you haven't got a place."

"I got a place," Johnny Rio says.

"I'll pay you," the man says, misunderstanding Johnny's reticence.

"You wanna suck me?" Johnny asks bluntly. His tone surprises him.

As much as he obviously desires Johnny, the man is thrown off. "Yeah, sure," he manages to say.

"Then do it, man," Johnny hears his own voice say. "Here, man. Blow me here!" His voice is hoarse.

Responding to Johnny's command, and perhaps excited by it, the man slips into the cavity of bushes and trees; he squats there, about to reach out to open Johnny's fly.

At that very moment a car like an angry wild animal rams into the road, its lights flooding the path.

Frightened, the man slides down the hill. Johnny turns away quickly. Is it the cops?

As he moves away at an even pace, remaining cool in case it is the cops—the car's motor stops. Its lights continue to bathe him for a long time: as if determined to imprison him in their glare.

Suddenly they shift.

Johnny looks back.

The car is backing out, into the street. It turns awkwardly and rushes away.

A drunk maybe, just making a clumsy turn, Johnny assures himself.

Feeling a pang of illness in his stomach, he realizes he's forgotten to eat tonight. But he returns to MacArthur Park.

At the entrance a man approaches him. The man is shabby and turns him off. Johnny merely says hiyuh and walks into the park.

The shadows are still cruising each other.

This time unquestionably, there comes a cop-car moving slowly through the park like a hearse, bright lights on, preparatory to driving everyone out now that it's almost midnight.

Defiantly—for the few minutes remaining before he'll have to leave—Johnny sits on the same bench as before, the one concealed by the large tree; and he's thinking:

Just one person, and I've been moving around for hours, just one person came on with me though lots wanted to, lots and lots, and it could've been two but that motherfucking shitass car had to come ramming in, it could've been two, just one person tonight, three last night, four altogether, three last night in the balcony, and that crazyman tonight, it could've been five, motherfucking shitass car, but it's four, four people in two nights, only one tonight, four.

Four.

SEVEN

YEARS AGO, a great fire swept Griffith Park in Los Angeles. It had been a dry, hot season; and the soil panted for water. Flames clutched greedily at the dry bushes, the trees, the sun-seared grass. At night an orange glow crowned the park, a glow visible as far away as downtown Los Angeles. The Cloud, swallowing the fiery smoke, was more orange than ever.

The blaze left horrid scars. Brown ashen patches, black skeleton trees—like something out of a dream of desolation.

Now the wounds, almost completely healed, have become a part of the vicissitude of the landscape. New trees, new brush, new grass, even new soil cover the razed terrain.

And how did Johnny Rio decide to come here?

Buried in his mind were breathless references to this park overheard mostly in Hollywood gay bars and always uttered in quickened tones of excitement: "You should have *seen* the numbers at *Griffith Park* the other afternoon!" . . . "Let's take a drive to *Griffith Park* and: See The Sights!" . . . "Her party was as crowded as *Griffith Park!*"

Then, however, Johnny (being, you'll remember, "strictly a hustler") wasn't interested in such parks—other than Pershing Square, of course, which was okay because it was hustling territory. (No actual sex-action occurred there; it was the place where such action was proposed, accepted, or rejected.) And so Pershing Square and Main Street and its two swinging bars, the bar on Spring Street and the one on Figueroa, and Selma Avenue (occasionally) and Hollywood Boulevard and the make-out bars off it—those were the boundaries of Johnny's jagged world, then. Now his boundaries were being redefined.

Even then, though, some part of Johnny's mind must have carefully filed the meaning of those aroused tones of voice, because, waking up late this morning and taking account of the dreary Sunday just passed (hours and hours and hours—and just one!—ironically, the weird hypocritical loony), those drowned references bobbed to the surface of his mind. *Griffith Park!* He knew immediately he'd go there this afternoon.

The park is much vaster than Johnny expected. It sprawls over several thousand acres—threatening to spill out into Los Angeles, Hollywood, Glendale, invading even the sky; its various roads spiral up hills high above the city.

Having approached it from the maze of the freeways, Johnny encounters the picnic grounds first, the zoo, the merry-go-round, the stables; families and troops of young boys and girls congregate noisily. Johnny knows this isn't the area he's looking for.

Though he doesn't know where that area is, he does know he'll recognize it the moment he comes upon it (not unlike the way he would recognize the hustling quarters of cities by their proximity to all-night two- and three-feature movie theaters). But finding it is becoming more difficult than he anticipated. Roads fork into one another in a series of seemingly endless Y's. A dead end at a bridle path. A steep blocked hill.

Johnny's radio is on: pouring out its mad, maddening cacophony, sounds ripped from the frayed edges of contemporary despair, often the slurred despair of those who are, emotionally, eternally children: who feel savagely but don't understand.

Now the Rolling Stones are conveying the sound of Johnny's anguish, speaking of the lonely blackness inside; and convoluted bastard sounds spawn convoluted bastard sounds, not finished, leading to others, also unfinished.

Johnny speeds along the curving road. Still he hasn't found the section he's looking for. Once he thought he had—when he spotted several parked cars in a cluster along a curve; but approaching them, he saw a man and a woman and a family nearby.

Not here.

Shit!

Johnny has reached the Griffith Park Observatory: that dome capping one of the park's many hills. Summer tourists wearing caps saunter about with cameras.

Dry with anxiety, Johnny parks his car, drinks thirstily from a water faucet. Hot, he removes his soaked shirt.

He goes into the men's room nearby. There's a mirror. Standing a distance back from it so he can see more of himself, Johnny squares his broad shoulders, smiles widely at himself—and knows that, once he finds the area he's searching for, he'll make out great.

Speeding determinedly along the twisting roads again!

Back down the same road!

The breeze kisses his bare chest coolly.

Golf course.

Crap!

Tennis courts.

Goddamn!

A greenhouse for special plants.

Motherfuck it!

And then the road exits into a long lane of attractive hybrid-California-Southern houses with wide green lawns.

Piss!

Johnny Rio turns the car around. Almost 3:00 in the afternoon, and he still hasn't found the area he's looking for! He's become tense, frantic.

I'm wasting time!

And then:

He sees a white car in his rearview mirror. Even from that distance and without having seen him before, Johnny "recognizes" something about the driver that comes through distinctly—he's a sexhunter.

Abruptly, Johnny swings his car to the side as if to park,

actually allowing the other (who looks back with interest) to pass him.

The white car turns to the right before the golf course. Johnny continues up so the driver won't think he's following him. When the car is out of sight, Johnny waits a few more seconds by the road. Then he makes a U-turn and takes a sharp left up the road along which the white car disappeared.

As if abandoned on the sandy margins off the road and near the brush, there are many empty parked cars here. No visible hikers nearby. Each such parking place soon discloses narrow paths leading to or around lush trees whose branches spread like hugging, possessive arms, creating, farther on, what must certainly be coves of twigs and vines and leaves.

As Johnny proceeds much more slowly up the swerving road, traffic thickens. Cars drive back and forth, making quick turns, parking. Men are getting out of their cars and moving into the thickly foliated areas and cavities of the park; they pause to look at those driving by. As Johnny passes them, they watch to see if he'll turn back.

But he doesn't stop yet; he's reconnoitering territory soon to be invaded, weighing the merits of one section against those of another for his purposes.

The road extends a long, long distance up.

At one turn, five cars are parked on a wide islet of sand about ten feet deep, bordered on one side by a dense grove of trees. On the other side, a broad path leads onto level land. Johnny marks that area in his mind.

As he drives up the same road, he notices many other islets of sand—islets big enough for several cars to park in, always hugged by the curve of the road, always leading

to tight paths down the side. . . . Treed sections before
cave-like hollows. . . . Men standing on dunes along the
road—like a periphery of an outpost overlooking the city.
. . . A high, high hill, three cars parked before it: signals
alerting others; at the top of that hill a growth of trees.

And all along the road: many, many parked cars, some
vacant, some occupied. Men waiting, sometimes singly,
sometimes in groups. Heads disappearing along paths.
. . . This is Monday's idle group, then—tomorrow there
will be another. It was so in Pershing Square and the
bars: the distinct shifts of idlers that a hustler relies on
to make it from day to day.

When the cars begin to thin out, Johnny drives back
very swiftly to the area where he saw the five cars. He
parks in the sandy fan and waits in his car a few moments.
He can see no one—but there's that cleared path narrowing very gradually into what must be several other paths.
And the cars—six now, and Johnny's.

All of a sudden, as it did at the landing of the balcony
that first night, Johnny's heart pumps cold blood.

But the iciness soon thaws into pulsing excitement.

Leaving his shirt in the car and lowering his Levi's,
typically, to his hips, Johnny gets out. Before taking the
wide path, he looks at his watch carefully (seven minutes
till 3:00)—as if he were about to execute a timed lap.

The branches of so many trees droop so thickly here
that the sun filters through only in tiny shifting sequin
points and jagged patches.

An atmosphere of eternal, sad twilight. . . .

Johnny has a feeling of having "been" here not long
ago—no: more a sense of having experienced this exact

mood. In the parks last night? Yes—and in the movie balcony. But other than that.

And then he remembers: the purple morning outside of Phoenix.

The wide path becomes several thinner ones, each narrowing even further, becoming circuitous, looping about trees, leading through clusters of bushes, to a slight ascent here, a decline there. And trees, trees. Still, no one.

It's like walking through a world of frozen green and gray.

At the edge of a strip of sun, Johnny sees the tip of a multicolored towel; and now: lying on it a blond youngman ostensibly sunbathing: "ostensibly," because the patch of light, drifting away already, is slightly smaller than the length of his body squared.

Coming on him so suddenly, Johnny is shocked to see him lying there in what appears to be complete nudity—shocked at first only because of the mind's unpreparedness. Before moving his eyes away abruptly (he couldn't allow that youngman, nor anyone else for that matter, to think he's interested—it's he who must be noticed), Johnny realizes the youngman is actually wearing a bikini, the kind with snaps on the sides. What made him appear naked is that he's unbuckled one of the two metal loops so that the front flap barely conceals his groin. Although pretending to sunbathe, he's already spotted Johnny and is leaning interestedly on one elbow, the flap of the bikini almost sliding off. Only a short distance away, another man, fully clothed, leans against a tree.

Noticing that Johnny is walking away, the blond youngman calls out hopefully to him: "Did you say something?"

Johnny Rio hardly glances back, turned off by the fact

that the youngman is obviously trying to attract attention
by his near nudity. (He doesn't attract *me!* Johnny thinks
defiantly.) "Nope" is all he answered as he walked away.

"Too bad," the blond youngman sighed wistfully, in
a tone that seems to indicate that he would come on with
Johnny on Johnny's terms. Nevertheless, Johnny moves on
because there's that other man near the tree. If, having
seen Johnny too, he still prefers the blond youngman, it
will depress Johnny very much. Rather than find out, he
moves quickly along another path circling the large round
trunk of a tree which could easily conceal someone leaning
against it, another kneeling in front.

The gray greenness is like mist.

Another pocket of sun. The sudden pouncing warmth
is a relief on Johnny's flesh.

Another man, young, dark, and wearing tan trunks, is
also pretending to sunbathe here. Johnny notices immediately—always weighing possible competition—that
the dark youngman is very handsome. Johnny suspects he's
looking for a mutually interested partner. So Johnny
doesn't even invite: never until someone expresses clear,
unequivocal desire on his one-way terms.

As Johnny moves through the green dusk along a gradually descending path which appears to lead to a kind of
grotto formed by overhanging branches, the dark youngman in tan trunks gets up. Johnny notices an older man
looking at them from a higher level of the path. Johnny
has seen four people here so far, and there were six cars
parked. Others are still about, unseen.

Indeed, there could be many more and you wouldn't
necessarily encounter them all, because this area extends
inward off the road for a depth of perhaps a short block—

then cascades down a hill. Looping erratically, the paths, made by feet that have walked them over and over—the dirt a grainy dust—might equal, unwound, several blocks, though the area itself is not nearly that wide.

Johnny feels as if he's walking—awake—through a dream.

The curving path he's on leads to the "grotto" created on the side of an incline by entwined twigs, vines, branches of trees, all dried and ashen on the underside from lack of exposure to the sun. There are "entrances" from two sides—like tunnels formed by overlapping branches.

Johnny spots the dark head of the youngman moving along this same path. Turning to the other side, which ascends to another grading, Johnny sees the blond youngman in the bikini (snapped on now) leaning with one hand on a tree, looking down at Johnny. The dark youngman, as if aware that the blond one may be preparing to advance toward Johnny, quickens his pace toward the enclosed section, into which Johnny has moved slightly back into the hollow. Waiting.

An opening of branches before the grottolike hollow reveals the awesome spectacle of the rest of the park as it yawns in lazy sunny stretches for miles.

Two other men are moving along the upper paths. Again the slow soundless movements of a dream; again the pervasive mood of silent trance where sexhunters gather for a specific purpose. Perhaps this gray mood is the opposite of that of gay bars, where laughter soars toward euphoria; or perhaps it's a further manifestation of it, just one degree higher: from laughter to euphoria to a hypnotized daze.

Johnny wonders which of the two youngmen would be more of a conquest. Both are goodlooking—the blond one very slim and boyishly flat; the dark one more masculine, his body solid. And then this shattering thought occurs: *What if they're cruising each other—and not me!* But no: The indications otherwise have been too clear.

Whoever gets to me first, Johnny decides.

But this happens—which causes Johnny Rio to turn in near desperation to the dark one:

The blond youngman, who is moving along the path, has fixed his cock so that its head protrudes over the bikini, and he's stroking it. Fiercely, Johnny turns away, resenting him deeply—hating him for apparently thinking that gesture would attract him. Frantically he faces the dark one, who, finally encouraged, moves swiftly into the grotto, touches Johnny between the legs—ignoring the blond youngman approaching. Johnny leans against the shell formed by the intertwined branches and vines.

The blond youngman moves swiftly to the entrance of the enclosure, to see better. This would excite Johnny if it weren't for that earlier gesture. Instead, he's apprehensive; but he doesn't move away because he's longing again for that sexual contact the dark youngman is preparing to make. He's unbuttoned Johnny's pants, which, being loose, slide down. Already shirtless, Johnny Rio is almost completely naked.

Leaning over, but sideways, the dark youngman is blowing Johnny—awkwardly in that position, his teeth chafing Johnny's prick. Johnny places his hand on the other's head, shifting it to the front. Squatting, holding Johnny's thighs, the dark youngman sucks him easily now.

The first one today! Johnny thinks. *I'm alive!*

But his sense of fulfillment is rendered imperfect by the fact that the blond youngman in the bikini has entered the grotto.

If he tries to rub against me or acts like he thinks I'll touch him, I'll bust him in his motherfucking face! Johnny decides, fists clenching.

Instead, the blond youngman reaches out—tentatively—to touch Johnny's chest, lightly. His fingers brush lower, to the edge of his pubic hair, brush his balls, touching Johnny's cock, holding it while the other sucks it.

Then the blond head bends toward Johnny—and Johnny, thinking the youngman wants to kiss him on the lips, draws back quickly, a knife of fear wrenched into him. But he's wrong again. What the blond youngman wants to do is this—and Johnny lets him: At the same time that he continues the light movements with the fingers of one hand and holds Johnny's prick with the other for the dark youngman to suck, he laps at Johnny's nipples with his tongue.

His attention drawn by a noise, Johnny turns and sees that the man who stood by the tree near the blond one earlier is surreptitiously nearing them. Afraid his discovered presence will stop what he obviously wants to watch, the man retreats for now.

After long moments during which he felt that, for whatever strange reason (perhaps the whirling thoughts), he wouldn't be able to make it—Johnny knows he'll come. His body stiffens. Alerted, the dark youngman plunges more rapidly with his mouth; the blond one cups Johnny's balls in his hand, his tongue flits in moist circles about his nipples.

In one sudden, jetting thrust, Johnny comes.

Immediately, he breaks away.

The two youngmen in trunks now turn to each other.

Having taken a wrong path, moving deeper into the area, Johnny feels an instant of panic—a panic, illogical, of being lost in the park, of remaining here forever . . . wandering. The feeling is quickly assuaged, and forgotten, when, taking another turn, he sees the striped towel where the blond youngman had lain.

As Johnny walks toward his car (at least eight more cars are in the cleared area now), another car—a long, shiny-new, brilliantly red convertible driving up—stops abruptly at the side of the road.

Johnny waits to see if the driver will get out.

But the man in the red convertible merely stares at him through dark, dark sunglasses.

Johnny drives all the way up the road. A long distance. This time he keeps going beyond where there are fewer cars and men—drives up until the road splits, and then he continues to the left. A sign nearby informs him the park closes at sundown.

Hands clinging to the steering wheel, he swerves to avoid running over a squirrel squashed on the road—a pulp of blood and fur. Cringing, Johnny's whole body responds in terror to the horrible spectacle. To draw his thoughts away from it, he raises the volume of the radio: Bob Dylan is singing in shanty defiance about the inevitable stoning the heart takes.

Discovering that this road leads back to the Observatory (the split in the road is the boundary of the sexhunt, then),

Johnny drives there again, parks to get a drink of water at the fountain. Again, he goes to the restroom.

Predictably, he stands before the Mirror. He looks beautiful!—as if the sex experiences are actually feeding him. He glows.

Suddenly he remembers the time, years ago, when he saw a vision of . . . corruption: that distorted face leering at him in the mirror—the face that sent him away . . . for three years.

Desire screaming, Johnny returns along the same road.

He drives past the hill before which he noticed several cars earlier (The Summit.)

Past the sandy dunes. (The Outpost.)

(His mind is giving names to the sexhunt sections of the park.)

An area he hadn't observed earlier: a flat spreading of scrubby land before which several unoccupied cars are parked. A crumbling iron tower, and, beyond, a veritable forest of trees. (He names it that: the Forest.) Across the road, an islet of sand, two more cars parked—each occupied by one man.

I'll explore that area later! Johnny thinks, anxious to reach what his mind has just named the Arena—within which is the Grotto, where the two youngmen came on with him earlier.

But when he gets there, there are no parked cars. The hunt has shifted to another area—perhaps the one he just passed. Yet he knows instinctively that one parked car will alert others; and his own goodlooking, slick car, with just the right degree of vulgarity—and its Texas license plates —will be an easily recognized signal of his presence.

And a car has already parked behind his.

Johnny walks into the Arena. It's even duskier now. He leans against a tree. Waits.

The eerie crunch of footsteps. The man who just drove up. A big, burly, goodlooking man, he might be a vice cop. Johnny will cool it. Instead of going to the Grotto, he explores another path down a slope. Unexpectedly, there's an opening into what appears to be a larger bower, large enough for several men—formed by arched branches, almost as if it had been carved. Johnny stands before it. The burly man is about ten feet up the path.

A few seconds later the man walks down. Johnny moves noncommittally aside. The man enters what Johnny will know as the Cave. Johnny can see the lower part of the man's body squatting on his haunches.

Johnny moves into the Cave.

Like the Grotto's, the Cave's wall, which forms the shell is dried twigs and vines, twisted. A thick low-hanging branch sags like a wounded arm. A darker grayness here.

The burly man makes an unequivocal motion with his tongue. Johnny stretches his lithe body, runs his hand down his own bare chest.

"God, you've got a beautiful body!" The man shatters the silence shockingly.

"What?" Johnny asks. He heard, but he wants to hear it again.

"Your body—it's beautiful!" the burly man repeats; and getting up, he touches Johnny's tanned body.

Bending over as he begins to unbutton Johnny's pants, he licks around Johnny's shoulders, his arms, chest, stomach—down, avoiding his prick for now, licking about his

upper thighs, even his knees, now his balls. And now he
sucks Johnny's cock, which is stiff and very hard.

One more! Johnny's mind says automatically.

He comes again, this time without difficulty.

"That was great, kid!" the burly man says enthusiastically. The sound of his voice—of any voice—in that near
soundless duskiness comes again as a shock. "I could suck
your dick all day!"

Johnny Rio smiles, dazzling the man further.

"You're a greatlooking kid," the man goes on, following Johnny out of the Cave. "You even smell sweet—taste
sweet! I'd sure like to see you again—maybe take you to
dinner. How about getting together tonight?"

With a shade of sadness—knowing that much has
changed irrevocably from the days with Tom—Johnny
says, "Oh, sure, man, I'll see you—around—some time;
you know, like if we run into each other."

The man understands this means no. "So long, kid," he
says, and adds: "And thanks a lot, hear?"

"Yeah, sure," says Johnny; he waits at the cleared portion of this area, letting the burly man go ahead—waits
there until he hears him drive away.

Johnny is deliberating whether to hang around longer.
He's come twice. But he's not sure he wants to leave yet.
He walks out of the Arena toward where his car is parked.

The drivers of two cars passing on opposite lanes turn
to stare at him. They'll come back, Johnny knows.

Suddenly he notices the long, shiny-red convertible he
saw earlier. It's parked once again across the road, several
feet away. The man in it turns toward Johnny. Johnny can
almost feel the black sunglassed stare. That's all he's really
been able to notice about the man at this distance.

Johnny waits by the road, again expecting that the man will get out, come to him. But he still doesn't—remains there, staring darkly at him.

Annoyed, Johnny drives down the road and out of the park.

EIGHT

JOHNNY RIO is wearing a faded-denim Western-style shirt unbuttoned all the way to his navel, sleeves rolled way up showing off his arms still pumped from exercising earlier, worn Levi's slung low. He checks his watch carefully as he walks into the green twilight of the Arena the next day: 2:26 P.M.

Back too—"sunbathing"—is the blond youngman in the snap bikini—one snap again unbuckled to create a pouch. This time, however, he's wearing something more: Wellington boots—either because he thinks they make him look more desirable or because they protect his feet from stickers.

Perhaps he's on vacation, or else he's one of the vast

wave of the perennially, or semiperennially, idle of Los
Angeles.

"Hul-*low!*" The youngman's greeting clearly indicates
he's still interested.

Johnny merely mutters, "Hi"—although of course he's
glad the blond youngman desires him again. But Johnny
doesn't want to make it with him twice. He doesn't know
why. He just knows it's so.

Last night, after returning to the motel, bathing, eating,
Johnny lay on a lounging chair for hours by the pool
(lighted fluorescent blue) until the Cloud deepened into
evening. A man, also sitting by the pool, kept inching his
chair closer and closer and gobbling him up with his eyes
—obviously trying to make him; he finally moved right
next to him and told him how much he admired a well-
made body. But although Johnny was, of course, pleased
by the attention, his cravings seemed to be— . . . What?
Suspended! Even earlier in the evening he hadn't been
tempted to go back to that movie theater, telling himself
that scene is too unpredictable. To Main Street? Yes: a
part of his life, always. But he didn't go there—and he
cooled the man cruising him by the pool—all because: It's
as if Griffith Park has become the arena of some unnamed
game, with rules not yet clearly defined.

Now as a scared child (and he was a very scared kid
though he put up a tough front), Johnny would often go to
bed saying a rosary (secretly, embarrassed that anyone
should know) in order to drive away the unfocused black
fears. Sometimes he wouldn't even actually pray the rosary,
he'd just count the beads over and over until he fell asleep.

In bed last night he remembered those childnights be-

cause once again he went to sleep counting—but, now, it
went like this:

Three people came on with me in the park this afternoon, though, sure, it's the same number as on the first
night in that movie theater, but in much less time, don't
forget, so that makes seven since Saturday night, and it
could've been eight if it hadn't been for that shitass car
in Lafayette Park last night.

Seven?

Or six?

He counted: the thin youngman in the balcony, one;
the guy in the men's room, two; the weird fucker in Mac-
Arthur Park, three; the two in trunks this afternoon, four
and five; the man who licked me all over, six. Six. I
must've forgotten one; I'm sure it's seven. Let's see: one,
two, three, four, five, six, and— . . . Just six. No, seven!
Yeah!—I forgot the man in the movies!—the first one who
sat next to me. He didn't really suck me, just tried to
through my pants—but he did grope me earlier and took
out my cock. I forgot to count him.

"Count"?

The word, looming large in his consciousness, startled
Johnny. Oh, it's not that I'm "counting" for chrissakes;
it's just that soon I'll have enough ("have"?) and then I
can stay away from the parks and everything ("enough"?).
It's not that I'm *counting!*

A vague game, emerging, vaguely.

Just in case the blond youngman is still tempted to
follow him, despite Johnny's curt dismissal, Johnny heads
for the Grotto but turns in another direction at a split

in this path, where it curls around trees (providing many secluded areas along the way), winding like a labyrinth.

The Labyrinth leads to an elevation abruptly sheer on one side like a cliff—high enough above the road to be invisible to passing cars. The elevation affords a long-range view of the Labyrinth and part of the clearing near the entrance to the Arena.

Johnny stands on the Cliff, waiting with cocky assurance for one of the several men he encountered along the way to approach him. He's begun to notice that although, of course, there are all types of men here, the park seems predominantly to attract the goodlooking and vigorous, the young and desirable.

Floating toward him like sailboats along the gray-green sea are three men—an adverse situation if each merely tries to outlast the other—the stalemate eating severely into his time. Though he certainly doesn't mind more than one person coming on with him at once—and others watching—several, gathering *before* any sex overture has been made, can thwart the whole scene.

Almost equally spaced out, the three form a triangle: a small, mousy man who immediately turns Johnny off; and the other two—young—one wearing a suit, the other Bermuda shorts. At another time—hustling—Johnny would have probably encouraged the small mousy man—spotting him as an easy mark. Now he wants to dissuade him and then decide between the other two. Unfortunately, the little man is the most aggressive; he's advancing more quickly.

It's 2:32.

Exasperated, Johnny moves away from the Cliff, along the Labyrinth—deliberately taking the path farthest from the little man and almost exactly halfway between the other two so they'll be encouraged to follow him. Along the way out of the Labyrinth, he encounters two other men cruising aimlessly (the mood of a trance, recurring . . .). Farther on, the blond youngman in the bikini and boots is posing while sitting on a low branch before an interested man. Approaching the Grotto, Johnny sees a man there rubbing his own cock. That doesn't necessarily mean that he wants to have someone come on with him—as Johnny learned yesterday when the blond youngman made the gesture that turned him off so bad and then came on with him on his one-way terms; but Johnny darts swiftly away anyhow—to the entrance of the Cave.

He's startled to hear the trampling of running feet approaching him.

Next to him panting, as though he'd sprinted several laps around the park, is someone who's either a college student or successfully trying to look like one. He's crewcut, and is wearing white shorts, tennis shoes, sweatshirt. Is he here innocently?

No.

He quickly gropes Johnny experimentally.

Both inside the Cave, "Whattayalike-to-do?" he asks Johnny.

"Nuthin, man—I don't like to do nuthin," Johnny answers curtly, annoyed, thinking the guy's implying a mutual scene.

"Ya wanna get blowed?" the guy in the sweatshirt says bluntly.

Johnny shrugs, pretending indifference.

"I'll blowya," the guy in the sweatshirt offers; and he does. A few seconds later he stops abruptly, stands up, unbuttons his white shorts, letting them drop. "You wanna fuck me?"

"Here?" Johnny asks after a few moments during which he decided that's not an insult, since he'd be assuming the man's role.

"Why not? . . . Cummon, fuck me. You don't know what you're missin if you don't," he says conceitedly.

"Naw," Johnny decides, bugged by the other's vanity. But: Was he even tempted? He's not sure.

"Suit yourself!" Once again he squats and blows Johnny.

After Johnny has come and is adjusting his pants, the guy in the sweatshirt says, "Another time you'll screw me, okay, stud?"

"Yeah—sometime," says Johnny, already moving out of the Cave.

"Groovy," the guy in the sweatshirt calls out.

Not even pausing to consider whether or not he's satisfied, Johnny's back in the clearing of the Arena knowing suddenly he needs to make it again.

It's 2:41.

One in less than half an hour! And: I could've made it in even less time if it hadn't been for that little man following me.

And goddamnit there he is again!—watching him from a few feet away. And there's the man in the suit, too, one of the earlier three.

How to get rid of the little man? I could tell him I'm hustling. No—that might just turn him on more and he'd wanna take me home. I could talk tough to him—that might turn him on too!

Hurrying to the Grotto. But, there—the unexpected sight jolts Johnny severely—the man who was playing with

himself earlier is blowing the blond youngman in Wellington boots and, now, no bikini. Johnny dashes away
quickly, curiously jarred. In his self-absorption he's forgotten that others—all over the park—are making it . . .
without him. (Too: Johnny Rio's morality, like his sex
scene, is at times one-way.)

Walking swiftly up the path, through the Labyrinth,
toward the Cliff, beyond it—passing other men (like ghosts
in a cemetery . . . drifting), not encouraging them for one
reason or another though they all stare at him. There's no
doubt he's the main attraction in the park.

He's moved in a narrow horseshoe almost exactly back
to where he started—and the mousy little man is there.

Damn!

Finally Johnny manages to dodge him long enough for
the suited man to gravitate toward him.

But this happens, shocking Johnny profoundly: Instead
of coming to him, the man moves to one side of Johnny.
Turning, Johnny sees the man in Bermuda shorts. The
man in the suit is advancing toward him, not Johnny!

Before the hideous feeling of rejection can descend on
him like an axe cutting him down, Johnny laughs aloud.
They were cruising each other! he thinks in disbelief.

He grasps for ready protection, for a "reason": Oh, hell,
they just felt more easy with each other, he thinks as he
watches them moving away together. They want to make
it mutually, and they gave up on me because they knew I
wouldn't because I'm so toughlooking, and they probably
thought I was hustling—because it can't help showing—
and they didn't want that scene—and then too the little
man was busting it up for me, and— . . .

Johnny's ego is intact this time . . . almost. What keeps

him from really feeling rejected is that neither of the two men was nearly as goodlooking nor as exciting as himself— and he knows that. Had either been really handsome, Johnny's heart would have been ripped.

It's 2:54.

There's the mousy man again!

On wayward inspiration, Johnny walks up to him, crosses his eyes crazily, and begins deliberately to tremble and shake, hands dangling at his sides quivering. That'll turn him off! he thinks, but he stops the contortions immediately when he sees someone else approaching:

A young kid: 18 years old—at the most.

Much, much too young, Johnny knows immediately, as he moves away (past the little man; is he finally turned off?), feeling a certain sadness for the kid, because he's so young and already here among the hungry hunters.

But the kid, crossing through the brush quickly, intercepts him on the path. "Wouldyouliketotakeawalkwith- me?" he asks breathlessly as if that's the only way he'll get the words out. A sandy-haired boy with blue, blue eyes, he'll be an awfully goodlooking man in a few years. "Will you?"

Jesus! He sounds so new at it! He reminds Johnny of someone. "I'm— . . . I'm in a hurry!" is all Johnny can finally think to say as he rushes out of the Arena.

Outside, there are nine cars—spilling onto the very road.

Inexperienced or not, the kid is persistent. He's followed Johnny. "Where are you going?" he asks him.

"Down the road," Johnny lies.

"Would you give me a ride please?"

"You mean you *walked* up for godssake?"

"Uh-huh."

"Get in," says Johnny.

No sooner are they driving down the road than the kid reaches out to touch Johnny's thigh, his fingers springing toward his groin.

For a split instant, Johnny lets him, thinking: He's not inexperienced at all!—maybe he's older than he looks; maybe— . . . He stops his thoughts, shoves the kid's hand away roughly. He's *still* too young!

"Ouch!" But the kid's blue eyes are beaming.

"Cut that out!" Johnny says—feeling awfully square— but fuck it! At the foot of the road, where the houses begin, he says "So long," to the kid.

"You mean you really want me to get out?"

"Right!" says Johnny, thinking, Am I gonna have to shove the bastard out?

"Then please: takemebackupagain," the kid says.

"Nope," Johnny says adamantly. "You'd better get out, I'm in a hurry." Convinced the kid shouldn't be in the park, Johnny is also determined to have his own way.

The kid gets out. Leaning through the window, he says, "Bye," looking at Johnny with eyes that hint of a fierce instant crush.

"Be cool!" Johnny attempts to erase the uncomfortable feeling of having come on square.

"So long!"

It's 3:09.

The little shit queered all that time! Johnny thinks, driving back up the road.

But he isn't really angered because all of a sudden he knows who the kid reminded him of.

Tina's boy.

On the radio, the mournful soul-tones of the Beatles, as Johnny, again shirtless, speeds to a place he noticed where three cars are squeezed tightly together alongside the road. He gets out.

A tangle of trees and vines like a tight clutch of wire. A narrow path leading to an even more tightly wound tangle, like a beehive. But: In the Beehive, there are already two men. Pants lowered, they lie on the dirt, face down, one pumping on top of the other. Either they didn't hear Johnny approach or they had reached a point where nothing would stop them. Johnny turns away instantly.

Back on the road, he notices another path. He takes it— only to discover that it leads once again to the Beehive, where the two men, through, are adjusting their pants.

Johnny drives away—fleeing the Arena when he sees the mousy little man standing before the entrance.

He parks before the unexplored area near the crumbling iron tower where he saw many cars yesterday—that area, flat and bushy for a few feet, soon becomes a dense forest. No cars outside the Forest now. Johnny's will be a signal.

So steep he almost slides down it, a path brings him to a tangle of branches and vines, like a giant nest lying on its side.

Inside, the Nest is even darker than the Cave. The sunlight hardly wounds the shadows. So strange. So strange to be just standing here among the twigs. Waiting. So strange and eerie. Like being alone in the world. Johnny feels as if he's been abandoned in a dream.

The sound of a car parking, a door slamming. Footsteps. Despite the vastness of this area, the many choices of paths, the number of secluded pockets, the man who has just parked is advancing ineluctably toward Johnny—as if some kind of radar leads sexhunters together.

Now that the man has looked at him with unmistakable hunger, Johnny executes his signal. The man advances.

Then: the crunch of twigs, of somebody losing control, slipping. They both turn, and there's the mousy man about ten feet away. God *damn!* Not even Johnny's loony exhibition turned him off!

Alarmed, the man who was about to approach Johnny has moved a few feet away.

Furious, Johnny drives away from the Forest.

It's 3:31.

Past the sandy Outpost. He's tempted to stop when he sees three men there; but it's too bare, too naked; they'd make conversation. *I'm in a hurry!*

Past the Summit. A few cars. But it would take too long to climb it. Another time, I'll leave it for another time, he thinks.

Finally, on a margin of the road, he parks. Anxious perspiration bathes his chest.

Noticing that beyond this islet of dirt a long steep trail leads way, way down toward what looks like an abandoned water tank, he gets out of his car.

On a slight mound he stands exhibiting himself before what he instantly names the Trail. In full view of the road, he'll attract those driving by. Knowing how his tanned muscularly slender body, shirtless, looks, he becomes semi-hard.

Then he sees it, long before it passes him, sees it along a curve as it ascends twisting more than half a mile away: the long, slick, shiny-new red convertible. Johnny feels instantly disoriented by it. *I'll turn my back to him!* he tells himself, immediately assuming it's the man he saw yesterday, the man wearing the dark sunglasses. But when he hears the insistent roar approaching, something compels him to turn. It's the same man all right!

Passing Johnny—the dark sunglasses turned toward him —the man stops his car several feet away. A slender man of undeterminable age, he looks back at Johnny.

Suddenly—blasting his honk very, very loudly, the sound chasing itself into the many hollows of the park— the man drives away, tires screeching.

Son of a bitch! Johnny thinks fiercely, sure the man was honking at him. But then he sees a car swerving closely around the curve; he could have been honking at it.

That car, also a convertible—white—cuts diagonally across the road and into the islet of dirt where Johnny stands.

A muscular man, roughlooking and also shirtless, gets out. Actually he's quite short, perhaps a few inches over five feet—but his chest is massive and sculptured. After appraising Johnny, who's still poised on the mound, the man turns as if to display two reddish X's, about six inches long, on his back. They're either tattooed or drawn on—Johnny can't tell—or they could be relatively fresh scars. There's something sinister about them.

Vaguely repelled, Johnny gets into his car and drives away—but only long enough for the man with the two X's to leave the area—which is too propitious to Johnny's purpose to abandon now. Returning (the man is gone), Johnny Rio exhibits himself again on the same mound of sandy dirt.

It's 3:47.

A sportscar, its top down, drives by: a man and a youngwoman in it. Turning around to look at Johnny as he applies his brakes quickly, the man says, "Wow!" Still staring at him, he's talking to the woman, who hasn't even glanced at Johnny. After a while, the man backs his car up, parks across the road, and gets out. Facing straight ahead, the youngwoman remains impassively in the car.

Dark and jazzy, the man approaches Johnny. "Lookin for action, babe?"

"What kind of action, *mano*?" Johnny asks.

"Like you're the grooviest; so choose your trip," the man says.

"What about her?" Johnny indicates the woman.

"She's a lez," the man says.

"You sure?" Johnny can't help asking.

"Couldn't be surer," the man laughs. "She's my wife. Well?"

They move down the Trail. The man sucks Johnny off. Aroused further by the fact the woman is so near—though she can't see them of course—Johnny came quickly. "Beautiful," the man says; "You blew my mind baby." They move out on the road together. The woman still hasn't glanced back. The dark man gets in his car, says something to her—and they drive away.

It's 3:58.

And Johnny Rio is ready to make it again.

One more and that's as many as yesterday and then I'll leave the park, he assures himself. Just one more to make it three. Like yesterday.

Driving up the road.

Cars back and forth.

Men staring.

Standing.

Moving.

Johnny parks near the hollow in a hill. Gets out.

The moment the man drives up, Johnny knows he won't make it with him.

"I'm hustling, man," Johnny tells him when the man approaches him—figuring that'll turn him off.

The man seems hurt.

Sorry, Johnny tries to make up for it: "It's just that I need bread for gasoline to get back home to Laredo," he lies. "I didn't wanna waste your time, man. Shoot, I can tell you're not the paying kind; I know you don't have to pay." He wants to make the man feel not insulted.

But Johnny was wrong. "How much?" the man asks.

Oh, no! "Ten bucks," Johnny says automatically from the past.

"I'll give you five."

"Fuck," Johnny says, insulted although he had no intention of making it with the man.

"Okay," the man reconsiders. "Ten. Why don't you leave your car here? I'll drive you—so you won't use up your gasoline," he adds slyly. He wants to make it at home.

"Naw," says Johnny. "I'll follow you."

When the man turns his car to the left, Johnny makes a quick right. He feels bad, sure. But: It would've taken so long!—and I didn't want him to come on with me!

In case the man will try to find him, Johnny drives to the Observatory. In the men's room a man is peeing. There for only that purpose, he's nevertheless taking his time. That bugs Johnny, who's impatient to be alone with the Mirror—he's beginning to think of it as his own.

When the man finally leaves, an obvious tourist walks in. Fuck! Johnny feels frustrated. The tourist finishes pissing. *Now* Johnny has the Mirror to himself.

Curiously—perhaps because all the interruptions made him nervous—he approaches it with hesitation, again remembering the distorted face which sent him away from Los Angeles. (Hell, I've got to get that out of my head; it happened long ago, when I was fucked up!)

I look great!

Impulsively, he kisses his own reflection.

A man standing before the Forest. The only one there, he's so unattractive—round, short—that no one else has stopped. Although he feels sorry for him, sure, Johnny too passes him by.

In the opposite lane, the man with the two X's on his back stops his car to see if Johnny will turn. He doesn't.

It's 4:33.

In the Arena: The youngman in the bikini is gone, towel and everything. Johnny has already attracted a man who is following him to the Grotto. I've made it again! But, almost there, the man hesitates. Another handsome youngman is standing on an upper level of the path. Is the man deciding between him and the other?—or is he just waiting for the other to go away so he can continue his pursuit of Johnny? And the handsome youngman—who— . . .? Johnny prefers not to find out. Rather than run the risk of feeling rejected, he moves out of the Arena. *I* left *them!*

It's 4:42.

In the Beehive: His face and hair as if dipped in blond

paint—as if the blondness had been smeared on, then chilled (but his eyes are intensely dark—perhaps black— or so they appear in the dimness)—the man stares at Johnny, who's entering from the path. In only a few moments, Johnny is looking down on the blond head bobbing back and forth between his legs. But Johnny is finding it very difficult to come. Determined, the blond man keeps sucking. Deciding this is the only way, Johnny pushes the blond head back, then down, indicating that he lick his balls while Johnny works his own cock to the point of coming. The blond man nestles between Johnny's legs. Just as he's about to give up, Johnny's aware of a sudden gathering at his groin. He pulls the blond head up, its mouth ready to receive the cum. While Johnny comes weakly in his mouth, the blond man jerks himself off.

Standing up, the blond man spits urgently, as if about to vomit. The dark eyes turn hostilely on Johnny. "Shit!" the blond man says.

"What the hell do you mean—shit?" Johnny asks indignantly.

The blond man stutters in obvious disgust: "I mean— . . . It's all so— . . . ." He rushes out, perhaps at the point of tears, nausea.

Depressed, Johnny sits in his car. He moodily looks at the sky shrouded by the gray Cloud. If it would only clear up—really clear up! he wishes. In Texas the sky— . . .

He smothers his thoughts with the loud blare of the radio, and the Lovin Spoonful:

> *Hot town! Summer in the city!*
> *Back of my neck! Gettin dirty an' gritty!*
> *Been down! Isn't it a pity? . . .*

It's 4:55.

There are even more cars in the park now. New people coming here from work.

Just one more! something insists inside of Johnny, although only minutes ago he had to force himself to come. One more to— . . . to— . . .

Why?

What "reason"?

Yeah! . . . —one more to make up for the one in Lafayette Park the night the car rammed in! Sure!—that's what's been bugging me! he tries to explain his franticness. That's all it is! I'll make it up and then I'll leave! he convinces himself, suddenly alarmed. Just—one!—more!

The sad ugly round man still waits forlornly before the Forest. Alone.

Back to the Arena. The Labyrinth. Standing on the Cliff, Johnny looks down at a bird smashed on the road. Johnny's body tenses at the sight; he walks away—to a tree that blocks that area of the road.

In his mid-20's, a youngman, goodlooking—and slightly swishy (and therefore somewhat out of place here since the effeminate, Johnny has noticed, generally stay away from the park)—stands very near him. But he's taking too much time! Johnny rubs his own prick, outlining it in his pants.

"Want to come to my place?" the swishy youngman asks quickly.

Engulfed by anxiety, Johnny almost gasps: "I can't! I'm in a hurry!"

"Oh, I don't live far," the swishy youngman says, "and I got a real nice apartment. I furnished it myself. Scarlet velvet drapes. I even got a statue of the Greek God Apollo in my garden. I'm going to have a fountain put in— . . ."

I'm wasting time! Johnny thinks urgently. Time, time, time! I can move away, there's another man I saw hunting nearby—but then all this time'll be wasted!

Finally, the swishy man gropes him.

"Suck me!" Johnny hears his own voice say, although he doesn't even know if he can get hard.

"Well!" says the swishy youngman, getting giddy, pretending innocence—although his fingers are on Johnny's prick. "I don't do that sort of thing. . . . In public." Sensing that Johnny is about to move away, he qualifies his statement: "*Generally* I don't" As he unbuttons Johnny's fly, he continues talking: "In fact, the first time I ever did it, I was forced." From his tone of voice and the way he rolls his eyes, it's quite clear he's evoking some kind of fantasy for himself, as he goes on: "This real butch number—cute, too, looked like you, come to think of it—well, he just grabbed my head in the steambath and said suckmebitch—kind of like you did except he said bitch. Well! What could I do? There I was with— . . ."

Johnny's urgency is boiling savagely. *Time!* He reaches for the man's head, forcing it down. It offers only token resistance.

Still indulging in the charade of inexperience, the swishy youngman gags—though Johnny's cock isn't even hard.

"Suck me, bitch!" Johnny utters the fantasy words: and instantly the swishy youngman swallows Johnny's barely stiffening prick to his balls.

Johnny breaks away—without even attempting to come —knowing suddenly he's got to leave the park.

Near his car and evidently waiting for him is the kid

he drove down the hill earlier. Johnny ignores him. Ignores the man with the two X's—driving by slowly, staring at Johnny. Ignores men sitting in their cars, others drifting like phantoms into the dusky green of the Arena.

Speeding away—cars multiplying along the road—Johnny has a feeling of having been involved in a ritual whose temple is Griffith Park.

It's 5:17.

NINE

JOHNNY RIO RETURNED to Griffith Park the next day. This time in the morning. Ten minutes after 11:00.

He had thought there wouldn't be much traffic in the park this early, but the funereal procession of slow-cruising cars had already begun; and when he parked before the Arena, there were five cars there already. It's summer, the season of indolence; and the subterranean reputation of the park draws people from everywhere.

Once again last night Johnny lay by the pool until he went to bed. And then it was as if sleep were a craggy, steep mountain he *had* to climb. . . . Eleven, eleven, eleven, his mind kept insisting—until, finally, he faded out.

It was still dark when he woke, startled, thinking he was in the park and it was night. . . . He got up, turned the lights on—to reassure himself. In the imagined night the park had looked like a graveyard, the bushes like stones.

I won't go back!

In the morning, he knew he would.

Long ago, Johnny saw a movie in which misty ghosts rose from their graves to prowl a foggy cemetery. He wasn't so much frightened as saddened by the silence and remoteness of it all—though at times the ghosts did fuse. Now, in the Arena—still struck by the sense of entering a separated world, and seeing the men here cruising the misty greenness—he's reminded of that movie—and of the awake "dream" he had last night. It's as if he's interrupted the walk of somnambulists.

As if to assert *his* aliveness, Johnny walked in like a warrior certain of victory.

The blond youngman in the bikini isn't here today, though he could be "sunbathing" somewhere else—his usual place is smothered by shadows.

Farther inside, Johnny encounters a very goodlooking youngman wearing a crazy sailor cap pushed back over masses of sandy curls that tumble down his forehead. (He can't possibly be a sailor, though, with hair so long it licks at his collar.) Cocky as hell, he's what queens refer to as "a real cute butch number." He too is dressed in Levi's, and a sweatshirt with the sleeves lopped off unevenly. Perhaps slightly shorter than Johnny, he's clearly competition.

In one sharp look—and only one—they became rivals, declare war. I'll show the fucker up! each obviously thinks.

Two other men in the area look from Johnny to the other, as if trying to decide which one to pursue (and it's clear both Johnny and the curly-haired youngman expect to be pursued). Of course, a clear-cut victory for Johnny would be for the two men to follow him to the Cliff, toward which he's swaggering.

Here comes one of them. And another!—a new one. Two on Johnny's turf. Only one on the other's. No, two; Johnny just saw a second one edging toward the curly-haired guy. Two and two—a draw for now. (But not really, because that other man cruising him hasn't seen *me* yet! Johnny points out to himself.)

Like in that movie in which ghosts materialized, new people keep appearing in the area—too many to divide into two camps. Others will be taking up different sections. Despite that, Johnny and the guy wearing the sailor cap are keeping track of each other—pointedly staying in sight, like generals gauging each other's maneuvers.

Okay then, thinks Johnny, I've got to make it before he does!—and let him know it—somehow!

From somewhere along the upper level of the Labyrinth, a youngish athletic man in a checkered shirt, like a lumberjack's, emerges. Johnny might have suspected him of being a vice cop if, ignoring the others preparing to approach Johnny from the other side, the man hadn't walked up boldly to him and said, "There's too many here, kid, I know a place down the path"—taking it for granted that he'll agree—which he does, admiring the other's to-the-point approach, especially since Johnny's in a hurry to make it before the curly-haired guy in the sailor's cap.

Ducking to avoid the snagging twigs, they hurry along the path. But Johnny's not sure the curly-haired guy saw

him going in here with the other. So: "Not here," Johnny
insists—moving (distinctly within view of the curly-haired
youngman—and he saw them) down the path in a curve to
the Grotto. There, the man in the checkered shirt is about
to bend down before Johnny when two men, one from
each side, move in to watch. The man in the checkered
shirt straightens up. Obviously he doesn't want spectators.

Exasperated—especially because as they moved away
Johnny saw that the curly-haired youngman was about to
be approached—Johnny slides down an incline—the other
following—heading for the Cave. About to go in, they back
out. Two men are in there already.

"I'll bust it up!" the man in the checkered shirt says.

"Naw, don't, man!" Johnny protests democratically.
Too late!—the man is in.

Johnny decides to move away, when two men come out
of the Cave mumbling angrily. Their anger doesn't keep
them from looking interestedly at Johnny, who discourages them.

"It's okay now," the man in the checkered shirt announces. "I just let them know I'd outlast them," he explains inside the Cave.

Now did the curly-haired guy see me coming here?
Johnny wonders. If so, he *knows* I'm making it. But maybe
he's making it somewhere, too! So a victory is questionable.

The man in the checkered shirt barely squats before
Johnny when: footsteps!

It's the curly-haired youngman!

Oh, wow!—does the fucker really think the guy I'm
with'll dig him better! Johnny thinks in outrage—
nevertheless experiencing an awful apprehension. A
groundless apprehension: The man crowns Johnny the

victor by pointedly looking away from the curly-haired youngman (after the first glance)—to send him away— while winking at Johnny, clearly preferring him. Trying futilely to swagger, the curly-haired youngman walks out in irrevocable defeat.

After he's come in the man's mouth ("Umm—that was good," the man said), Johnny Rio moves back up the path, feeling jubilant. (I won, and that cocky bastard knows it!) He looks around for the curly-haired youngman, spots him, goes out of his way to strut past him—and smiles dashingly to announce his triumph. When the other pretends not to see him, Johnny can't help saying: "Later, *mano!*"

In his car, he glances at his watch—although he resolved this morning before coming to the park that he wouldn't keep track of the hour as he did yesterday (time running out without action makes him panic too much) and that he wouldn't stay in the park long. But it's almost noon. And I'll just drive around till 12:00, he decides. Then I'll eat, really *see* a movie later—or go to Laguna Beach. But maybe the City Authorities have invaded it, too.

Now I'll just drive around the park. Till noon.

The Beehive. Two cars.

The Arena. Six.

The Forest. Three.

The Outpost. One.

The Summit. One.

Back again. Several other cars cruising both lanes.

The Summit. Three cars.

The Outpost. None.

The Forest. Six.

Johnny gets out.

The man in the checkered shirt does a double take when he sees him. Whatever he thinks about his still being around after just having come, the man wants to make it with him again: "How about it?"

"No, man," Johnny says quickly, thinking: Not him twice. "I'm just killing time now," he offers feebly.

"Well, if you get stiff again, kid . . ." the man extends an open invitation as he heads hopefully toward the Nest.

Johnny explores the interior of the Forest. The silence is almost physical. A gray shroud. The near-noon sun creates filigreed patterns here and there. Otherwise the thick trees choke the light savagely. . . . Johnny turns back when uncomfortable thoughts threaten him.

The curly-haired youngman with the sailor cap! (Did he recognize my car? Johnny wonders.) And another man approaching. The rivalry flares again: to see which of the two this man—important only because that rivalry—will prefer. Watching the man moving toward him, Johnny feels twice as cocksure—but prematurely. Because: Catching sight of the curly-haired youngman, the man entering turns abruptly away from Johnny and goes to the other.

Johnny feels the world collapse.

Now—as he goes off, with the man following—it's the youngman's turn to swagger (and he does—in long, tough strides)—glancing back and smiling triumphantly at Johnny. The bastard even strutted back a few steps to call out, "Later, mahn," to Johnny.

Your fat loss, motherfucker! Johnny puts that other man down in his mind.

Typically he grasps for support. It rushes, tumbles to his rescue like this: Okay, so the man chose him, but the man in the checkered shirt didn't—and what about that man who was cruising him when I first came into the park?—he preferred me—and anyhow we're different types entirely (not so), and that guy just happened to be more this man's type, that's all—so it's not that that guy with all the screwy curls is sexier than me, for chrissake—*he can't be!*

Johnny is floundering badly. None of these "reasons" has satisfied his deflated ego. He wishes, so much, that he'd left after the smashing victory of the Arena. He's never been able to reconcile himself to the fact that no one in the world, no matter how desirable, will *always* be preferred.

He drives to the Observatory. To the Mirror. It's becoming part of a Ritual. Is the face back? No. He's handsomer, more desirable every day. (How the blind hell could that mothering son-of-a-bitch prefer that other guy to *me!*)

Without preparation—as unexpected as the first bolt of lightning in a sudden storm—this thought strikes:

Why am I here!

To stop the flow! A stasis in time! A pause! The liberation of orgasm! Over so quickly! Only in retrospect!

Johnny is grasping for an important "reason" in his sudden chaotic and contradictory thoughts.

Pushing those thoughts away, he surprises himself in the Mirror. He's caught a glimpse of another face. Not the distorted one that grimaced at him so hideously three years ago. Not the lean, sensual, dark-angel face either. Another face: a face he's never seen before.

A face marked by enormous, bewildered sorrow.

By the time he finished lunch he was feeling great again.

His spirits began to rise when, leaving the park, a man followed him determinedly for blocks along Los Feliz Avenue, probably to find out where he lives. Johnny finally dodged him. In addition, at the coffeeshop where he ate, three youngmen kept turning to look at him with giddy interest; and the waitress (and *that*'s really something!) flirted with him and asked him insinuatingly is there *any*thing else he needs. Johnny gobbled the admiration. He even found the perfect bandage for his scratched vanity: That cheap bastard went after the curly-haired guy because he was sure I was hustling and the other guy was for free!

Okay. That's that!

After he left the restaurant, he took a drive to Hollywood. Either he'd forgotten what it looked like (or never really "saw" it)—or the Boulevard too had changed: unbelievably trashy and shabby, like a blocks-long remnant store in smog-tinted technicolor. And Selma Avenue in the afternoon looks like a skimpy movie set. (So much of my life buried in these streets . . . late alert nights . . . early dazed mornings.) Back on the Boulevard, even without getting out of his car, he got cruised at stoplights. That much, then, hasn't changed! (And something else which pleases him: the tribes of hippy "flower children," young men and young girls in beautiful costumes. . . .)

Feeling as desirable as he does now, he *has* to return to the park. (Just one more!)

The blond youngman in the bikini is back in his spot. "Hi!" he calls out, to indicate his undimmed interest.

"Hi-yuh!" Johnny says. And pauses. Why not? Why not let that guy come on with me again? After all, he didn't suck me, just held it for the other guy, remember? If I let him blow me now, it'll be like two *different* ones. No, he decides; that's cheating.

"Cheating"! That word weighs heavily—disturbingly—in his mind—just as the word "count" did the night before last.

Now: a still-vague game—but with vague rules . . . and in a clearly designated arena.

Along the Labyrinth, a man follows him. Johnny immediately decides: Not him.

The Cliff. Another. No.

The Grotto. Two men playing with each other.

To the Cave quickly. A pair of legs, pants at the ankles; two knees on the ground. Johnny flees.

He drives to the Beehive, gets out. No one there except him. He waits among the shadows. Minutes. No one. The feeling of isolation. Trapped so that the thoughts he avoids are threatening him. They scatter: Johnny is no longer alone.

Two men flank him, entering almost simultaneously from opposite sides. They must have recognized his car from earlier because they came toward him with a certainty that implied they knew who was here.

One says quickly, "Let him, I'll watch out for you!" He means he'll look out for intruders—but he'll also be watching, of course.

Bugged for a second ("Hell, I don't care," he answers), Johnny finally figures what the hell, the guy prefers looking.

Perhaps the other man overheard because he acts quickly, lowering Johnny's pants, going down on him. After staring raptly for several moments, the man who

spoke to Johnny abandons his role as watcher. He eases
the other one away, and now *he* sucks Johnny's cock de-
vouringly. The other watches for a few moments, and then
he squats and rims Johnny, who comes in a quick
eruption.

Outside, the two men get into one car. They were together all along.

Johnny returns up the road. He's about to get out at
the Arena (though he's just come—and twice today)—
when a heavy, square camper autobus drives up. Out
comes a youngman and his girlfriend, laughing, carrying a
lunch basket as they run into the treed section. Because of
the many cars there, they must think this is good picnic
ground! Johnny waits in his car to see what'll happen—
amused as he imagines the startled men inside the Arena
when they see the man and his girlfriend preparing to: *picnic!*

Here they come!—the youngman and his girlfriend:
rushing out!—driving away as fast as the lazy lumbering
camper can go.

Johnny laughs aloud—laughter which is partly released
tension, partly genuine humor—and a fleeting sadness,
disguised.

He decides to drive to the Forest. As he nears it, he sees
a parked red car. The red convertible! But no; it's a hardtop—not new. Just thinking of the man with the dark
sunglasses angers Johnny—the way he looks at him but
won't approach him; the way he seems to follow him
around. He's glad the bastard isn't here today; he's probably at work.

Seeing the man in the checkered shirt in the car behind
him, Johnny drives away from the Forest, somewhat em-

barrassed. Approaching the sandy Outpost, he immediately notices the curly-haired guy again!—standing there with his shoulders hunched, fingers looped inside the waist of his pants: trying to look hoody and tough. Shit! And two men cruising him. (So what? Johnny asks. *I'm* not there; if I was, they'd be after *me!*) Johnny slows down, about to stop and get off—absolutely sure he can easily bust up the guy's scene with those two (who would certainly prefer me, Johnny repeats): but he decides not to, figuring the guy's so cocky he might think he's trying to come on with him! . . . Why the hell is he still here, anyway? Didn't he make it with that guy in the Forest? (Cheap son-of-a-bitch!) But then I've made it with three guys and come twice—and I'm still here, he reminds himself.

As Johnny drives by, he and the curly-haired youngman wearing the sailor cap look at each other—and—two of a kind—they both turn away immediately after.

As Paul Revere and the Raiders groan over the radio:

> *Hungry for those good things, baby,*
> *Hungry through and through;*
> *I'm hungry for that good life, baby—* . . .

Johnny parks in the islet of dirt and sand before the Trail. As before, he stands exhibiting himself on the mound there.

The first person who stopped annoyed him badly. "Are you a dancer?" the man asked him through the window of his car.

Johnny changed his stance quickly. "No!" he said curtly, deepening his voice, irritated at being taken for a dancer.

"An actor?" the man persists.

Oh, for chrissake! "No, man!"

"It's just that you're so goodlooking and you've got such a beautiful body." The man senses Johnny's annoyance. That calms him down somewhat.

But the man bugs the scene again. "Is that really all tan?"

Now what the hell does he think it is? Johnny decides to ignore him.

"I bet you're a 'traveling salesman,'" the man persists, his meaning unequivocal: He's pegged Johnny as a tramping hustler.

The man continues to sit in his car staring at him. Johnny continues to ignore him, still exhibiting himself on the mound so someone else will stop and hopefully drive this guy away.

Suddenly Johnny realizes the man is jerking off looking at him. He pretends not to notice, but it pleases his vanity; and he flexes his body exhibitionistically for the man, who, after a few seconds—evidently having come—drives off.

Then: Long, long minutes elapse.

A longer time.

Johnny avoids looking at his watch.

Cars pass, pause, move on.

More empty time!

I'm looking too rough! Johnny reasons. Indeed, since the man took him for a dancer, he's been clenching his fists. Because: a dancer wouldn't stand *that* butch!

"Please!—just stand over me and let me jerk you off on me!" the man pleads, thrusting himself on the dirt while Johnny straddles him (with difficulty because of his

pants dropped down over his boots). They're by the water
tank at the base of the Trail.

The face Johnny looks down on radiates desire.

The man has Johnny's cock in his hand, trying to jerk
him off in that position. But Johnny can't come that way
right now—he's only semihard. Bending at the knees, he
tries pulling himself off into the man's open mouth. At last
he comes: on the other's tongue—weakly.

A few moments later he's standing by the road alone
again.

Now Johnny has come three times, four people have
made it with him and many more have wanted to, one
jerked off just watching him. And what does he feel? A
screaming need still unfulfilled.

He panics when he finally looks at his watch: It's 4:30!
He's been here since morning—longer than yesterday—
and he's made it with the same number.

I'll stay around and make it just one time more than
yesterday, and then I'll leave for sure, he tells himself.

Driving down the road. Now that he's familiar with this
area of the park, it doesn't seem so vast as it did at first;
he moves like an animal in his jungle. (He's even begun
to recognize some men by their cars. Like: the white convertible: the scary man with the two X's; he's back, probably just got off work.) For these three days the park has
become his world.

My world!

Shit, no! he rejects the thought.

Not mine!

To prove it, he decides to leave the park now—skip the
fifth.

But as he drives past the Forest and sees two cars, he thinks:

Five.

He waits in the Nest.

The curly-haired youngman swaggers in. Shirtless too now—but he's still wearing the sailor cap.

His car, which Johnny would have recognized, wasn't one of the two parked outside by the road; and so Johnny wonders if he saw *his* car and actually came here looking for him.

Suddenly Johnny knows there could be no more decisive triumph in this crazy battle they've been waging since morning than for this youngman to come on with him.

But neither is looking at the other. They just stand there—although: To someone else looking on impartially they might seem to be swaying sideways toward each other. In fact, the curly-haired youngman has let his knuckles touch Johnny's. Casually: as if it Just Happened accidentally.

Okay, okay, thinks Johnny, remembering what Danny said on the beach about wrestling, *guys* touch knuckles. But he breaks the contact after hardly a few moments. He begins to rub his own cock; the curly-haired youngman rubs *his* own. Johnny looks away; the other does too. Like children playing follow-the-leader. Boldly, Johnny brings out his prick, works it up, enticing the other. Instead of reaching for it—as Johnny clearly wanted him to—the curly-haired youngman brings *his* prick out and begins to work it up too. (That doesn't mean anything! Johnny reminds himself quickly. Remember the blond guy in the bikini, how he played with his own cock and then— . . .)

But, now, Johnny's victory or defeat is *contingent* upon whether the other touches his cock. *It's got to happen!*

Johnny wins: The curly-haired youngman wearing the sailor cap is holding Johnny's quickly stiffening prick—but lightly, as if undecided, evidently expecting that, now, Johnny will take his. When he doesn't, the youngman reaches for Johnny's hand, clearly to coax a mutual act. Johnny jerks his hand away angrily.

"I don't dig that, man!" he says gruffly.

The curly-haired youngman releases Johnny's cock instantly. "Naw?—then what do you dig, mahn?" he asks him.

"Getting blown," Johnny says.

"So do I, mahn." But, sadly, the cockiness is fading. "If I blow you, will you blow me?" he blurts hurriedly.

"Hell, no!" says Johnny with incredible outrage.

"Then me neither!" the youngman says.

Cocks stuffed indignantly into respective flies; flies buttoned hurriedly pretending they hadn't gaped open only seconds before.

"Fuck it," Johnny says—stalking furiously out of the Nest.

"Yeah—fuck it!" the other calls out angrily.

Anyway, Johnny thinks, *he* played with *my* cock—and *I* didn't touch *his!*

And yet— . . .

Johnny doesn't feel happy with his victory. He can't help wishing it had stayed a tie.

In his darkening motel room.

Five! (For a curious moment, he hesitated over including the curly-haired kid of this afternoon; but then, firmly, he insisted: *Five!*) Four yesterday! Three the day before! Just one the day before that. . . . God*damn* that shit-ass car in Lafayette Park! (He's beginning to think of that incident as though it had been deliberately planned: *Is it possible?* Of course not! Some silly-ass drunk, that's all. But— . . . Someone from the other park, maybe—from MacArthur Park! The man I scared away by coming on tough—or—yeah!—the loony who ranted about "love" and then sucked me and didn't even say so-long-buddy! . . . Oh, wow, *mano,* he tells himself, you're too much! Some drunk makes a weird U-turn, busts up your scene, and you think he was aiming for you on purpose—oh, wow! Cool it! He tries to ridicule his potential obsession.) . . . Five, four, three, one. And three before that!

For godssake!—I haven't included Tina! No. Not her. Why? Just because! A reason! Well, she's a girl—that kid's mother, for chrissake!

Three, one, three, four, five. Three and one—four! And three—seven! And five— . . . I mean, *four*—eleven! And five—sixteen! *Sixteen!* . . . Wait! That real young kid yesterday—I pushed his hand away and didn't want him to (so it's not my fault!)—but he *did* grope me! Hell, I wouldn't include him anyway. He's too young. Anyhow he didn't really touch me—only through my pants. . . . Only if someone actually touches my cock, directly— . . .

A rule! A definite rule. Rule One.

And it can't be the same one twice.

Rule Two!

And if— . . .

Oh, God!

Shocked suddenly by his feverish thoughts—jolted as if

someone had shaken him unexpectedly—Johnny left his room impulsively to do this:

He drove downtown, parked, walked to the corner of Broadway and 7th.

She's back!

The Negro woman proclaiming doom dispassionately is back!

Okay.

Okay.

We're still not doomed.

TEN

"JOHN! You look simply smashing!"

Sebastian Michaels hugged Johnny warmly. Johnny is so glad to hear his own name (the first time in— . . . !) that he doesn't pull away as he usually does, instinctively, when anyone, male or female, tries to embrace him unexpectedly.

Indeed, it was partly to restore his own identity that Johnny called Sebastian.

A few minutes after 10:00 this morning Johnny Rio was automatically on his way to the park—when a furious rebellion against going there raged within him.

A powerful fear seized him.

Impulsively—just as he had called Tom—he telephoned

Sebastian. "Oh, please *do* come over!" Sebastian said enthusiastically. "For dinner."

Not early enough for Johnny: The fear persisted, increased; and the hours till evening stood before him like an unbudging gray rock. Determined not to go to the park, he exercised until he was exhausted; he sunbathed, read, listened to the radio, watched television; but as with an addict in withdrawal, nothing soothed his shrieking nerves: He felt a physical demand for the park—a craving as commanding as those triggered by hunger, thirst. Finally it was time! Avoiding the familiar streets, he drove into Santa Monica.

"It sure is good to see you, Sebastian," he says.

A small, slender, grayish-blond man in his 50's, Sebastian Michaels is a famous writer of fine, serious, often beautiful, books.

They sit in Sebastian's lovely house in the Santa Monica Canyon. An enormous open window greets a lush vista of Malibu and the magnificent ocean.

"But I simply can't get over how wonderful you look," Sebastian says. "Frankly, one expected you to have faded."

"Why?" asks Johnny—but he knows: People generally expect that those who flash brightly will dim quickly.

Sebastian explains it more nicely: "One hardly expected you to become better looking in three years; few people do."

Johnny's ego soaks up his words. And he does look "smashing": A pale-blue silk shirt—two buttons open at the throat—clings to his body so sensually as to suggest nakedness. He exudes sexuality and knows it.

Though the evening is warm, a fireplace stacked with wood warns of the chill California nights.

It was on such a cool night, before that fireplace, that Johnny first got to know Sebastian.

Introduced to him earlier by a mutual acquaintance on whom Sebastian happened to drop in one afternoon, Johnny—on a murky day when the sun doggedly refused to shine on the beach—accepted Sebastian's invitation to call him.

After dinner at a nearby restaurant, Johnny and Sebastian sat drinking by the fireplace. Tony Lewis—Sebastian's young companion for several years—was away at art school. In rebellion against the hustler's life, which relies on silence in order to readily fit *any* prospective client's sex fantasy—and impressed by Sebastian's fame as a writer of sensitivity and perception—Johnny talked freely about his frantic life, even about his increasingly complicated relationship with Tom. Sebastian listened with serious attention. Both very high—almost drunk—Sebastian invited Johnny to spend the night in the guest room—accompanying his invitation with what seemed a more-than-cursory press on Johnny's thigh. Johnny declined; he knew that if Sebastian came on with him he'd be convinced the famous writer had listened to him only because of a sexual interest and not—as Johnny wished—because he wanted to be an understanding friend. Johnny needed the latter much, much more than the former.

Very late that night Johnny hitchhiked from Santa Monica—and made it (parked by a dark abandoned filling-station) with the man who gave him a ride—and five quick bucks. Then Johnny asked the man to drop him off one block from Tom's house. Waking Tom up, Johnny told him, "I just had a strong urge to sleep here tonight."

After that, the ambiguous incident with Sebastian was ignored; and Johnny would drop in occasionally from the beach to talk with him. Subsequently, Johnny even met Tony Lewis.

"Tony will be out presently," Sebastian is explaining now as he sets golden drinks before them. "And some friends of yours and ours will be coming over soon."

Johnny knows who they'll be: two writers he met through Sebastian. Creative and sophisticated—and at times sexually chauvinistic—they represent still another aspect of the homosexual world—a world as vast and complex as that of heterosexuality.

"Emory Travis," Sebastian is naming the people who'll be over, "and Paul Blake and his actor . . . friend." In saying "friend," Sebastian didn't quite use the inflection which makes the word a euphemism for "lover"; he did, however, pause before it—as if he's not certain.

And so again it's six days of Saturday and one of Sunday. That's how Johnny remembers his life among people who keep no definite hours.

"What have you been doing, Sebastian?" Johnny asks, longing for conversation.

"Oh, they've finally seduced me into doing a screenplay—and from some absolutely ghastly bestseller: *The Pope Goes to Heaven*. Simply a trashy, irrelevant book—but if I camp it up, it might be rather fun!" Sebastian says. "Oh, here's Tony!"

Once preciously pretty, Tony Lewis in his 30's has become a goodlooking man. "John!—how *well* you're looking!" They're greeting each other warmly when Emory Travis arrives.

"Oh . . . *John! So . . . good!*" (They've never called him

Johnny—perhaps considering that to be his hustling name.) "You look absolutely ravishing! Ummm!" Emory is a tall, skinny, fastidious-looking man of about 45. Soon after they first met, through Sebastian, he made a pass at Johnny—a pass which Johnny quickly discouraged for the same reason he declined to spend the night at Sebastian's. Now Emory camps up his interest in Johnny as though he's simply languishing from unrequited love.

Emory, Sebastian, and Tony kiss in greeting.

They've hardly sat down when here are Paul and his actor . . . friend. Kisses for Paul. But not for Paul's friend, whom Sebastian, Tony, and Emory have apparently met before.

"John!" Paul greets him with a handshake. "How very good!" An intelligent face compensates for Paul's lack of goodlooks. "This is Guy Young," Paul introduces his friend. "Guy—John Rio."

Johnny Rio and Guy Young glance at each other—and quickly away.

But in that one glance Johnny sees that Guy is neither tall nor short—about Johnny's size: a very handsome dark youngman with curly black hair and enormous brooding eyes rimmed by thick lashes. Despite his name—which is probably only his actor's name—he looks distinctly Italian. Automatically weighing him as competition or otherwise, as he always does with others who are goodlooking, Johnny acknowledges a certain sensuality about him, especially in the pouting lips, the unruly black hair—which make him resemble a rock-n-roll singer—or, more, one of the moody dark youngmen who play (inevitably in black T-shirts) sad, sensitive, rebellious gang leaders in movies about Brooklyn or Chicago.

They sit about a square table while Sebastian makes drinks for the others. Johnny waits for Paul (whom he doesn't know as well as he knows the others, having seen him only a couple of times or so and never alone) to comment on how very fine Johnny looks.

Instead, Paul asks him: "And how long will you be in southern California, John?"

Johnny is actually startled by the question. "Oh—ah—I— . . . oh, a few days," he finally stutters. For those moments he forgot he's returned for ten days. "And what have you been doing, Paul?" he asks suddenly, to change whatever disconcerting course his thoughts hinted of taking.

"Oh, I've got a book coming out—I'll probably have copies when you come over— . . . Sunday? Will you still be here then?"

"Sure," Johnny says quickly, no longer disoriented; "I'm leaving Monday—before noon. I came back for only ten days. I'll be here four more."

("Oh, so soon!" pined Emory.)

"Then Sunday—for dinner." Paul invites everyone.

All agree—yes, fine, marvelous, wonderful.

"And I'm working on a screenplay," Paul continues. "Really a *great* bore. Stifling! But it might be fun."

Johnny remembers: In the land of technicolor, life, if it's fun, is good; when it isn't, it's a bore.

"And *you* Emory?" Johnny asks politely, intending then to ask Tony.

"Oh, darling, how *nice* of you to ask. I'm doing a simply maddening screenplay—the most completely *boring* thing in existence: *When the Swans Come Home to Roost.* . . . About a revolution in South America. . . . But *you*—

what have *you* been doing? You've always led *such* an exciting life!"

"I've been Away—in Laredo—leading a very, very quiet life." He wants to indicate to them that in Laredo he hasn't been involved in the turbulent life they all know he lived here—the life Emory's words implied just now. "I left Los Angeles in a hurry," he reminds them.

"Oh, I quite remember," says Sebastian. "I didn't know what had happened to you until I got your postcard with a picture of a . . . cactus?"

"*I* pined for days!" says Emory.

"He really did," Tony confirms.

Sitting facing Johnny—but pointedly looking away (just as Johnny pointedly looks away from *him* each time their eyes meet accidentally—and they do so recurrently)—Guy Young has just poured himself another large shot of liquor, as if to quench a moody restlessness which is already apparent.

"You've been in Laredo *three years?*" Sebastian sounds incredulous, perhaps because he knows so much about the turbulent life Johnny led here. "But whatever can you do there?"

"I work for my father's brother. In the evenings. At home. In the day I exercise a lot." He flexes; the silk shirt protests lovingly.

"Oh, my, it does show!" says Emory. "I *should* exercise," he says somewhat distractedly.

"And here—now that you're Back—for ten days?—are you still leading: 'a very, very quiet life'?" Sebastian asks.

Now as a kid, Johnny Rio loved to go to confession—rather, he loved the feeling afterwards of purity. Now that he no longer believes in God, he's replaced strict confession with a compulsive honesty about his sexual activities, but that leaves him without absolution—without a substitute for salvation. . . . Johnny confesses: "No—I've been back only a few days—since Friday—and I've already made it with 16 people!"

"Sixteen! Oh, I am envious!—and heartbroken," says Emory.

"I'm terribly impressed!" says Tony.

"Marvelous!" says Paul.

Sebastian said nothing.

Aware that he hasn't made it clear that he spoke in despair when he mentioned the 16 people, Johnny tries to clarify the matter this way: "But it *shouldn't* be like that—not this time. I mean: Like I wasn't too happy when I was hustling and fucking around. (You know that, Sebastian.) That's why I left—I just knew I had to. And I kept away for three years. But—just like I knew I had to leave—I knew I had to return; I guess because I had to know if I'd really changed in those three years—changed inside—and to find out if I could stop hiding like I have been in Laredo—scared all the time even when I didn't know it."

Swallowing his second drink, Guy looks openly at Johnny for the first time since they were introduced. "But now— . . . Now— . . ." Johnny goes on. "And it's not for money any more—just for kicks!" He feels infinitely frustrated. He doubts that he's been able to convey the mysterious seriousness this has for him. He had wanted to verbalize the strange fear he felt today. "Something's 'off,'" is how he attempts to describe it again.

Still, Paul is already chiding him, though gently: "I'm sure all this has to do with the fact that like all so-called immoral people you're much too moral, John. Too bogged down in guilt."

Tony: "Imaginary guilt."

Paul: "I'm absolutely convinced it merely has to do with all that nonsense about original sin—which was clearly devised by the impotent to outlaw fun!"

Emory: "How clearly you've convinced me!"

Nevertheless, Johnny tries again, floundering, wanting to indicate that it doesn't have to do with guilt so much as with something out of control: "And I haven't screwed around every one of those days. Like today, I actually forced myself not to go to the park."

"Of *course* you mean Griffith Park," Emory says; admitting: "I've heard *all* about it. It's supposed to be the most divinely *wild* place in the world!—but too much for me! . . . And did you read some time back about the hermit who was discovered to have been living there undetected for two years—sleeping on leaves, eating whatever he could find?" he asks everyone.

Johnny remembers how the park looked in the darkness of his awake dream. He shudders at the thought of someone "living" there. "It's possible—it's a hell of a big park," he says. "I'm sure he wasn't in the same sections I mean, though."

Guy continues to drink silently.

"Anyway! Why did you force yourself not to go today?" Tony wants to know.

"Because— . . ." Johnny was about to say: Suddenly I was afraid! But he feels the futility of trying to convey the strange, mounting horror of— . . . Of what? Being swallowed.

"Perhaps you should try—only because you imply there

should be something else—and only because of that—perhaps you should try . . . a fuller range of experience," Sebastian fills the silence for Johnny.

"You mean why don't *I* come on with somebody—mutually?" They all know what his one-sided sexual scene is: the single homosexual act which is his symbol of sexual power: to have his body adored.

"In a general sense, yes," says Sebastian, "but more what it leaves unsaid."

"If I wanted to, I would," Johnny says staunchly.

"It may be that, among all those numbers of people, you've been looking for *the* number," Emory suggests.

"But *the* number is death!" Sebastian surprised everyone by saying—though he smiled and said it lightly.

"Oh, how dreary and black and morbid and— . . . *boring!*" Emory laughs. "I very clearly meant *the* one *person!*"

"Anyway!" says Sebastian to Johnny. "Your ten-day period of discovery isn't up yet. And the discovery of a lifetime can occur— . . . in one second!"

At the candlelit dinner table, random conversation:

Sebastian on using real people in novels: "It's axiomatic: One can say anything one wants about a person's morals—describe them as black as black—but *never* anything disparaging about his physical appearance!"

Paul: "I'm unswervingly convinced!"

Emory on camp: "I wish that giddy woman who started the populace fussing had shut up. My butcher the other day offered me a 'campy leg of veal.'"

Tony on movies and women: "It was marvelous! For once they allowed the woman to tower over the man. That way she even *looked* like a man-eater."

Emory, as if grading an essay: "Perfect!"

Sebastian on heterosexuality: "It's brought about the downfall of all the great civilizations."

Tony: "I've never doubted it for an instant."

Paul on Sodom: "I'm convinced the real reason Lot's wife looked back is that she wanted to make sure the city was razed—otherwise, she'd go back to join the fun. She turned into salt in simply absolute boredom at the prospect before her!"

"Oh, the poor dear," says Emory.

Johnny is reacting to the mixture of wine and liquor; he hasn't drunk in so very long. The conversation at the table is beginning to float in and out of his awareness.

Sixteen.

Out of nowhere he "heard" the number in a part of his mind, which then "said": It could have been 19 or 20 or 21—if you'd gone today.

Dinner over, they sit in the living room drinking.

Sixteen! Johnny's mind insists. The Labyrinth, the Cliff, the Trail. . . . Where are the people who were there? —now that the park is dark, black, closed, dark? Where? The Nest. . . . And where's the curly-haired guy wearing the sailor's cap? I should've at least said so long to him. That might've helped. He must feel rotten. . . . And all, all, all those people. Without names.

Suddenly the Fear chokes Johnny with iron fingers.

I'll never go back again!

The sudden resolution is so strong, the Fear so encompassing, that he can hardly wait for tomorrow to prove he won't return to the park.

All at once he notices that everyone is staring at him in what appears to be either apprehension or shock, as if awaiting some angry response from him—all except Guy, who's merely looking at him. Johnny realizes that someone just asked him something. "What?"

"With all those people—did you ever have . . . several at the same time?" The question came—completely unexpected and in thick, liquored, slurred tones—from Guy. It's the first time he's addressed Johnny since they mumbled a few words on being introduced.

Now Johnny might have resented the blunt question from someone he's just met, and with others around, if it weren't that he perceived no real malice in it; it was obviously an expression of fascination released perhaps by the liquor. Rather than angering him, the fact of that fascination saddens him in a curious way.

The others are still looking on in disbelief—not realizing that the question didn't bother him. In fact, he would have answered; but Tony said quickly: "John, may I show you my recent drawings?"

"I'll come too," Emory says, flinging a look like a dart at Guy.

Guy merely takes a long, long swallow of his drink.

In Tony's studio. Outside the main house. A cool sea breeze assures Johnny he's not drunk at all.

"Of course, I *did* want to show you my drawings," Tony is saying as he brings them out—black-and-white portraits, mostly of writers, dancers, actors and actresses, "but I also wanted to stop Guy from going on so rudely."

Emory: "It's a bore. . . . What an interesting expression on Marla Hedwig's face. That's the first time anyone's ever pictured her not showing her legs."

By deliberately emphasizing the eyes and mouths and merely sketching in the other details in his portraits, Tony

has achieved a haunting, haunted effect, to which Johnny
immediately responds. Each face seems to be on the brink
of self-discovery.

Tony: "Yes, I quite like it myself. . . . I'm sure Guy
won't stay at Paul's after he starts acting again."

Emory: "I'm absolutely convinced he'll move out immediately. As much as we all *love* dear Paul, we're not
blind—and whatever one may think of Guy, he *is* very
goodlooking—and, well, after all, his lovers have been
people like Tim Story, who's the rage on Broadway."

Determined not to mention Guy, Johnny makes com-
ments on Tony's drawings as he exhibits each.

Emory: "*Do* notice what Tony does with the eyes! Oh,
that's Barbara Banner!"

Tony: "Her famous nose gave me the most difficulty."

Emory explains to Johnny: "Now that Guy has con-
descended to work on television and films, he's been staying with Paul." To Tony: "You did catch the nose just
right."

Now it's perfectly obvious to Johnny that they don't
like Guy because they suspect he's staying with Paul only
out of convenience until he gets work. Instinctively,
Johnny "knows" Guy's scene: two or three relatively long
affairs with men—always very handsome—and as many
shorter interludes with others: a completely "safe," if po-
tentially emotionally complicated, scene—the antithesis of
the tumultuous worlds Johnny has known.

Tony: "And, you know, Guy is quite a good actor. I
saw him on Broadway in *Dusty Moon;* he played the
young romantic lead."

Emory: "I'd be the last to say he's not talented—probably—but, oh, he can be so aggressive—like just now with

John!" Struck by a pang of let's-be-fair-though, Emory adds: "Of course, he must be under terrific pressure. I mean, his career—leaving the stage for films."

Tony: "Yes—and he's rushing—in more ways than in his career. There's something else driving him. He's on fire."

As if they've become much too grave, Emory adds quickly: "Well! Whatever it is, it's an absolutely devastating bore!"

Then: Johnny felt sorry for Guy. Even sympathetic. . . . On fire . . . rushing . . . driven. . . . Johnny Rio might have overheard that about himself, though his life is so different from Guy's.

Back in the living room with the others—and out of the cool breeze—Johnny knows the sobriety was spurious; he's quite high.

"And how many will there be . . . this time?" Guy asks immediately, as if he's been waiting for Johnny to return. "You know—how many? People. You said . . . 16? . . . in . . . few days. What's your . . . goal?"

Again, Guy's question was asked in abject fascination, a disturbed fascination; again without malice, with just that saddening, exacerbated, drunken fascination with Johnny's scene.

In a strange state of inexplicable franticness (and—adding to the sudden quandary—at the same time that he knows for certain that he won't return to the park because a serious threat exists)—Johnny reaches quickly—desperately—for a number: "Thirty," he says. It seemed to have been on the edge of his awareness, waiting to be summoned. "Thirty in ten days," he repeats, as if that will enable him to understand his reaction.

"Why 30?" Sebastian is interested.

Johnny shrugs. He still doesn't understand what made him answer what he did (though his mind suspects there's a "reason")—especially since at that very moment he knew without doubt he'd never return to the park.

Guy seemed about to continue his strange questioning of Johnny. But:

"We *must* be going!" An embarrassed Paul gets up abruptly.

Suddenly—exactly like this—while the others stand by the fireplace saying goodnight—Guy sits next to Johnny on the same couch.

Looking lost—curly black hair over his forehead, one hand resting there—and terror very clear in his voice, a note of doom—Guy is saying to Johnny: "I *know* too— but in a different way— . . . When you said 'scared'— . . . Like there are times when I can't sleep at all, I'm so fuckin afraid."

And Johnny, hearing his own words as if someone else were speaking them: "Yeah—like someone shook you and you're suddenly awake—alone, but with yourself— . . ."

Guy: "And everything's so . . . *weird!*"

Johnny: "And even when it's going right, you know there's something all, all wrong."

Guy: "Especially at night— . . ."

Johnny: "But even on the brightest after-goddamn-noon!"

And Guy: "Like time is fighting you—and there's never enough!"

And Johnny: "Yeah—but at the same time there's too much . . . time— . . ."

Then they were both silent, until—grasping for lucidity

out of the drunken spell which engulfed them without preparation—Johnny Rio muttered: "We're gonna regret this tomorrow, man"—and he means getting drunk, the confessions of dark fears, the revelation of possible vulnerability.

Guy says: "Only if we don't make it tonight."

Johnny has grown used to the fantastic occurring in his life. It's become the expected. But now he wonders if he heard right. "What?" he asks.

"Make it." Guy whispers so the others can't hear—but he forms each word distinctly: "I. Gotta. Make. It. With. You."

Johnny hears himself ask: "How can we?"

"I'll walk away from Paul's car," Guy says, "and I'll wait for you. I know a place—we can walk there."

"Okay," Johnny hears himself say.

"Okay," Guy echoes.

The night is foggy. The Cloud is hovering lower than usual.

By his car, Johnny says so long to Tony and to Sebastian. ("You're sure you can drive?" "Yes, of course!") As if belatedly understanding Johnny's earlier franticness— if indeed he didn't before—Sebastian invites him to come up whenever he wants: "We'll have a long talk—if you care to," he offers earnestly.

"And *do* call me!" says a tipsy Emory, driving away jerkily.

Across the street—shadows—Paul and Guy seem to be arguing.

Reeling, Johnny gets into his car. Paul into his. Guy waits on the street a few moments. A desolate outline in the dark mist. Johnny starts his engine. Guy walks ahead.

Paul calls out to him. Guy waits—and then he gets into the car with Paul.

Now the two cars rush away in opposite directions.

Jesuschrist!

Would I have gone with Guy?—hurt Paul? Johnny asks himself over and over.

He keeps reaching dead ends in the canyon, backing up, taking wrong roads. Finally he's on the Malibu highway.

No, I wouldn't've! I would've driven away. Then why the hell did I ask, "How?" when he suggested making it.

He parks his car near the shore as the world threatens to tumble blackly on him.

Hell, *Guy* propositioned *me!* he reminds himself.

The ocean roars like an echo of something infinitely more turbulent.

Of course I won't go back—not Sunday, not ever!

He leans back on the seat of his car, shutting his eyes tightly as if that will also shut out his thoughts.

I just asked, "How?" figuring he knows his business, he's hip to my one-way scene, and if he wants to— . . .

Dawn is breaking the fog in a lightening arc at the edge of the starless sky.

ELEVEN

ALWAYS BEFORE, at each crisis of his life, the only salvation Johnny Rio has found from total, shattering anarchy has been the grasping for and finding of a reason for his actions—no matter how ugly, no matter how wild those actions: a frame to contain his fantastic existence. Whether or not it's the real reason (he has never looked too closely)—*a* reason has always emerged to save him from disorder, to keep him from surrender to chaos, from complete disintegration. (When he hustled: I go with men only because I need the money they give me. And so on: the entire Myth of the Streets.)

Erected on such a flimsy foundation, then, his life, like a pyramid of playing cards, requires perfect balance: for every action, a reason. One without the other can topple Johnny's whole world. Like a row of dominoes.

Although he can function for a time in a state of suspension—as he has for the past few days—inevitably a questioning takes place.

Like now.

As he stands in the Arena of the park.

Yesterday, he was struck by the anonymous horror, the emotional carnage of the sexual hunt in the park; and he resolved never to return. But today he merely got into his car and drove here—although the fear that kept him away yesterday has not abated. Until he felt the Fear of the park so acutely, no reason for his actions was needed; there was no crisis. But now an action exists without a reason—with, instead, many reasons against the action; and this signals a crisis.

Of course he's aware of all this only as a festering irritation, something which blisters his consciousness and makes him feel that he's "floating"—drifting, afraid, in what has become a hostile but deceptively welcoming sea: the Park.

It's Friday afternoon, a few minutes after 1:00. Late—because Johnny Rio woke up slightly before noon—miraculously without a hangover and curiously relieved to find he couldn't remember what Guy Young looked like. No, not at all. In fact, the incidents of last night are like slides projected in rapid succession on the screen of his memory: sharp images changing instantly. Like this:

Sebastian and Tony. Clip! . . . Emory. Clip! . . . Tony's drawings. Clip! . . . Myself as I know I looked. Clip! Clip! Clip! . . . Paul and— . . . No, he can't "see" Guy. He remembers only: curly black hair over a face covered de-

spondently by a hand; and: a note of doom wounding
his voice.

Fleeing the scattered, shapeless thoughts, the empty
awareness of today—trying to stop the persistent sense of
mental drift by physical motion—Johnny has just moved
down the path that leads from the clearing of the Arena
to the Cave, wondering which of several men cruising him
will be the first to reach him. He's in luck: the Cave is
vacant. Perspiring in the unusual warmth of this afternoon, he waits before it.

Soon: A man is standing a few feet behind him. Now
another—right next to Johnny. In a quick backward
glance, Johnny notices that a third is higher up on the
path. All three are clearly cruising Johnny.

Three at once! The thought excites him, but beyond
that he figured: I'll make it a total of 19!

But the three have assumed stationary posts, trying to
outlast each other; and Johnny's already been in the Arena
about ten minutes. If this becomes a stalemate—instead
of making it three in one, he'll have to start over again
somewhere else and lose all that time.

Time!

I'm not going to look at my watch! he tells himself. But
he measures approximately three more minutes of the
standstill. He ducks into the Cave. But before he does
that, he looks at each of the three men for a few seconds—deliberately encouraging all three.

Surprisingly, the man who stood farthest away on the
path enters the Cave first. Johnny sits on the low-hanging
branch, one leg propped, the other stretched before him
in invitation. As if apprehensive the others will still get
to Johnny before him, the man advances quickly:

He licks the sweat off Johnny's shirtless chest, licks his shoulders, under his arms. Like a child with an ice-cream cone! it occurs to Johnny—but he blocks the image.

Having opened the top buttons of Johnny's fly, the man inches his mouth to where Johnny's pubic hair begins—kissing the lower part of his stomach so softly that his lips feel like feathers. The tongue withdraws to Johnny's chest again.

Through the opening of the branches that form the Cave, Johnny sees the other man is still there. Even more obsessively now, Johnny wants all three to express their desire for him at one time. Soon, two pairs of legs; a third man has come down the path. What if the two outside the Cave are playing with each other? He refuses to accept that. His mind repeats prematurely—as if to make it so: nineteen, nineteen, nineteen!

The man has lowered Johnny's pants to his calves. Methodically his tongue outlines each of Johnny's thighs—down and up in a U, always avoiding the groin. Again the chest; again under Johnny's arms.

Impatient, Johnny pushes the man's head downward. When it resists, he pushes more firmly—until his prick touches the man's lips, which are nevertheless tightly closed, clenched. In exasperation, Johnny reaches for his own pants. Warned he's about to leave—and having apparently been playing a game of deliberate delay—the man opens his mouth and swallows Johnny's cock.

The second of the three enters the Cave. A tall, good-looking youngman, he stands there tentatively. By glancing first at him, then at his own cock, Johnny indicates he wants him to come on too.

Kneeling, then bending his head and edging the first

man slightly to one side, the tall youngman is able to lick Johnny's balls while the other continues to suck.

As if Johnny's determination has pulled him into the Cave, the third man enters, stands there looking for long moments during which Johnny's mind keeps insisting: Nineteen! . . . Finally, the third man advances to the side of Johnny, licking his chest as the first one did earlier, tongue flitting over his nipples now, then along his back, down, rimming him, while the two others grovel at Johnny's crotch.

Nineteen! he counts exultantly. Three in less than 20 minutes!

He comes. Still, he feels aroused. His cock isn't softening at all. Having felt his jetting cum, the man who sucked him has swallowed and withdrawn his mouth. The other one, however, pounces on the still-hard prick, while the third man bends to lick the lower part of Johnny's stomach. Still kneeling, the first one looks on in amazement as Johnny pumps into the other's mouth.

Only a few moments later, Johnny came again.

He pulls away, adjusting his clothes. The man who entered first is now fondling the tall goodlooking youngman. Now he's going down on him. Johnny rushes out to his car.

As he turns the key starting the ignition, it strikes him with depressing impact:

The one who entered the Cave last—he didn't touch my prick!—just kissed and licked my body: almost but not quite my prick!

I can't count him!

It isn't nineteen!

It's only eighteen!
Shit!

He's become so familiar with the Park he can tell the approximate hour by its changing appearance as the shadows flee the sun: mistier in the morning, actually darkening in the afternoon.

Driving beyond the boundary of the hunt, he's even more disturbed by the increasing sense of drift—as if he's succumbing to the trance he's sensed in others.

To set things at least superficially in order by executing a phase of what has become a Ritual, he drove to the Observatory: to the Mirror.

Now there are two faces he doesn't want to encounter: the leering one of many years ago, and the sad one of the day before yesterday.

Before confronting his image in the Mirror, he smiled widely. . . .

It's all right.

He dazzles himself.

But even that pleasure fails to sustain him for long. Today, there's a mountain of emptiness inside him. He needs a catharsis from the Fear. Desperately.

I'll make it one more time, and then I'll leave!

A few minutes later:

In shorts and carrying a towel as if he's going to sunbathe (and seeing him, Johnny realizes that the blond youngman in the bikini isn't back today), a youngman follows him into the Nest—where, the day before yesterday, Johnny and the youngman cockily wearing the sailor cap had their disturbing encounter. For a few moments it looks as if something of the day before yesterday will be duplicated as both stand there with their pricks out, working them up, Johnny looking away from the other in pointed indifference. But moments later, the youngman is jerking Johnny's cock with a saliva-moistened hand.

"Let's go to that place where we can take all our clothes off!" the youngman in shorts invites him.

Johnny of course resents the suggestion that he'd be interested in the other's nudity, but he asks, "Where?"— telling himself he wants to keep oriented to the Park's total geography.

"Up there—on that hill; we could drive to it, then climb." He means the Summit. "There's not too many places—so it could be crowded, but we could try."

"Naw," Johnny rejects the suggestion.

"Okay, then," says the youngman with the towel. He's lowered his own shorts and is playing with himself with one hand while he jerks Johnny with the other. "Say, can I screw you?" he asks Johnny.

Johnny feels a surging anger. "Hell, no, man!" he says gruffly, reaching to bring up his pants. "What the fuck's the matter with you?"

"Okay, okay," the youngman placates him. "Actually I really wanted to ask you if you'll screw me."

Johnny pauses, long, before answering no.

"Okay," the youngman says. Then before Johnny can stop him, the youngman has placed his own stiff prick on Johnny's to jerk them both off with one hand. Johnny twists away furiously. "Cut it out, man. I don't dig that!"

"Okay, okay," the youngman placates him again—by going down on him. But the youngman in shorts isn't very good at sucking, and Johnny's having a difficult time coming.

Still, the other continues to blow him determinedly, at the same time playing with himself.

Johnny still can't make it. "Why don't *you* come?" he suggests; that would be one way of ending it.

"No," the youngman says. "I think I'll just wait and find someone to blow me later."

That bugs Johnny enormously—that the youngman in shorts would prefer to come while someone sucks him rather than with Johnny Rio's prick in his mouth.

That, however, settles it: Johnny fakes coming—increasing his breathing, thrusting his cock far into the other's gagging throat.

Soon after, they take different paths out of the Forest.

So much intimacy and . . . you . . . just . . . walk . . . away . . . without a word, Johnny thinks suddenly. All these people. What are they really like? Does anyone ever get to *know* anyone else? Does anyone ever want to? I don't know anybody's name. . . .

Yet: here I am!

And that's only part of the Fear.

He's thinking that and driving away from the Forest when in his rearview mirror he sees, trailing him in the red convertible, the man wearing the dark sunglasses.

"Mother-bitching-fucker!" Johnny says aloud.

What the piss does he want? Who the fuck is he? Why the hell is he following me? . . . *Is* he following me? Could it be some wild coincidence? Jesus, is he a cop? No. Just some guy with some odd perversion bugging him, something real weird he wants from me.

Johnny slows down, edging to the side of the road, allowing the red convertible to pass him so he can see the man more closely, more clearly. But the man with the black sunglasses continues to trail him. Johnny parks suddenly, intending to get out and confront him angrily— but the man accelerates his car. It growls up the road.

I'd like to ram my cock in the fucker's mouth and choke him!

Fury is transformed in Johnny into an intense longing for sex. Suddenly it swells inside him. He's made it with four people (no: three—he can't count the one who only licked and kissed his body), and he's come twice in quick succession. Yet he longs again for the excitement of the act: for the precious moments when his body poises at the instant of ecstasy and then life surges in orgasm. But it's over so quickly that it's almost as if it exists only in retrospect—or in anticipation.

The wave of excitement has drowned the terror, has calmed the sense of drift.

But only momentarily.

Today it all seems wrong. He feels very sad. He's drifting toward nowhere.

One more!—to make it four today!

As if in preparation for what must be the hecticness of the weekend, there are even more men than usual in the Park today. Cars hurl themselves up and down the road. Johnny imagines the Park devouring them.

But he hunts for more hunters in the Arena. Two men are milling in the clearing. One won't do. The other will—but he looks familiar. *Did I make it with him some other day?—or did he just cruise me?* He can't remember. Rather than run the possibility of having already "included" him (not the same one twice!), he discourages him, and the other one as well, by looking down as he winds along the Labyrinth. Alerted by footsteps, others materialize out of the green. A youngish man follows him to the Cliff. But there, two men are—were—playing with each other's cocks. Johnny hurries away, along the extension of the Labyrinth from the Cliff. The youngish man is trying to keep up with Johnny, who darts along the branch-formed tunnels—paths tangling in and out—to the Grotto. In the Grotto, a man hurriedly straightens up before another. Johnny cuts quickly through the brush— not really caring that he lost the man who was following; not caring because there are many, many in the Park and he attracts new ones as he moves to the Cave. Predictably, it too is taken: Two youngmen kissing (squeezed so far against the back wall of the Cave that Johnny didn't see them until he was already inside) don't even start at the accidental intrusion.

Too many in the Arena today.

So he drives to the Forest. No one parked there.

At the Outpost, three cars. He slows down, considering this area. Too open. You'd have to make the contact here, then walk across the road and down an almost-concealed path along which two men are already moving.

On the radio the Standells:

> *Yeah, down by the river . . .*
> *That's where you'll find me . . .*
> *Along with lovers, muggers, and thieves. . . .*
> *Well, I love that dirty water— . . .*

Cars at almost every islet along the road. Some of the men merely sit inside, talk to each other through windows.

No one before the Trail. Johnny parks there.

In only a few minutes a car cruises in. From where

Johnny stands exhibiting himself on the mound of sand, he sees a shirtless, tightly muscled chest on which a good-looking face, though somewhat askew, like a boxer's, is mounted. Ordinarily Johnny would have considered this man to be searching a scene like his own—or a mutual one—and to be therefore incompatible to him; but he's no longer apprehensive that way, having been wrong too often—with the notable exception of the curly-haired youngman wearing the sailor cap; and even then, he—... (He rejects the memory, which, oddly, is followed by a fleeting remembrance of Guy's wounded voice.)

Not in a whisper but as loudly and casually as if he were asking the time, the man with the boxer's face and body calls out to Johnny: "Hey, kid, you wanna blow job? ... Just stand by the window, I'll blow ya, cummon."

Aroused by the words, Johnny moves to the man's car, which is flush against the mound. He stands on a slight rise so that his groin is even with the window and almost with the man's face.

In shocked surprise, Johnny sees that the man in the car is completely naked.

Johnny is about to move away quickly, to indicate his disinterest in the other's nakedness, when the man reaches out through the window to unbutton his pants. Oblivious of being seen, the man doesn't even pause when a car drives by: a rashness that in itself is exhibitionistically exciting. He's already got Johnny's cock out and is sucking it through the window.

Cars pass. Whether or not they see what's going on, or whether they think the two are just talking, they slow down, look. But that's ordinary.

The man has opened the door and is sitting on the edge

of his car seat (a pair of trunks lie next to him) in order to reach Johnny better.

Jerking Johnny's moist cock with one hand while with the other he arouses himself, the naked man asks in a desire-shaken voice: "How many cocksuckers you been with, kid?—do they lick your balls too?—and stick their tongues up your ass?—how many, kid, huh?—how many times today?"

An unwelcome memory evoked: Going to confession and telling the priest you've comitted such and such a sin—like telling a lie—and the priest insisting, in order to determine penance, "How many times? . . . Estimate how many times. . . . How many times?"

"How many, kid?" the man with the boxer's face is going on. "I've seen you several times—but I never had a chance till now to get near you. You're driving everybody in the park crazy. Jeez, you're a sexy number!—but you know that, don't you, huh, kid? . . . Cummon, tell me how many tongues you've had up that cute ass of yours. Tell me— . . ." He pauses in the rush of words every once in a while to lick Johnny's crotch. "Let's go to another part of the park, kid!" the man says. "I wanna go all the way with you, let's go down the road to that place where there's lotsa people, I wantem to see me lick you all over, from your toes to your neck, I want to eat your ass, I wantem to see you spit in my mouth, jerk off on my face, I want you to piss all over me, I want— . . ."

Johnny stops the crazy words by pushing his cock in the other's mouth.

The driver of a car passing by *did* see them; he jammed his brakes suddenly, backs up. The naked man doesn't seem to care; would certainly welcome the other's watching. "I want you to— . . ." he starts again. But Johnny buttons his pants quickly, gets into his car, and dashes away.

I must be looking mean today; that's not my scene— that way-out stuff, he protests to himself.

Seeing that the naked man is following him, Johnny speeds up the road toward the Observatory—but he makes a quick left—through a tunnel that takes him to another road leading to the lower part of the Park.

Something else! There's got to be something else!

Johnny implied that last night at Sebastian's—and he's thinking it as he stands at the Outpost only a few minutes later, looking down at the city. But his thoughts are pushed aside by the fact that a well-dressed man in a suit and a tie has just driven up cruising him.

One more!

Leaving his car parked by the sandy rim, Johnny crosses the road automatically, toward a giant umbrella of trees— completely automatically, by reflex, as if now one movement inevitably sets off another. (And this, too, is only part of the Fear!) He descends the grading off the road, along a brambly path down the slope. The man who cruised him on the Outpost soon stands in front of him in a hollow of branches as Johnny rubs his own cock. Now the man raises his hand as if to touch Johnny Rio's face gently . . . tenderly.

But the gesture is quickly abandoned by him and, at the same instant, rejected by a sudden movement of Johnny's body. Simultaneously rejected by each, that gesture implies too much affection, too much tenderness: it's too far beyond the realm of desire.

The man goes down on Johnny. Afterwards, he spits out whatever of Johnny's cum there was.

Johnny Rio looks down where his sperm creates a small spot of mud on the ground.

Twenty-one.

Twenty-one!

The horror that he *is* counting, accumulating numbers aimlessly, strikes his consciousness like a sniper's bullet.

He sits in his car before the Forest.

And so it is a game—but a game that can't be won because it's limitless. Only *It* can win—the game itself . . . and the Park. The Park, which is suddenly his enemy— his opponent in this mysterious game.

That's the terror!

I'll leave for Laredo tonight! Leave before the Park wins! But if I do, I'll have gone back defeated—to hide again. But *how* can I win?

Thirty!

The number he grabbed for yesterday when Guy asked him his goal re-enters his mind. Thirty. . . . Where did it come from?

Lurking . . . waiting to be spoken. Unconscious calculations now becoming conscious:

Feverishly: I've been away three years. . . . If I hadn't left, I would have made it with, say, 300 people in one year. . . . In three years 900. . . . I'm behind 900. . . . How long would it take to catch up? . . . The least I've made it with in one day in the park is three. . . . At least three a day . . . into 900. . . . that's 300. . . . I could catch up in 300 days. . . . But I came back for only 10 days, and that's exactly how long I'll stay. Ten into 300— . . .

Thirty.

That's it!

Thirty!

That's the goal!

Now partly from having been raised a Catholic—and
partly from the fact that he's long fled self-examination—
Johnny has always relied strongly on symbols to exter-
nalize whatever bewilders or troubles him. Outlandish as
his symbols—like his "reasons"—may be, they have never
failed him. And so, now, having limited the anarchy by
choosing 30 as the symbol of his triumph over the park, he
feels suddenly resurrected. As usual, he doesn't look too
closely at his deductions nor his conclusions. He was battling against chaos, and all that matters is that a symbolic
"reason" has again emerged to save him from disintegration. Now that the game has a winning score, the horror
of counting toward no limit—of being swallowed by the
Park—is actually gone.

Johnny Rio is sure—unequivocally sure—that when the
ten days are up and he returns to Laredo it will no longer
be to the imposed isolation of those three years. No, his
victory over the Park will end that; and, he tells himself,
in Laredo or anywhere else, he'll finally be able to live
peacefully without fear that that devouring world of rampant sex is stalking him, luring him back.

That's why I came back to Los Angeles! To free myself
completely!—because it has to be *me* that's through with
that world—I had to know *it* still wants me but *I* don't
need *it!*

And so 30 is his symbol—both of that world's desiring
him as well as of his liberation from it. Thirty: It wanted
me for all those years and it still wants me. Thirty: I can

walk away from it—freely, and not feel confused as I have in the past.

Suddenly it's as if an iron band had been removed from his mind.

He can think calmly: and so, nine to go and the game's won. . . . He's about to enter the last inning of this strange game which he will win at the symbolic score of 30.

I can easily add four tonight, in that theater balcony, he thinks.

But no.

He knows that the score of 30 must be won only in the Park. Those in the movie theater before and the one in MacArthur Park are okay. He can count them because they occurred before the rules of the game were clarified. But the rest *must* all be in the Park.

But he won't begin now—because it's late and he's hungry—and because he wants to cherish the sudden peace—a peace shaken only momentarily by an awful, glancing doubt:

What if I don't make it! What if something happens!

What for godssake?

Something!

No. Nothing can. Absolutely nothing. Because:

I'm in control again.

Nine to go.

For the first time Johnny Rio drove out of the Park completely happy.

And that night—still in high, high spirits—he went to downtown Los Angeles, knowing the Negro woman would be at her corner.

She was.

TWELVE

SATURDAY. Ten-thirty in the morning. An alternately sunny, cloudy morning. The day which begins Johnny's victory over the Park. "Begins"—because he hasn't yet decided whether to rush, accumulating all nine today, or to go slowly, savoring victory into tomorrow.

Nine to go.

Monday he'll leave Los Angeles. Before noon. Exactly ten days. I'll pack Sunday, he reminds himself as he drives past the Arena reconnoitering the Park.

Sunday. . . . There was something— . . . Paul's invitation, Johnny remembers. I couldn't face him. I'll just call. No. Not even that. Guy might answer. Guy's voice. He still can't remember his face. But the sound of the lost voice haunts him.

There's a serenity about the Park today . . . the greens so varied and gentle . . . a serenity he'd never noticed before. He laughs as he remembers that in the dark of his room last night he actually convinced himself that, at that very moment, in its own darkness, the Park itself was girding for the last lap of the game!

(Johnny exercised vigorously this morning as if in preparation for his victory.)

The weekend waves of men have already inundated the areas of the hunt, spilling beyond what is usually the boundary. Despite the recurrently cloudy sky, several men sunbathe on the shoulders of the road—sometimes lying across the trunks of their cars. Others pretend to read, books propped on steering wheels.

Johnny decides to try the Arena first.

In this last inning of the game, he'll be even more selective "choosing" only the very most desirable. Of course—it isn't that *he* responds to physical appearance in males, he reminds himself: Attractiveness in those who want him has merely become what money once was in hustling: a further indication of his own desirability. Already he's rejected several today.

From among the many here, he finally encourages two, who were cruising each other before he walked in.

In the Grotto, the one who reached him first asks, "You wanna come to my place?"

"Naw, man," Johnny says, "I gotta be somewhere in a few minutes, I wanna make it here." He's anxious to count 22. Having called the game and determined the winning score, he had expected there would be no franticness today. But already he feels nervous, apprehensive.

"Too bad," the youngman says, "cause I don't mess around in public—too dangerous cause of the vice cops— but if you wanna come to my pad, I'll ball you."

"Can't, man—sorry."

Turning away without another word, the youngman goes to the one he was cruising before both began following Johnny. If they go off together, it'll depress Johnny severely; he'll feel rejected by the one who hasn't approached him. He readies a "reason" in that eventuality: Hell, the guy who just talked to me will have told him not to make it with me because—because— . . . whatever he'll invent. Or maybe the other guy just wants to get blown and knows—of course—that I won't. . . . But Johnny doesn't have to grasp for a "reason," because, very soon, the *two* youngmen are with him in the Grotto. The one who spoke to him earlier is saying, "He'll suck you off, I'll watch out for you."

This annoys Johnny only at first—that he'd give him up so easily—until he reminds himself the guy wants someone to go home with, doesn't like to make it in public—and so what's wrong with his having gone to get the other guy and offered to guard against any possible hostile intruders? Besides, he suspects the guy likes watching.

Before he unbuttons Johnny's pants, the second youngman is outlining the shape of Johnny's hardening cock with his mouth. Impatient to count 22—and he can't until direct contact is made—Johnny quickly opens his own pants. His prick is already erect. The youngman sucks it.

Instantly at the contact Johnny counts: Twenty-two!

He resists an urge to come: If he decides to make it with all nine today, he'll have to hold off; and so—because the other is determined, putting his hand firmly under Johnny's balls, pushing his cock farther out—Johnny fakes it, apparently successfully: He thrusts way into the other's throat, his body jerking in imitation of orgasm.

Afterwards, the two youngmen went off together, probably to make it mutually at home. Since they both preferred him *first*, that doesn't bug him at all.

Eight to go! he begins to count backwards.

In his car, minutes later, he stops by a place he hasn't explored. Five cars are parked flush against the side of a hill. He gets out. A path leading steeply up is all but obscured by the thick brush. No one around. After a long climb, he reaches a scrubby section of more or less level land.

In a pool of sun two men lie side by side naked.

By a different, shorter, but steeper route than the one he's often noticed, Johnny has reached the place on the Summit which the youngman with the towel mentioned yesterday. He moves away quickly through more thick brush. A few more patches of sun, all occupied by large beach towels—but no one on them. Ahead, branches separate just barely enough to reveal two men, shoulders bare, standing very close.

"Why don't you take *your* clothes off?" A goodlooking crew-cut youngman—propped on his elbow and lying on an army blanket in another small island of sun—is looking up at him. Less daring than the others, he's concealing his nudity with a small towel draped loosely about his middle. Quite likely he pulled it up when he heard footsteps. Dogtags about his neck indicate he's a serviceman.

Since he was trying to cut through the bushes to the path by a route that wouldn't take him past the two men lying together, Johnny didn't notice the youngman until he heard his voice.

"Cummon—take your pants off!" he coaxes Johnny. "Want me to help you?"

Johnny avoids looking at him, especially now that the towel has slipped off.

Encouraged by Johnny's silent acquiescence, and by his not having moved away, the youngman sits up—and unbuttons and lowers Johnny's pants. "Sit down so I can take them off." Johnny does, on an edge of the army blanket. The youngman pulls Johnny's boots and pants off—and even his socks, which he places neatly inside the boots. Lying flat on his stomach, he buries his head quickly between Johnny's spread legs—and Johnny's apprehension at this flagrant scene thaws in the heat of making sex, naked, under the sun.

Seven to go! he counts.

And he stretches back on the blanket as the youngman licks his body from toes to neck. Raising Johnny's legs so they straddle his shoulders, he rims him, at the same time jerking him with his hand. Aroused by the double sensation, a sensation further augmented by the sensual warmth of the sun emphasizing their unsheltered nudity, Johnny comes readily, his cum spurting on the other's face. Wanting it in his mouth, the youngman takes the squirting cock just in time, pulling himself off.

Johnny dresses hurriedly—keenly aware of the rashness of the scene, now that it's over.

He descends the steep decline of the hill back to his car, not bothering to take the regular path. Suddenly he bumps his foot on a large stone, loses balance—and slides several feet down the slope of the hill before he recovers control at the very edge of a sharp drop.

Heart hammering, his shoulder bleeding from a scratch, he looks down—many feet down. Directly below, cars cruise swiftly up and down. A few inches more and he might have plunged into their midst.

Never clumsy—and profoundly superstitious—Johnny reacts for cold moments as if there had been some deliberate action behind his fall. As he stands wiping the blood with his handkerchief, the beginning of a horrible thought shapes: The Park! What if—...

Oh, wow, he chides himself hastily. I'm at it again like I was about the car that busted my scene that night at Lafayette Park. An accident happens and I'm running wild. Oh, wow!

But he proceeds very, very carefully down the hill.

He wouldn't admit it, but he was so shaken by that incident just now that he left the park "for lunch" although it was still early and he'd had a late breakfast. He also stopped at a drugstore and put a bandage on his scratched shoulder: which made him feel even more attractive—the white, white bandage on his brown, brown skin.

Now he's back in the Park, but his nerves are still hopped-up by his reaction to the fall.

To occupy his mind with other thoughts as he drives up and down looking for a propitious place to park and make it six to go, he tries to remember *all* the numbers he's collected till now—all 23 so far.

Number one: the man he stood before in the movie

theater, who tried to suck him through his pants; number
two: the youngman who made him come, who was so
very expert at blowing; number three: the very goodlooking guy who sucked him in the restroom; number
four . . . who? Oh yeah: the dark youngman in the tan
trunks here in the Park. Oh, and the blond one in the
bikini who held it for the other—that's five. Then there
were several at once: the two in the Beehive, who alter-
nated: numbers six and seven. And there were the three—
but he can count only two because one never touched his
cock. That's eight and nine. And today he's made it with
two. So that's 11. Eleven. . . . There's 12 more. Oh, and the
naked man yesterday: number 12. And also yesterday: the
guy carrying the towel; he's 13. And . . . of course . . . the
curly-haired youngman in the sailor cap. . . . (Johnny
again hesitated counting him; but— . . .) He's 14—and the
total is 23 so far. Nine more.

Nine he can't remember now—no matter how hard he
tries to squeeze them from his memories.

Nine, lost in his mind.

Because there are too many hunters in the other places
today, inhibiting quick action, he's decided to concentrate
for now on the islets of sand off the road.

To his annoyance (though he doesn't know exactly *why*
he's annoyed), the man with the heavily muscled chest
and the two red X's on his back—again shirtless—parks
near his car by the Trail. Actually, he's a goodlooking guy;
it's the weird reddish X's that make him seem strange.

"What are you looking for?" the man asks Johnny, who's
standing on the mound of sand.

"Nuthin," says Johnny, deliberately acting dumb.

"Wanna good time?" the man asks.

Johnny shrugs. His mind counts prematurely: six to go. He'll ignore the two X's, which he hasn't actually seen today. Maybe, if painted on (but why?), they aren't even there today.

"Let's go down there." The man indicates the path to the water tank.

To avoid seeing the other's back, Johnny goes ahead.

By the water tank: Unexpectedly, as if a triggered switch had transformed him, the man pulls his own belt from the loops in an ominous *thrash!* and, holding it out to Johnny, he begs suddenly: "Hit me with it!" And he turns his back expectantly to him.

The two X's are there: scars, either slashed or burned on.

Wincing, Johnny looks away, genuinely puzzled by the man's desire to be hurt. "That's not my scene," he says softly. "Man, what made you think I'd— . . .? I mean, what made you take it for granted that I— . . . ?" He's honestly perplexed and bothered. It's the second time in two days he's been similarly approached, although this time it was much more overt.

Obviously verbalizing rehearsed dream words from a wild, perverse fantasy, the man says, in a voice broken by his pain-craving desire: "Because you've looked cruel from the first time I saw you—like a merciless, dark angel. Like a beautiful executioner! I was *sure*— . . ."

Johnny feels cold. "I'm not *any*body's executioner!" he says angrily—though of course he knows the man doesn't mean it literally.

The strange man follows closely as Johnny walks away. Halfway up the Trail, Johnny whirls around instinctively.

The man makes an abrupt movement. Something flashes silver.

A knife!

But no: The man has merely taken out a metallic cigarette lighter.

I've gotta cool it! Johnny resolves as he drives away. I'm getting too psyched-up.

Still seven to go.

Parked on another shoulder up the road, he's approached by the handsome dark youngman who sucked him the first day in the Park—the first one of all here. "You wanna?"

Johnny doesn't want to hurt him—after all he was the first one in the Park—but how can he explain he can't count him twice?

Okay, okay. They move off the road to one of the ubiquitous sheltered sections. The dark youngman blows Johnny. Johnny pretends to come—though he's not at all sure the other was fooled.

Okay, I let him, Johnny thinks. But I can't count him. It's still seven to go.

Irrelevantly he remembers one of the nine "lost" numbers in his earlier inventory: the man who was going to touch him so tenderly yesterday and then withdrew and later spat out the cum.

He's driven to the Arena, parked, walked to the Cliff. There aren't as many cars before this area as there were earlier—so the chances of quick action are good.

A slender, pretty youngman is trying to come on with him. Very nervous, he's about to open the first button of

Johnny's fly when they hear what may be footsteps or a branch shifting in a breeze. "What was that?" the young-man says. "Nuthin, man," Johnny assures him, anxious to count six to go, "Go ahead." "You watch carefully!" the youngman exhorts him as he starts once again to unbutton Johnny's fly. From somewhere along the Labyrinth, another sound. "Oh, my God, this is nerve-racking," the jittery youngman says, "I heard the park is crawling with vice cops lately." "Go ahead and suck me!" Johnny insists, pulling out his own cock, his mind insisting: six to go—six to go—six— . . . Still, the youngman is much too apprehensive. Johnny is about to say to hell with it and leave when the youngman bravely takes Johnny's cock in his mouth. "What was that?" He's heard another noise. Now Johnny does say to hell with it—and he moves away; but brief as it was, the contact was made; he can count: Six to go.

Only six more! He's already experiencing a hint of the liberation he knows he'll feel on reaching his goal of 30.

Even more so: now that—a little while later, in the Forest—he's about to make it five to go, and it's still early in the afternoon.

A lithe, blond youngman—the type referred to in some effete circles as "a great beauty" (not effeminate, but reedily slender and delicate-looking, with enormous beautiful eyes that any woman would envy)—keeps following him throughout the Forest while still others pursue them. Finally, they're alone, Johnny leaning against a tree.

The blond youngman says, "Will you screw me?"

"Suck me!" Johnny says.

"*I* don't do *that!*" the blond youngman protests indignantly.

And so all that time and no scene.
God damn!

"Don't you ever wear out, man?" asks the wise-assed young guy who's built like a very solid wrestler. "Jeez, you must've made it a dozen times today!"

"So what, *mano?*" Johnny asks. They're in the Arena, and he figures the guy resents him as competition because those who were cruising him began cruising Johnny as soon as he came in.

"You're a conceited bastard, aren't you?" the squat youngman says. "You think everyone's after you."

"They are," Johnny says cockily. "Including you," he adds, but only because he's sure that'll bug the guy enough so that he'll leave him alone and he can make it five to go.

"Shee-it," the squat youngman says contemptuously.

Minutes later, in a momentarily secluded part of the Arena, the squat youngman, surprisingly, became number 25, though he only attempted to jerk Johnny off—unsuccessfully, because, pulling himself off at the same time, he came before Johnny even got completely hard.

Five to go! Johnny counts.

And he remembers another of the "lost" numbers: the man who licked him all over, who wanted to see him again, who hinted— . . . that he too, like Tom, might make him feel like a prince.

In his car. The radio. And Donovan slurring acid-head images about Superman, Green Lantern, and a velvet theme.

It's become a gray, progressively darkening afternoon that hints of rain. The shadow of a heavy black cloud smears the Park ominously.

In the Forest: A man insistently wants to know how big Johnny's cock is. Selective as he is, Johnny wouldn't have made it with him anyhow; but his questions and remarks turn him off even further, since he wants to be desired for his whole appearance—not the size of his cock. The man is going on like this: "I met this guy here . . . week ago . . . like a stud horse . . . bigger'n my fist . . . thought I'd never get it out— . . ." Johnny leaves him talking.

Later: Standing by the Trail, he bounces a key ring in the palm of his hand—a reminder of Laredo, because on that ring is the key to his apartment there.

Very quickly he has attracted three men, almost simultaneously: and so the small islet is crammed with cars. Even so, a fourth man parks almost on the road. Although he won't make it with any of them, rejecting each for one reason or another, he allows himself to bask in the obvious adulation of the four—until, finally—suddenly wanting urgently to make it four to go—he dissuades them, one by one—or tries to. The one who parked on the road moves quickly into the place on the islet vacated by another who gave up.

Johnny is still bouncing the key ring in his hand—impatiently.

"I bet those keys belong to just a *part* of the many hearts you've broken."

Hustling, Johnny would have spotted the man who said that as an easy mark—the kind who gets an instant crush and is a pushover—though Johnny never took as much advantage of the type as he could have. The man is very insipid and unattractive. Johnny won't encourage him. He doesn't want to hurt him, either.

Finally, "How much?" the man—apparently used to asking this—wants to know.

Though Johnny has no intention of going with him, he can't help feeding his own vanity by asking, "What makes you think I'm hustling?"

"You're too sexy to be giving it away," the man said.

Johnny had expected something of the sort. "Thirty bucks!" he tells the man.

"Whew!—you're awfully *nice* and all that—but that's simply *too* much for me! I'll give you ten," the man barters.

"Naw. Thirty," Johnny says.

This is how he planned it, and it worked. Before he drove off, the man said, "Hope you get your 30"—startling Johnny, who at first thought he meant his goal rather than 30 bucks.

Suddenly he remembers another of the "lost" numbers: the man who drove up with the woman. Only six unremembered now.

Driving past the Beehive, he sees a man, who just came out along the path, get into a car where a little boy—about five years old—has been waiting. The man's son? Johnny feels an outrage that almost nauseates him.

Ten cars outside the Forest. But inside, Johnny sees only two men—one, tall and well dressed, coming toward him. It's much too open here. Johnny retreats farther into the Forest.

Number 26: The tall, well-dressed man licks Johnny's balls while his hand works Johnny's cock to the point of shooting. Johnny's about to come, when someone—who looks very much like a vice cop is supposed to look—

approaches. The tall well-dressed man begins to withdraw. "Take it!" Johnny says urgently. Ignoring the man advancing, whether or not he is a cop, the tall man takes Johnny's cum in his mouth. But if the other is a vice cop, it's his day off and he likes to watch.

Four to go!

Clouds glower blackly.

In his car once again, Johnny swerves to the left at a twist of the road to avoid hitting a squirrel running across. A car approaching on the opposite lane barely manages to squeeze past. Brakes! Honk! . . . Sounds of panic.

Jeezuss! I could've smashed into that guy! I'm really getting nervous!

Large drops of rain on the windshield.

Rare for this time of year, the rain can't last long. It's not the season of the long, dreary Los Angeles rains—when it pours during eternal, infernal days.

Johnny parks off the road.

The rain increases.

Scattered by the shower, men drive up and down in their cars in that exhilarated mood generated as if electrically by sudden rain. Some wait along the road to see if it will pass soon.

Through the rain-smeared windshield, the top of the highest hill (distorted to Johnny's vision as he sits in his car) seems to tremble in wrath. Crazily, Johnny imagines God perched with his heavenly rifle on just such a height to "catch" those whose numbers are up:

Pinggggggg! God shoots!

And Number Infinite-billion, Six Million, Eight Hundred and Sixty-six Thousand, Three Hundred and Seventy-two crumples over.

And now Number Infinite-billion, Six Million, Eight Hundred and Sixty-six Thousand, Three Hundred and Seventy-*three* runs for cover!

But God—the expert sniper who *never* misses—aims his rifle. Unswervingly.

Pinggggggg!

Another's number coming up!

Suddenly depressed by these images, Johnny drives to the Mirror at the Observatory, to be ritualistically dazzled by himself. But the rain has brought several tourists there for shelter. He can only glance at himself. But even that glancé is enough to reassure him.

Slowly, he drives back down the road and parks before the Forest.

His lefthand window is open; rain splashes on his bare chest and shoulders.

"Hi!" A man stops his car beside Johnny's. A handsome man—like the hero in a historical movie.

"Hiyuh," Johnny answers. Three to go, three to go, he counts ahead impatiently.

"Lotta rain!" the man calls through his open window.

"Yeah—lots!" Three to go.

"Why don't you come sit in my car till the rain stops?— better than being alone!" the man says.

Three to go, three to go, three to go.

Now Johnny sits beside the man in the man's car. The man is rubbing his own cock. Johnny looks out the window to indicate his lack of interest in the other's motions; he's getting ready to return to his own car. But again he needn't have been concerned. The man has reached over and cupped Johnny's cock.

Three to go! Johnny counts.

As the man goes down on him in the car, Johnny looks out the rain-waved windshield, again to the uppermost part of the Park. The hill still seems to tremble angrily. (*Pingggg!* The Heavenly Sniper strikes!)

Back in his own car (he didn't come just now—too cramped—and he hadn't felt like running out into the Forest as the man suggested), he can't help feeling a measure of pride at the realization that he's made it with six in one day—more than on any one of the previous days. (And if he could have counted the same one twice, it would have been *seven!*)

The rain hasn't stopped.

As he's about to drive away, in his rearview mirror he sees the cocky, curly-haired youngman of Wednesday's disastrous interlude dash from his car into the Forest. Today he's not wearing the sailor cap. But there's no confusing the exorbitant mass of curly hair, even wet and at this distance. And Johnny recognized the car, too.

Instinctively, Johnny begins to get out—despite the rain, telling himself: There're lots of sheltered places, and I could make it two to go. But he knows the real reason he's about to get out is because the curly-haired youngman is there.

But *why* do I wanna see the guy? he asks himself. . . .

All he knows is that he'd like magically to "set things straight." Not by reciprocating—no, of course not. But just by— . . . being friendly, he explains to himself; by making the guy feel less bad about the scene in the Nest the other day.

Even now, though, he's not entirely sure what's goading him on; but deciding that the rain is relenting anyway (it isn't), he gets out of his car and rushes into the Forest—

past the startled look of the man he'd just sat in the car with.

The rain penetrates the Forest only in streaks, as if through a leaking green roof.

Scanning the area, Johnny notices several men leaning against trees as if to escape the falling drops of rain; but he doesn't see the curly-haired youngman—and he's as much relieved as disappointed. Then he spots him standing deep in the Forest. Not knowing what he'll say to him, Johnny approaches, his heart threatening to escape.

"Howdee, *mano!*" Johnny says cheerily to him.

But the youngman misinterprets Johnny's friendly approach—perhaps even thinks Johnny has come to gloat: Johnny deduces this because, as he nears him, the curly-haired youngman turns pale, then red—and he immediately walks away, very quickly, out of the Forest. There wasn't even the slightest swagger to his walk.

Okay. So that's that. Period, Johnny thinks, not knowing what he feels.

Then he remembers another of the "lost" numbers: the man in MacArthur Park who ranted about love and then blew him.

All at once, he decides definitely to leave the last three numbers for tomorrow.

By the time he reached the motel the sky had cleared as suddenly as the storm had come up.

And that night, on the eve of his victory over the Park, stars are visible and the air is pure as Johnny Rio, exultant, completes this day's ritual by going to the corner of 7th and Broadway.

The Negro woman is there.

Only— . . . Only she seems even more listless than before. Her eyes droop mistily. And as Johnny Rio moved away, she seemed to see him for the first time.

THIRTEEN

SUNDAY. A miraculously clear day. His last in the Park.
The Cloud has all but disappeared. For the first time since
Johnny returned to Los Angeles, the sky is pristine blue.

Three more, and the game is won.

Fresh after the rain, the Park is glorious. Young: and
green and yellow. Shadows lie softly on the ground. The
sun carves blue figures on the hillsides. For the first time,
Johnny notices the delicate veils of gold and lilac flowers
spread gently on the slopes.

Like yesterday, there are many in the Park this morning,
cruising even outside the Arena, the Forest—some standing beside their cars, others driving by slowly. As his car
moves up the road, several men look hopefully at Johnny.

With extreme care he'll choose the last three numbers to be desired by. Packed and ready to leave tomorrow morning, he can go as slowly as he wants today.

Not him.

Not him.

Him.

A youngman standing by his car off the road. Light-haired and athletic-looking, wearing white shorts, tennis shoes, and a faded-yellow T-shirt, he looks like one of the young models who advertise summer softdrinks for a "cool generation." He stares very long at Johnny as Johnny drives by slowly. Even if there hadn't been two men cruising the youngman in shorts, Johnny wouldn't have stopped, since he never advances first; but he does do this: He looks back very long and smiles at the youngman staring at him.

Already shirtless, Johnny parks by the Trail (fortunately it was unoccupied), sits in his car with the door open to allow the warm sun to nestle on his bare chest. He waits. Cars slow down, pause. He looks away. One stops. Not the youngman in the white shorts, Johnny notices through half-closed eyelids: his strategy in order to keep away those he doesn't want. If someone turns him off, he'll pretend his eyes are closed—as he's doing now to discourage the man who drove up, got out, and is standing in front of him looking at him as if he's an object on display for his pleasure.

And damnit if at that very moment the youngman in shorts didn't drive by, obviously looking for Johnny—and because of the other's presence there, he drove away.

After eternal moments of just standing staring at Johnny—while Johnny steadfastly kept his eyes closed, or pretended to—the man finally gave up; but another takes his place immediately, parking almost parallel to Johnny's car.

Not him.

Gone.

Another.

Not him.

Since the youngman still hasn't returned down the road, Johnny gets into his car and drives up—to show him, wherever he is, that he's still around. And there he is: on another margin of the road—and a man is cruising him. Certain that the youngman noticed him, Johnny makes a U-Turn and returns to the Trail—still luckily unoccupied.

Parked there, lying on the seat of his car, the door open to admit the sun, he waits again: convinced the youngman he chose is looking for him at this very moment. To Johnny's great annoyance, though: Undaunted, the same man who stood staring at him earlier has returned! Johnny just lies in his car looking away: up at the soft outlines of the hills crowned by velvet-green trees. Beyond, the azure sky stretches in an extension of the Park's new peace. A lovely peace which Johnny begins to feel a part of.

Hearing the near approach of a car, he sat up. It's him. But the man—an irritating nuisance now—again thwarted the other's stopping. Johnny's got to get rid of him. But he doesn't want to leave the Trail, because it's too propitious and the other places are very crowded. Also, he's sure the youngman will be returning soon. . . . So he continues to ignore the man until it works—just in time. As the man drives away, the youngman drives in.

Leaning against the trunk of his own car, Johnny is

bouncing his key ring in the palm of his hand. Kicking at the dust idly, the youngman in shorts is just-hanging-around. Like Johnny, he seems to be waiting to be approached, merely making himself available. Suddenly it occurs to Johnny that the youngman expects a mutual scene: So determined was he to include him among the last three numbers that he encouraged more than he usually does—or so it seems to him in retrospect.

A car driving in to cruise either or both of them—and thereby threatening to make it more difficult between them—goads the youngman to this much action: He takes a few uncertain steps toward Johnny, to indicate to the third man that they're together. Understanding, the other drives away.

Though standing close to each other now, they're both still silent, looking away. And Johnny is becoming more and more convinced the other has taken a mutual scene for granted.

To find out definitely, Johnny moves down the Trail (cautiously: the near-disaster of yesterday, as he descended the Summit, branded into his mind), sure the youngman will follow. He does.

They face each other, like boxers about to challenge and be challenged.

Johnny touches his own cock. The youngman reaches out lightly for it. But when Johnny doesn't reciprocate, the other withdraws his hand quickly.

"I don't go for trade," the youngman tells Johnny. "It's gotta be a two-way scene."

Neither surprised nor angered—but just disappointed that he won't be one of the last three numbers—Johnny shrugs. "Sorry, then, *mano*." He turns to move up the Trail.

"Wait," the youngman calls.

Perhaps his announced stance was just his way of sounding Johnny out, a gambit to see if he'd make it reciprocally. Or perhaps he really is new to this particular scene but is impulsively going ahead with it. Whatever the reason, the youngman slides down on his knees, hugging Johnny tightly about the thighs, his head nestling between Johnny's legs. Johnny places his hands on the youngman's shoulders—not in embrace, he tells himself, but to support himself standing. For many moments they seem to freeze in that intimate closeness: like two children playing a way-out game of statues. Then Johnny withdraws his hands from the other's shoulders. "Suck me, cummon," he coaxes.

The youngman does—very clumsily, using his teeth and taking just the head of Johnny's prick. And so he *is* very new at this scene. Maybe his first time this way.

Thinking that, Johnny stops him abruptly. "Don't do it unless you really wanna, man." His own words surprise him—and his accompanying action, too: He actually began to draw the other up by his shoulders.

"I want to," the other says. "Don't you?"

"If *you* wanna," Johnny insists.

The youngman does: continues sucking, so awkwardly that Johnny can't possibly come that way. He eases the other's head away, directing it to his balls. Now Johnny works his own cock to the point of coming. "Okay!" he alerts the other. The youngman opens his mouth, and Johnny comes in it.

Swallowing the cum, the youngman leans softly against Johnny's flat stomach; and Johnny hears himself ask: "You wanna come too, man?—I mean, like it's okay if you wanna jerk off." When the other assents, Johnny Rio offers the only thing he knows how to offer—his cock. With it in his mouth, the other jerks off.

Johnny had actually forgotten to count until he was in his car again.

Two to go.

Driving down the road, he sees the man with the red X's cruising by in his white convertible. As if hoping Johnny will have changed his mind, he pauses, looking back; but Johnny continues ahead. Johnny's also seen others he's made it with before—though some he's not absolutely sure about: Did they actually come on with him, or did they just cruise him? . . .

Again, he tries to remember all the numbers so far. Beginning again: Number one—the one in the movie balcony, the one I stood before, who— . . . Number two . . . number three . . . number four . . . number five . . . number six . . . number seven. . . . But now the numbers are hopelessly scattered. Remembering some he'd forgotten and sure he's forgotten others he remembered in his original inventory of yesterday—and feeling almost unfaithful to be able to recall some so vividly while others fade away—he gives up.

Breathing deeply of the rain-purified air, he's struck powerfully by the beauty of the Park. And on his last day here it's a dazzling spectrum of green shades.

But the hunt goes on frantically. Cars jam the main sections. Seven cars parked near the small area of the

Beehive. A dozen by the Arena—perhaps even more since they extend up the road toward the Forest, where there are at least as many more.

And other cars plunge up and down the road like an army against an invisible enemy.

Acutely aware of them at this moment, Johnny thinks: The season of sex and death is about to end.

Death?

Why did he think death?

The superstitious part of him is chilled by that odd slip in his thoughts. He tries to find a "reason" for it. . . . The crushed bugs on the windshield, the birds smashed on the highway: the specter of death that marked his entrance to the city of lost angels. . . . And perhaps he meant another death, too—the death of that part of him that could have surrendered to anarchy after the spurious years'-long isolation of Laredo. Yes, certainly *that* death.

Completely sure that nothing can thwart his victory over the Park, seductively beautiful as—almost perversely —it appears now (but only physically so), Johnny feels "outside" of it already. Or almost so: like one who has wakened from a trance but remains—momentarily— among those it still claims.

And yet— . . .

Yet he can't help feeling it's all going too easily—as if the Park is only waiting to spring its trap.

Laughing, he catches himself before his imagination carries him too dangerously far.

Fulfilling the ritual of the Park—a ritual which will soon end: He's at the Observatory now. Looking into the Mirror.

The face there is the one he wants to see.

The leering one, and the sad one—they're gone. Forever, Johnny assures himself.

Even in the euphoric mood his image has put him in, anger swells when he sees the familiar red convertible parked obliquely parallel to his car outside the restroom. Because of the dark sunglasses the driver always wears, Johnny can never tell definitely whether he's actually looking at him. It's mostly a strong feeling that he is. He decides to ignore him. But as Johnny gets into his own car, he can't keep from looking at the man; and he sees him much better this time than ever before:

Deeply tanned, he's slim—and well-dressed in the casual style of southern California—a blue sports jacket, a striped shirt unbuttoned at the collar. What makes his age difficult to determine is that his hair could as easily be white as very, very light blond; the wide sunglasses, concealing what is usually an age-revealing part of the face, augment the difficulty. He's handsomer than Johnny thought.

Oh, no!

Suddenly, uncontrollably, Johnny remembered the car that intruded that night at Lafayette Park—its lights glaringly fixed on him. Could it be? Of course not! That other car was dark. But it *could* have been red, dark in the night. No—the other car was a hardtop. Was it? It *could* have been a convertible—with the top up! No!

That's really crazy, *mano,* Johnny tells himself, driving away quickly. Now that *really* is crazy—it would have to be a near-impossible coincidence. . . . *Unless he followed me to the motel that night—out of Lafayette and then MacArthur, and then here!* he persists. And it *was* a new car, the one that night; it gleamed like one even in the dark. . . . Oh, hell, *mano,* he chides himself. Get it out of your mind!

And he almost does.

Like this:

Two to go.

And the radio floods his senses as the Yardbirds wail a hopped-up dirge gone mad, lamenting the relentless continuation of all things.

Despite the many cars parked there, Johnny decides to try the Arena. Although there are too many men here to divide into strict camps, he quickly notices that the floating attention is focused mainly on himself and a very muscular youngman (in Levi's and formfitting T-shirt), who quickly establishes his desire for Johnny with an unambiguous look. Inviting him with a backward glance, Johnny moves into the Grotto, which has just been vacated by two youngmen evidently through.

As if to show off *his* chest (Johnny's, of course, being still bare), the muscular youngman removes his T-shirt as he approaches Johnny: a slight annoyance to Johnny: a hint they're still competing. But that doesn't mean he won't come on with me one-way, he reminds himself from past experience.

Hungry, others circle the two; but Johnny and the other together look so formidably "tough" (they're trying hard enough to—flexing for each other) that others are kept from approaching them here—or were—because without their having noticed him a man has descended from the upper level of the broken path, and he's offering to suck them both off.

"Shag ass, man!" the muscular youngman tells him gruffly.

Alone in the Grotto again, they face each other.

Putting his hands on the loops of his own Levi's, Johnny pushes them very low on his hips, almost half-way to the triangle of hair. The heavily muscled youngman does the same. Johnny rubs his own cock, hardening it—so does the other to his own. And now they're playing a familiar game of follow-the-sexual-leader, determining who'll be the one to break it. Soon both have their pricks out, stiff. But there is this difference: Whereas Johnny is looking away from the muscular youngman, the other is looking straight at him, which, however, makes this possible: Soon after the muscular youngman took Johnny's erect cock in his hand, he put his own aroused prick under Johnny's, Johnny's cock now lying on his; and clasping both firmly with one hand, the muscular youngman is jerking them off simultaneously.

For a few moments, Johnny doesn't react (it happened so fast I was thrown off balance, man, he'd explain), and the other continues working both cocks—pressed tightly together—back and forth. Then Johnny withdraws from the compromising contact. Now the youngman bends down and sucks him and jerks himself at the same time. Obviously about to come, he stops pulling himself off, wanting Johnny to come first in his mouth. Johnny does, and the other releases himself too, into his own hand.

As they leave the Grotto, the two actually smiled at each other. Almost shyly.

Only one to go.

To the Mirror again, to prepare for his triumph.

Perhaps because his face is exulting in the imminent

liberation, it seems to glow in its reflection. Victorious. Elated.

Realizing he hasn't yet eaten, Johnny left the Park; and he ate with much appetite, flirting outrageously with the same waitress of the previous afternoon. As he re-entered the Park, two girls, young and cute, gave him come-on smiles as they waited to cross the street; and Johnny dazzled them with his.

Returning to the area of the hunt, he slows down at each familiar place: he's searching for the person he'll choose to be the last of the numbers, yes—but also he pauses along the road in a premature farewell to the Park.

So much buried here. In this city. In this Park. To be left behind. Soon. No, never left behind entirely. Always with him in his mind: remembered. Along with: Tom and the crushed memories of an earlier time. And Tina and her sad child. And, strangely, Danny, too—and the desolate, wrecked, haunted, sad beach. And, yes, the youngman with the sailor cap. Of course. . . . And Guy. No: Guy's *voice*. The moment of shared dark fears. . . . And all the numbers. . . . Unexpectedly, all his life—he knows it—they'll enter his mind, singly or together, demanding not to be forgotten.

Memories of that season of sex and death. A season almost over.

In the afternoon light, the Park is even more radiant. The colors are so vibrant they seem to flee the shadows.

In the Forest.
One more and the game ends.
Now.
Leaving behind the many he's discouraged, he's drifted

far into the trees, lured by the Park's newly noticed beauty; and he moves along the elevated rim of a ravine, looking down at the intricate tangle of sandy outlines created by yesterday's flow of rain.

Someone is behind him—he can tell by the crunching twigs.

Because he hasn't seen anyone here he wanted to encourage, he turns prepared to reject him too. He starts. For a wild instant he thought it was the cocky curly-haired youngman who fled from him yesterday after the earlier day's crushing interlude in the Nest.

It isn't him—but he resembles him a lot, mostly in the way the sandy unruly hair curls over his collar. A very goodlooking youngman wearing Levi's and a shirt open to his navel—sleeves rolled very high—he must have come from deep within the Forest.

Him, Johnny thinks immediately, choosing.

He moves into a secluded cove of trees. He waits there. The other approaches.

They smile at each other.

Silence.

"Hi."

"Hiyuh," Johnny answers.

They smile again.

More silence.

But they've moved closer to each other. And now, standing side by side leaning magnetically toward each other—as on that other afternoon Johnny and the curly-haired youngman with the sailor cap did—they let their knuckles touch. But this time Johnny doesn't break the contact immediately. Instead, he allows it to continue as the young-

man, turning slightly, touches Johnny's chest with the
fingers of his other hand. Lightly and tenderly.

"You too!" the youngman whispers.

And Johnny touches the other's chest. Lightly too. And
tenderly.

Now Johnny would say that the reason he did so is
that there was an imploring note in this youngman's
voice—a need implied—similar to that he heard, and rejected so harshly, in the voice of the curly-haired youngman. Perhaps. Also, perhaps Johnny sensed this youngman
needed the barest token of reciprocation before he could
proceed on Johnny's terms. And perhaps, too, remembering the look of hideous rejection on the face of the cocky
curly-haired youngman, and his own subsequent deep re-
morse, Johnny wanted to prevent a recurrence. And—
maybe—this way, he wanted to stamp the last number, 30,
indelibly in his mind.

Whatever the true reason, Johnny Rio does reach out to
touch the other's chest, letting his hand slide down the
smooth flesh on which tiny hairs shine gold; allowing the
movement to continue to just below the other's navel,
which is where the other stopped too on Johnny's body.
And then Johnny withdraws his own hand.

The youngman leans slowly toward him, unequivocally
to kiss him on the lips.

Johnny doesn't move—until the crucial moment when
their mouths would have touched, then he turned his head
away quickly, and the other kissed him on the neck.

And from his neck, the youngman's mouth moves down
gently, kissing Johnny's stomach softly, tongue brushing the edge of his pubic hairs: as if, indeed, he required

that bare token of reciprocation to goad him. Having lowered his own and Johnny's pants, he runs his hands caressingly down Johnny's slim hips.

Johnny was hard long before the other's lips enclosed his cock. And he came that way. But he remained standing there until the other, head leaning on Johnny's bare chest, came into his own hand. Very slowly, Johnny eased his body away.

Thirty.

The game is over. Johnny won.

He drives out of the Park and he doesn't look back.

FOURTEEN

"I'M SO GLAD you came! I wasn't sure you'd remember my invitation—we were all a bit high that night," said Paul Blake, admitting Johnny into a handsome house nestling against a heavily treed escarpment just blocks away from Sebastian's. "Guy . . . here's John Rio."

Guy Young emerges from within the house—extending his hand to Johnny. "Hi!"

Johnny had forgotten Guy's face so completely that if they had met somewhere else he would not have recognized him.

Paul shot a look at Guy that warned as much as it implored—or so it seemed to Johnny.

"Hiyuh!" Johnny said. Withdrawing their hands im-

225

mediately after the initial contact, Johnny and Guy hardly touched.

Paul leads Johnny into a large living room whose walls are almost covered with portraits and drawings—some by Tony. Guy follows with a drink already in his hand.

They sit in a triangle about a rectangular table, Johnny next to an unlit fireplace; and he faces a portrait of a woman clutching her throat as if to stifle a scream or drown out laughter.

Paul is saying that Sebastian and Tony will be over soon, and: "Emory is heartbroken that he might not be able to come. His *mother* descended unexpectedly on him from Oklahoma this morning, and he's absolutely disconsolate."

Now Johnny isn't sure what he feels on seeing Guy again. Or Paul. His reaction seems to be waiting for the embarrassment to pass before becoming definite.

And why is he at Paul Blake's this Sunday evening?—having resolved not to come here.

It happened like this:

As he drove out of the Park this afternoon, a wonderful peace descended on him immediately.

But soon the feeling was followed by another.

A powerful pain.

A pain which was the sum total of all the numbers. And the pain lingered.

When he reached the motel, however, he felt triumphant again—and free!

Triumphant and free as he went downtown to complete the ritual. (And, deliberately, he didn't shower—in order to leave the "stamp" of the last three numbers on his body for a longer time.)

The Negro woman wasn't at her corner.

Johnny's thoughts flowed defensively to drown the weird feeling of disorientation which ensued. Sure she's bound to miss a day!—everyone gets a cold!—a headache! Besides, it's still early. And she wasn't here last Sunday, either, remember? So she just doesn't preach on Sundays; that's like her day off. That's all. It. Doesn't. Mean. Anything. . . . Yet he couldn't help recalling that, the night before, she looked tired, sad, shriveled, the raisin face even more wrinkled.

To avoid going back and forth obsessively—as he did once before and as he knew he would again if he stayed around—he drove impulsively to Santa Monica. And he did that for two other "reasons": He "just knew" he had to let Paul know he had nothing to feel guilty about concerning the other night—though he's not sure how much Paul knows. And—more important—suddenly: He needed urgently to announce his victory over the Park—to announce it in the canyon, where he first verbalized his "goal" in answer to Guy's heated questioning.

And so; here he is in Santa Monica facing Guy Young and Paul Blake.

And silence has descended on them like an iron lid.

In an attempt to lift it Johnny asks Paul if the copies of his new book have arrived. Paul says not yet—what a bore.

The heavy lid of silence closes in even more oppressively.

Finally—after even more uncomfortable moments— Paul decides to bring up the source of their obvious embarassment. He said, "Oh, let's do stop being so somber, shall we? . . . John, I know all about what happened, or almost happened, the other night. I was somewhat aware of it even before Guy told me that— . . . that he'd made a proposition to you and that you'd indicated . . . it might be possible to . . . get together." Still haltingly, he goes on: "But— . . . that night . . . for whatever reason—or reasons . . . it didn't happen. . . . Now why don't we forget it? It's over. Finished!" he said staunchly.

Admiring Paul, Johnny can't help wondering: Is he pretending not to be hurt? Does Paul . . . "like" . . . Guy so much he can easily overlook what happened, flagrant as it was? Just like that? . . . (The way Tom overlooked my going with others. But that was different, he quickly tells himself.)

As if to indicate his firm belief that that's that and nothing will—can!—recur, Paul excuses himself, to check on dinner.

Guy is fixing fresh martinis. During the first silent moments, the tinkling of ice in the pitcher is like the gong of a bell.

Left alone, both sit trying to avoid the slightest overtone of the earlier scene—Guy talking very rapidly about a party he'd been to earlier at the home of an actress he might be playing opposite in a movie.

Though Johnny isn't really following the words, he is listening closely to the voice. And the broken note of despair to which he responded that other night—it isn't there now. Not at all. And so, he assures himself, what had drawn him to agree that they might get together that other night—the implied knowledge of mutual fears—doesn't exist now. Having convinced himself of that, Johnny feels the tension dissolving.

He stops listening even to the sound of Guy's voice, his mind drawn insistently to the Negro woman. Is she there now? He keeps reminding himself she didn't turn up last Sunday either. And: What difference does it make now, *mano?* he asks himself. Today, I won in the Park!—think of that instead. . . . But it *does* have to do exactly with that: as if, had she been there, she would have mirrored his victory.

". . . —not as if it could happen again, or we'd even want it to. Besides, nothing *did* happen—so I told Paul about it."

"What?" Johnny asked, coming in on Guy's last few words.

"Paul. I told Paul about what happened, because— well— . . . I mean, what happened—well—I was awfully drunk. . . . Sober, it wouldn't've—of course."

"Right, man," Johnny agrees emphatically.

They hear Paul greeting Sebastian and Tony at the door. Johnny wonders how much these two know about what happened the other night. He can't tell by their greeting of him or of Guy.

"John!" says Sebastian. "One wondered whether one would see you tonight—or whether the park would have swallowed you!"

Whether or not he said that only humorously, Johnny felt a chill: That's exactly what he escaped from; that was the alternative—being swallowed—if he hadn't won. He's anxious to announce his victory. He'll wait, though, until there's a lull. Now Paul is explaining Emory's lamentable predicament.

Tony says mothers can be such a bore, can't they?

They've hardly sat about the rectangular table when Sebastian says to Johnny: "Now tell us about the park!"

Tony: "I'm absolutely agog with interest."

Guy swallows his fresh martini, serves himself another, and refills Johnny's glass. Paul serves the others. They wait in silent expectation for Johnny to answer.

He's about to announce his victory when they all hear a car parking, a door slam.

It's Emory—here after all.

"Oh, the simply maddening horror of mothers!" he tells everyone. "She just descended upon me from the air—not by broomstick, by airplane—but only because that's *faster!* And she insists on staying with me, though I've offered to put her up at the Luxury Palms Hotel in Bel Air. In the presidential suite if that will keep her away! . . . Love!" he calls meltingly to Johnny, nodding coolly to Guy after kissing the others. "I do honestly believe she's here to spy on me in order to blackmail me—her own son! (She always did want a daughter!) . . . And on top of *that!*" he goes on documenting his woes: "The script of *The Night the Sea Exploded* (yes!—they've changed the title of *When the Swans Come Home to Roost*) is undergoing simply major, ravishing revisions: The leader of the revolution is a woman now—to avoid controversy. And that alters simply everything, unless they let me make her a Lesbian! . . . In the meantime: Oh, *do* let me *drown* in one of these!" he says, reaching for a martini.

After everyone has commiserated with Emory ("We've *all* had mothers, Emory dear," Paul empathized), Sebastian reminds them that he had just asked Johnny about the Park. But before Johnny can tell them of his victory,

Sebastian surprises him by asking: "But tell me first, John: did you ever work on a newspaper?"

Bewildered by the seemingly irrelevant question, Johnny answers, "Yes—when I was a kid—I was a copy boy—for a while. Why?"

"And you must have looked absolutely darling in one of those cute vizored caps," says Emory.

"I think only editors wear them," Tony points out.

"Well, he looked darling no matter *what* he wore!" Emory insists.

"Because of your . . . goal—30," Sebastian clarifies his question. "It occurred to me later—and I told Tony—30 is a printer's term for The End."

Of course. Johnny should have remembered that. But there was the real way he arrived at 30 the hurried multiplication and division that gave him the "numbers" to be accumulated in ten days.

"Oh, isn't that terribly significant!" says Emory. "But please, dear, dear Sebastian, I absolutely forbid you to be morbid and boring about it."

"Have you reached it yet—30?" Guy asks. As on the other night, he's been drinking steadily—and refilling Johnny's glass.

And now it comes. Johnny tries to sound casual; but his breathing increases, choking his voice slightly. "Yes. The game I was playing—and I was playing a game—it's over. I won over the Park." Now the victory has, in effect, been recorded; the announcement made where the winning score was stated—even if not understood, then. But because their reaction isn't what he wanted, he clarifies: "That means I'll never go back to the Park." Even so, they don't seem to respond. "And I'm all packed and ready to leave tomorrow before noon," he flounders before the mute reaction.

Something clearly went wrong. His announcement didn't have the impact he expected. Not at all. Perhaps because they don't know how very strongly he relies on symbols: difficult for them to realize that it took that symbolic goal, that symbolic victory over the Park to liberate him from the world of rampant sex. Not understanding any of this, perhaps they don't even sense yet how firmly he means it all—how completely certain he is of his victory.

"I'm simply crushed that you're leaving so soon again," Emory breaks the silence. "But *do* tell us much, much more about the numbers and the park."

But Johnny won't discuss the Park in detail. The numbers belong to him. And to his past. "I reached the goal, and the game is over," is all he says.

"And how many days did the 30 take you?" Tony wants to know.

They're interested, yes—but they don't *understand*. "Ten," Johnny answers. But that's the official number, he reminds himself. Actually it took less than that. His mind counts automatically: I got here Friday. . . . (The strange suicidal birds outside of Phoenix, dazed.) But I didn't mess around that night. . . . (Tom—and the shadow he made against the lighted door. . . . And: My Room.) And Saturday? . . . (Tina's kid—the sad, blue, lost eyes.) It began Saturday night. . . . (The yellow light floating in the darkness of the balcony, the beginning of the numbers.) And it continued Sunday. . . . (The black, loveless parks.) And Monday and Tuesday and Wednesday. . . . (The Park: the Arena . . . the Grotto . . . the Nest. The mouths.)

Saturday, Sunday, Monday, Tuesday, Wednesday: five days. Not Thursday. . . . (The Fear.) And then again Friday and Saturday and this afternoon. . . . (*Thirty!* . . . The three last . . . numbers. . . . The Negro woman. Is she there?) "No—eight days, actually," he corrects himself aloud.

"Were you there today?" Guy asks. There's a spark of the excited tone that flamed last time as he fired the intimate questions at Johnny.

"Yes," Johnny answers, remembering—vividly—the three he was with today. Already, he feels the liquor—but not so much the liquor, he tells himself, as the headiness of victory.

Guy fills his own glass again, swallows. "And what is the grand total?" he asked immediately, as if the liquor had made the question possible. "I mean, like, there were many, many before you started counting this time, right?" His fascination with Johnny's scene is once again roaring, obviously—perhaps deliberately—fueled by the liquor.

Paul cuts in quickly: "Guy, I *do* think— . . ."

But Guy doesn't even look at him. "How many would you say, John?" he insists. "Hundreds?"

Paul blanches visibly. A vein trembles nervously at the side of his nek, like a worm pinned there squirming.

"Over a thousand?" Guy persists excitedly.

"Yes," Johnny answers quietly, saddened as on that other night, at Sebastian's, by Guy's burning interest in that sad, lonesome, anonymous world.

Guy, obsessively: "And will you go for three?—four?—five thousand?—or have you already reached that?"

"The game's over," Johnny Rio reminds him.

"Of course it is," says Paul quickly.

"But how intriguing to conjecture," Tony says. "*If*—just a wild 'if'—*if* you *had* continued—*if* you *hadn't*—as you say . . . won— . . . The numbers simply accumulating until— . . . What?"

Sebastian, somberly: "Until the *other* 30—The End. . . . Of course," he went on gravely, "one could make it 31—beyond death; but then, 32 and 33 would be even further away—but never far enough— . . . Always, really, *closer.*"

"Oh, how maddeningly boring and morbid—and—and —well, *serious!*" Emory said snippily. "You're simply obsessed with death, Sebastian. I'm absolutely convinced you should go out and have more *fun*. . . . Even if John hadn't . . . won, as he so charmingly puts it—couldn't you think of a divinely romantic ending for our sweet John Rio and his numbers?"

At dinner the conversation was as before—aphorisms and theorems concerning homosexual life—all presented for ready approval over glasses of wine. But when they returned to sit about the rectangular table in the living room, the conversation shifted back to the numbers.

"And so do you think it's all over now, John—just like that?" Sebastian asked.

Tony: "Like giving up smoking—all you do is stop?"

"Does that mean you won't have *any* homosexual contact—at all? None?" Emory asks. "If so, oh, what a loss!"

His black hair rumpled and over his forehead as on that other night, his eyes half-lidded, the liquor taking effect, Guy looks steadily at Johnny.

Even more strongly than before, Johnny has the impression they don't understand at all about the game—nor how exactly he won it—nor what it is he won. This impression is so disconcerting that suddenly he wants to rush to the corner of 7th and Broadway. *She'd understand!* he thinks crazily, feeling the liquor even more. Instead, he decides to explain the matter of the numbers and his victory: carefully and clearly like this:

"I'd probably be lying if I said, no, I'd never make it with a man again. I guess maybe all my life I'll need that contact. But not in the Park— . . . nor in any other park."

Sebastian: "You're sure of that? Never again?"

Johnny, with emphatic certainty: "I'm *sure*. Never, *never* again. Not in the Park, nor in any other park, nor in movie balconies. It'll be only with people with identity —men *or* women—people I know, not people without names—not just 'numbers.' *That* was the spooky part; that's what the Park was all about . . . and the numbers. Losing control and losing identity. But I'm in control again, and that's what I won. I won't even have to keep myself alone like I did in Laredo these last three years— because now I can stay in control. No, I'll *never* accumulate 'numbers.' Not again. That's what 30 meant. See, the Park, it was beginning to pull me down—*under*—until I set a goal after which I could walk away, free. If I had stayed— . . . If I went back— . . . *It* would have won, and I— . . . Well, I'd lose control."

From their silence, Johnny can't tell whether they've understood him or not; but for those moments at least, they seemed to sense the seriousness of the furious struggle he had waged.

And then, with kindness, Sebastian says: "But you still haven't explored . . . a further country, dear John. And until you do, you'll never know if *that* is *it*: yes, what could, just possibly could, make you happy. Until you do,

you simply can't be completely—truly—free of a world
you've explored only in part—and I do know you yearn,
truly, to be free within yourself."

"What further country?" Johnny asks, knowing the
answer.

"The country of sharing mutually of course, one for
one," Sebastian answers. "And—perhaps—of finding *one*
. . . number."

And so again the recurrent echo: the unexplored
country.

"But haven't we gotten somber!" Emory says.

"And we should have celebrated John's . . . victory,"
Tony says.

"A victory is its own celebration," Sebastian says. "Besides!—it's late: and we must be going."

They all stand up. Emory decides to leave too.

"Goodbye for now, John—and good luck," Sebastian
says seriously.

"And do come back again before three years pass this
time," says Tony.

From Emory: a sudden, tight hug and an almost teary
farewell.

Paul sees the three to the door.

Guy pours another drink for Johnny and another for
himself. From his pocket he brings out two pills, which
Johnny instantly recognizes as benzedrine. They swallow
both liquor and pills quickly as if anxious for their effect
—and to seal a silent pact.

Now the fantastic will once again become the expected
in Johnny's strange life.

Guy says: "We'll *have* to make it tonight, man, okay?
Together—*tonight*—*okay?*" And there it was—the tone of

urgency, an urgency that, whatever its source, hints of that deep sense of desolation, of doom, of the despair and desolation which Johnny intercepted that earlier night.

"Okay," Johnny Rio says.

"After you say goodbye to Paul, just wait outside for me—okay?"

"Okay," Johnny repeats.

Returning—and seeing Johnny and Guy standing close together—Paul immediately understands. His face has the look of someone who insists, "This isn't happening"—while he sees it happen.

Johnny says, "Paul, goodnight—I'm leaving— . . ."

"No, wait!" Guy calls out urgently to him, as if not sure Johnny will wait for him outside.

Johnny stops.

Guy says to Paul, "Paul, I got to."

Paul looks at both of them in wild hurt, and then he disappears into another part of the house.

"I *got* to, Paul," Guy whispers.

Outside.

They walk up steps leading along trees to a terrace— very dark, invisible from the bottom—halfway between Paul's house and another many many feet above, on a higher level of the canyon. Trees are like black lace against the dark gray of the Cloud, which, after the bright, triumphant day, has returned to obscure the stars.

Johnny and Guy climb into that darkness: along that terrace—like the darkness of movie balconies, the seclusion of hunting parks—into the darkness where the darkness suffocates itself and ceases to exist: but, also: toward a further, symbolic country whose outskirts Johnny Rio knows intimately but whose interior he has left unexplored.

Guy leans toward Johnny. Their lips touch.

Drunk, swaying—the pill that was meant to nullify the effects of the liquor not yet having acted—they take off their clothes.

Smothered by the night, the Cloud, they spread their shirts and pants on the moist ground. Now, in the dissolving darkness, they study each other's nakedness—Guy, Johnny's tightly muscular body; Johnny, Guy's slender and flat body like a boy's.

Again they kiss. But this time their lips open, their tongues thrust in and back, into and out of each other's mouths—as if both are alternately hesitant and anxious to enter a depth beyond themselves.

Instantly aroused, cock erect, Guy reaches for Johnny's prick, which is soft—not even hardening.

Caught in a trembling wave of dark, to avoid falling they lie on their clothes, side by side, clinging to the contact of their lips; their bodies—shivering in the moist air and straining—pressed tightly as if to touch as closely as their lips.

Shifting his body around, Guy takes Johnny's soft prick in his mouth, and after long moments—quickly—Johnny takes Guy's in his. And Johnny doesn't know what he feels, no, not at all—although they remain like that, sucking each other—quite clumsily—for long moments: until Johnny turns his head away, and Guy shifts his body again, pressing sideways, his prick against Johnny's buttocks as if to enter him; and Johnny allows just that much only because he knows that he won't let the actual act of penetration occur; knows instinctively that this is a perfunctory action required by Guy before he'll allow Johnny to enter him.

And Johnny is right. Immediately after Johnny twists around to end the gratuitous, barely implied act, Guy turns over on his stomach, his body stretched waiting, his legs an inverted V. Still soft, Johnny mounts him.

It's as if they were involved in a ritualistic battle in which each must at least have attempted to pierce the other—like combatants in a symbolic mutual slaughter—although: In that position—Johnny pressing his soft prick against the opening at Guy's buttocks—they kiss again: Guy turning his head sideways to meet Johnny's mouth with his.

Wanting very much to penetrate him—but his prick refusing to harden—Johnny remains straddling Guy, and he tries—wants—to insert it—even soft. Giving up, he merely lies on top of Guy.

After a long time, Guy turns over. They lie sideways again, again very close, still kissing: thighs to thighs, chest to chest, mouth to mouth—Guy's hard prick against Johnny's still-soft one.

Their bodies parting barely enough to allow the action, Guy attempts to jerk both off simultaneously. Then Johnny tries it, holding both cocks; but his prick refuses to harden. Now Guy, aroused to the point where he must come, is pulling himself off, his free hand exploring Johnny's body.

Determined to come with him, Johnny stands over Guy —and they stare at each other as if to remember indelibly —and Johnny is trying very hard to work his own cock up, to come when Guy will; but he still can't, and Guy comes before him, lying there almost motionless afterwards while Johnny strains to make it.

Long, long moments later—straddling Guy, Johnny Rio came, too—at last. Came on Guy's chest. And came still soft. As if even then his cock refused to commit itself.

Then he lay down beside Guy, and they kissed gently. And with finality. As if kissing something *away:* knowing that nothing further is possible, ever, between them, that each has acquired what he sought needfully in the other: Guy, vicariously, the total, in Johnny, of all Johnny's numbers. And Johnny, an intimate knowledge of that further country. They remained lying there side by side for what may have been a long time or only moments—almost sleeping, drawing warmth from each other; and then they roused themselves.

Crushed leaves cling to their clothes as they dress.

They went down the steps without a word.

"Goodbye."

"Goodbye."

In his car, the world spins in a dark vortex for Johnny. He waits for the whirling to stop.

A light goes on in the upper story of Paul's house. Framed by the window, two shadows confront each other.

As Johnny drives into the Cloud, which has now descended as turbid black fog, he thinks or says drunkenly:

That other—that further country . . . I just . . . explored it. And . . . it isn't mine.

Nauseated, he stops the car; and he vomits convulsively out the window.

That country— . . . he thinks. It wasn't mine.

FIFTEEN

THAT WASN'T IT! That wasn't it! That's not my world, and it never will be! He thinks that for the hundreth time since leaving the canyon many hours ago—and it was his first thought after waking. He neither exults nor regrets— he merely took a journey with Guy and discovered the explored territory is not his. . . . Already Guy's face is fading in Johnny's mind.

It's not quite noon.

And again Johnny Rio is passing cars anxiously on the freeway, zigzagging frenetically from fast to faster lane. Rushing.

After throwing up into the whirling dark of the canyon last night (or was it already morning?), Johnny actually drove—crazily—to the corner of 7th and Broadway. Of course: The Negro woman wasn't there—nor had he rationally expected her to be—not then, not in the deep, deep quiet of the night. It was just that he couldn't resist the strong compulsion.

In his car he paused in the trafficless street. Briefly and sorrowfully. As if at somebody's grave.

He reached the motel just as the sun began to stare bleakly at the world from behind the Cloud.

Not even a sleeping pill could tame the wild thoughts. Giving up on sleep, he got up and checked to see that everything was packed, ready for his leaving this city of doomed angels before noon.

Very suddenly the sleeping pill seized him, pulling him into a dark pool of sleep—from which he emerged only a few hours later feeling powerfully exhilarated: as if the benzedrine—momentarily vanquished by the sleeping pill and the liquor and the events of the frantic night—was in complete control: woke so exhilarated that he exercised in that febrile state: repetition after repetition, set after set.

Impatiently now he passes another car as he speeds along the curving freeway, and the car ahead moves to the right, sensing the urgency with which Johnny Rio is driving.

The exit at last!

His heart races faster than his car.

Had he really expected to find it razed—like the Biblical cities?

Whether he did—insanely—or not: There it is:

Impassive. Apathetic.

Griffith Park.

And so on Monday, almost at noon, Johnny Rio returned to the Park after all.

He stands before the Arena. The sky is rubbed over as if with chalky ashes.

And what of his adamant resolve never to return? What of his victory over the Park?

Only minutes ago—ready to load his suitcase into the car—he stared at himself in the full-length mirror of the motel room. Having just exercised—his muscles taut with blood—he looked glorious to himself, and he remembered the Mirror at the Observatory.

It began then.

Like this:

A coldness in his heart. As if it had ripped and the warmth was flowing out. Then a tightening of his throat. Followed by a breathlessness which rendered each gasp like a swallowed piece of ice. And panic invading his body. His heart paused uncertainly at the top of each beat.

All the symptoms of fear. Yes. And of terror.

Except that: In Johnny they became a craving to be desired. All those manifestations flowed into a starved longing which burrowed insistently into his groin: a fire there: a harsh demand for sex: a self-contradictory *cold* excitement.

He set his suitcase aside. He got into his car, and it was suddenly as if a force beyond himself was pulling him physically to the Park.

And he felt:

That coldness. And:

A sadness. A heavy weariness. A breathtaking pain. A terrible resignation. A bottomless emptiness.

And then, as he entered the Arena:

A terrified excitement, screaming.

And because he has no reason for being here—no, especially not after his staunch resolve never to return; not after his stunning "victory" over the Park; not after achieving the symbolic 30 which was to set his life in order and make him free: because he doesn't have that necessarily powerful reason—and that announces a dangerous crisis—he feels an amorphous need like immediately before he consciously set the goal of 30; and his mind flails anxiously awaiting that "reason" to rescue him from the edge of chaos and surrender—as it has miraculously over and over and over. Again, he's aware of all this only as a nebulous disorientation; aware of something askew, unbalanced.

No "reason."

And so Johnny reacts: He removes his shirt and walks along the Labyrinth past several men, rejecting them, past others already involved; finally choosing a lithe goodlooking youngman who is following him.

To the Cave. Taken. But not for long: The man who was in it—alone—came out. Johnny went in; the lithe youngman followed quickly, groping him immediately. Johnny pushes the youngman's head impatiently downward.

"No—fuck me!" the youngman whispers, his voice shattered by desire.

Johnny begins to leave the Cave.

But he doesn't. Suddenly he wants to penetrate this youngman—as if to end something begun last night.

"Get me hard first!" he commands the youngman.

Understanding, the youngman sucks him.

Thirty-one! Johnny counts automatically. (Thirty-two? . . . Guy. . . . No. That was in a further country.)

It's obvious the lithe youngman doesn't like to blow, is doing it only to harden and lubricate Johnny's prick. That accomplished, the youngman pulls his own pants and shorts down. His back to Johnny, he leans over the heavy diagonal branch that splits the Cave.

Fiercely, Johnny pushes his cock into the other in one savage thrust. The youngman utters a gasp which softens into a long sigh. Pumping angrily in and out of the other's tight opening, Johnny comes immediately.

Leaving the youngman bent over the branch whimpering, Johnny rushes out, feeling a flaming rage without conscious object as he drives to the Observatory.

Before he looks in the Mirror, he washes his prick obsessively with soap, over and over (though there was no trace of the act), so obsessively that he hadn't noticed until now that there's another man here—looking curiously at him as Johnny washes his own cock.

Alone in the restroom now, and having moved a few feet away from the Mirror into a clearer light, Johnny faces his image. He's as goodlooking, as exciting as ever.

But— . . .

Something is different. Vaguely. A look. The eyes. No. The mouth. No—it *is* the eyes.

He drives down the road, fleeing.

Familiar cars. But new ones always.

Just one more number, and I'll leave! he tells himself.

By the Trail. Two cars drove in simultaneously, each man rushing out to reach him before the other. Johnny walks down the Trail to the water tank. One of the men tumbles down the incline off the path, sliding, determined to get to Johnny before the other, who's ahead. The other intercepts the first and shoves him roughly away.

Exploding in Johnny's already troubled mind with overtones of loss of control, the scene drives him away quickly, leaving the two behind.

A reason!

None.

To the Forest. So involved they didn't see or hear him approach—and he was so deep in his own clashing thoughts he didn't notice them until he was almost in the Nest—three men seem to have been frozen in deadly combat: One is standing while another penetrates or tries to penetrate him from behind. Another sucks the one in the middle. Like animals feeding on each other!

But the disgust he suddenly feels isn't enough to send Johnny away. A fever flares inside him—and a battle between ponderous weariness and kinetic excitement.

Just one more!

In the Forest a man approaches him. But he turns Johnny off. Another one. No. The two he rejected move away together.

Again, insistently, his mind demands a reason; like this: Johnny is acutely aware of drifting in the twilight green of this area: more, of drifting in that peculiar mood of *frantic* trance which the Park creates: actions automatic, reactions beyond control—all speeded up to rapid motion: a mood rapidly enveloping Johnny Rio.

Unless! . . .

A reason! Or:

Get out of the Park *now!* Drive away! Leave! Go back to the motel, check out quickly! So what if you came back to the Park today? You won Sunday! It's only if you *stay* that you need a reason! There are many—oh, many, many —for leaving!

But— . . .

There's a youngman staring at him.

And now a man cruising which one? Johnny.

In a hollow bowl created by the drooping branches of trees, the man goes down on Johnny.

Thirty-two! Johnny counts, waiting anxiously for the youngman also to touch his cock so he can count 33 in rapid succession.

But the man sucking Johnny reaches at the same time to take out the prick of the other youngman, fondling it with his hand while he blows Johnny. Now the man draws the other's stiff cock very close to his own face as if impossibly to put both pricks in his mouth at the same time. Resent- ing the intimacy that attempt would result in—the two cocks touching— Johnny breaks away abruptly, fleeing the Forest.

Moments later in the Cave: A man squats there, Johnny goes to him, pulls out his own dick, the man opens his mouth, Johnny sticks his prick into it, the man sucks it, Johnny comes, the man swallows the cum, Johnny moves away.

Thirty-three!

As Johnny left the Cave, another youngman entered, advancing with his pants already open toward the still- squatting man.

And this thought lacerates Johnny: Am *I* a number to him, too? Do those who suck me turn their mouths im- mediately to others just as I turn my cock? Are they col- lecting numbers too?

A reason—quick! his mind insists: by making Johnny feel as if he's *sinking* into the Park.

And because his mind can't find the sought reason, he thinks in terror and excitement: This is what I'd like to do all my life! Until— . . .

Until!

Leave the Park!

Just one more number.

But first, back to the Observatory.

The Mirror.

Now he knows that still another face has emerged: A composite of the three others, it bears the lean sensuality of the one he knows so well; the deep knowledge of corruption, without the ugliness, of the one that sent him away from Los Angeles three years ago; and the crystal-souled sadness of the one discovered in the Park. Strangely, the new face is the most exciting of them all.

Driving down the road. Men drifting everywhere. Caught in the trance that is inundating Johnny.

And—incongruously—all around, the Park's green peace.

At the Outpost. Standing. These thoughts race beyond his control: In ten days, more than 30; in 30, more than 90; in 12 months, more than 1000! And in— . . . No!

The largely sleepless night . . . the liquor, the wine . . . the opposing pills at war with each other. . . . Johnny's vision blurs off and on. His heart pounds audibly.

Suddenly he notices a peculiar shadow lurking on the highest hill of the Park.

God the Heavenly Sniper!

And so whose number is up?

Will He aim at the man in that car passing by?

(Whooosh! Pingggg!! *Cuhrrrash!!!*)

Or at the man walking with another down the path across the road?

(*Pinggggg!* . . . Oh, my God, He shot him dead!)

Or at the one climbing up the Summit?

(Ping! Eeeeeeee-*ugh!* . . . Dowwwwwwwwn!)

Whose number is up!

Johnny drives swiftly to a secluded part. He parks, gets out, lies down on a patch of grass, looking up at the ashen sky.

Heavily, his eyes close. Numbers race madly through his mind, tumbling over each other. One-hundred-and-12, 113, 114 . . . 5117, 6118, 7119. . . . Numbers, numbers, numbers, numb— . . .

He must have lost consciousness for a few moments because when he sat up startled, a man was standing looking down at Johnny's bare chest.

Johnny thinks: What if I'd been dead and lying here and he thought I was resting and he'd be standing there wanting to suck my dick? What if he'd even— . . . ?

The morbid thoughts turn him off. So does the man. Johnny drives away.

A reason! Something to explain why he's here—after his victory. A reason for his not being on his way to Laredo.

A reason for there being no peace.

A man enters the Cave, where Johnny is waiting. To rush the scene, Johnny rashly takes his own cock out. The man slides down eagerly.

Thirty-four!

But Johnny's prick is so numb it feels soft between the other's lips. He looks down, assuring himself visually of the contact.

A youngman enters. Neither Johnny nor the other man start. The youngman looks familiar. But the numbers are losing even their few vestiges of identity. Maybe I made it with him before, Johnny thinks. If so, I can't count him twice. . . . All of a sudden, he decides to change the rules: He'll count contacts—not people!

The youngman tried to hold Johnny's cock for the other to suck, and Johnny was ready to count 35; but the first one pushed the youngman away harshly before the contact was made. Moving behind Johnny, the youngman licks his shoulders, tongue sliding downward so that Johnny expects the youngman is going to rim him. Instead—straightening up without warning—the youngman presses himself intimately against Johnny's body.

Furious—outraged—Johnny turns swiftly, knocking him down with a fist. "Cut that out, motherfucker!" Johnny blurts angrily.

The youngman was sent crashing against the dried twigs.

Johnny stands menacingly over him, fists clenched ready to strike him again.

"Let me suck you!" the youngman begs.

In a fury, wanting to choke him with it, Johnny bends down and pushes his cock into the youngman's mouth, which was open, waiting.

Thirty-five!

The first man has crawled on hands and knees back to Johnny, and groveling in the dirt, he shoves the youngman away and takes Johnny's cock again in his mouth. The

youngman remains sprawled, looking on hungrily, arousing himself.

Johnny pulls himself away—not coming—feeling a
rage that goes far beyond the youngman's unwelcome
movements—a seething rage as he staggers dizzily out of
the Cave.

Coming out into the feeble sunlight, he feels as if he's
emerged from a subterranean depth of the Park.

Then:

An eerie moment. No one else in the Arena. The two
men are still in the Cave. Johnny stands alone in the
Grotto, and he looks through the trees of the Park—
beyond the falling hills and toward the ghostly city, which
is impassive and unconcerned; another world: locked, like
the sky, by the heavy mist. And he no longer notices the
Cloud: It's become his sky.

A silence shrieks at him: *Eeeeeeeeeeeeeeeeeeee!!!
Eeeeeeeeeeeeeeeeeeeeeeeeeeeeeeeeeeeeeeeeeeeeeeeeeeeeee!!!*

Running, he stumbles on a broken pipe. Water trickles
out through a small hole. He bends down, trying to get
enough of the leaking water in his cupped hands to throw
on his heated face.

A blackness outlines his vision, threatening to seal it.

Recovering, he sees the familiar red convertible parked
across the road facing in his direction.

It was the same car that night in Lafayette Park! His
raging brain has convinced itself at last.

Outside the Arena, he crosses the road hurriedly; and
impulsively he approaches the man in the red convertible.
"Say, man!" His voice is thick. It could have come from
someone else.

"Yes?" the man wearing the dark sunglasses says.

"I— . . . I wanna ask you . . . something . . . man." A sudden disorientation beyond the general feeling of imbalance makes him forget momentarily what he wants to ask.

"Of course, youngman," the man in the red convertible says eagerly, apparently not at all surprised by Johnny's having come over to talk to him. "Anything! What is it?" Even handsomer than Johnny had thought, the man has a soft, cultured voice; he speaks each word euphonically. Quite definitely he's in his middle—no, upper—20's. No, his 30's. No— . . .

"Why? have? you? been? following? me?" Johnny is so weary he forms each word carefully to make sure he's speaking it.

The man laughs. "But isn't that just too extraordinary! *I've* had the distinct impression that *you've* been following *me!*" He focuses the sunglasses on Johnny. They're not black; they're mirrored. Johnny sees himself clearly reflected. Two faces, trapped, very small, one in each pool of the glass.

"I don't— . . . don't follow— . . . nobody!" Johnny says toughly. "And if you— . . ." He tries to verbalize a threat. But speaking is too difficult at this moment—the battle between sleep and alertness for control of his body is too ferocious.

Angrily, Johnny turns away, crosses the road; and he gets into his car, thinking:

Weird motherfucker—that *is* his scene—following people!—and he's following me cause I'm making out like crazy, and that's how he gets his kicks.

But Johnny Rio is convinced the man is hunting some strange, ineffable, truly unnatural perversion.

To drive him out of his mind, Johnny thinks:

Just one more number!

It's one of those recurrent moments in the Arena when the wave of hunters has flowed from one area to another. Returning after driving away from the man in the red convertible, Johnny is here alone.

Was.

A toughlooking youngman with tattoos on bulging biceps has driven up on a growling motorcycle. A cap cocked crookedly, long sideburns, no shirt, wearing a laced-up vinyl vest, engineer boots, he spots Johnny immediately and descends after him into the Cave.

Inside the Cave, he throws himself suddenly at Johnny's feet, licking Johnny's boots. Although this has never been Johnny's scene, it excites him powerfully now; and he remains standing, though unsteadily, over the other. Having pulled Johnny's Levi's and his own down, the toughlooking youngman throws himself back on the dried twigs and dirt. Yearningly, adoringly, he stares up at Johnny; and the other's radiating desire inflames Johnny, even as he struggles to retain his physical balance.

"On me!—here!" the toughlooking youngman with the tattoos pleads desperately. "On me—*piss—on me—here!*" He indicates his own aroused cock.

Although a perverse excitement at the other's exhortation sweeps Johnny, still a part of him—the same part repeatedly demanding a reason—clings to control and causes him to move back, shaking his head in protest.

"Cummon—piss—on me!" the toughlooking youngman begs, his body writhing with excitement on the dirt. "Cummon, cummon! *Please!*"

Fighting the part of him that resists—as he feels an unfocused anger rushing to find *any* object—Johnny suddenly tries to force the liquid out as he straddles the toughlooking youngman. At first it won't come, then it barely trickles, finally it flows.

"In my mouth—quick!" the tatooed youngman gasps, rubbing the liquid over his own cock and balls.

Johnny bends at his knees, toward the other's face.

Gurgling frantically in order not to allow it to escape, the other's mouth receives Johnny's piss, the flow uninterrupted until suddenly Johnny's cock grows very hard; and the flow of liquid stops. Pumping brutally and for a long time, Johnny forces himself to come—thrusting his cock over and over into the other's mouth.

Thirty-six!

Groaning, the youngman with the tattoos comes too.

Johnny stands up dizzily—bewildered by what he's done —as if he acted in another's dream—another's nightmare. He looks down at the other's wet vest and pants, wet face—and quickly away as if he were viewing himself through the other's eyes and seeing a savage part of himself which he prefers not to see—not to exist.

Outside the Arena, the two stared at each other with the blazing anger of bitter enemies.

And Johnny Rio feels very depressed. That's not my scene, he protests to himself.

The depression is compounded by the fact that there's still no "reason" to prop the swaying structure of his existence—compounded even further by the fact that the man with the two red X's branded on his back, slowing his car when he noticed Johnny, would have clearly stopped if Johnny hadn't driven away hurriedly.

That guy's still after me and he thinks eventually I'll make his weird scene.

The thought lashes at Johnny.

Just one more!

Parked by the Forest. Sitting groggily inside his car.

As if that will resurrect him, Johnny breathes very, very deeply; and the odor of the Cloud, which is smoke and fog—the odor of the city of lost angels—accosts him:

It's the odor of something burned—but not yet final like ashes.

And at that precise moment—on a threshold of his mind just barely below the level of his consciousness—Johnny Rio finally knows this:

There never was a reason, I'm just here and that's all.

And thinking that, he's grasped by an enormous craving whose demands are already multiplying, squaring themselves, burgeoning geometrically—a craving that expects no surcease.

Johnny *feels* an emotional howling.

I'm afraid! his mind shouts.

Turning quickly toward the Forest, he sees a man standing a few feet away, obviously waiting for him. Johnny opens the door of his car and he gets out automatically.

The dark shadow lurking on the highest hill of the Park draws his attention again.

He looks up.

Swaying toward hallucination, feverish, Johnny closes one eye; and cocking his finger in imitation of a rifle, he aims at the Heavenly Sniper.

"Pinggg!" he says aloud.

Now he goes to the Nest, and the man cruising him follows swiftly.

Johnny Rio leans against the trunk of a tree. The man bends down before him.

Thirty-seven!